M

Flippin' the Script

Flippin' the Script

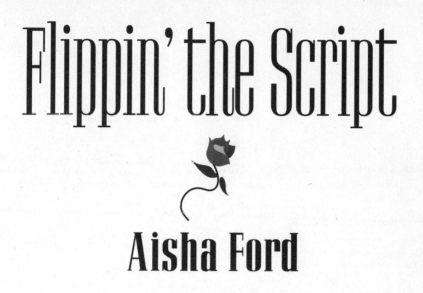

Aisha Ford

Walk Worthy Press

West Bloomfield, Michigan

WARNER BOOKS

NEW YORK   BOSTON

Published by Warner Books with Walk Worthy Press™

WARNER BOOKS

Time Warner Book Group
1271 Avenue of the Americas, New York, NY 10020

Walk Worthy Press
33290 West Fourteen Mile Road, #482, West Bloomfield, MI 48322

Visit our Web sites at www.twbookmark.com and www.walkworthypress.net.

Printed in the United States of America

First Printing: October 2004
10 9 8 7 6 5 4 3 2 1

Library of Congress Cataloging-in-Publication Data
Ford, Aisha.
    Flippin' the script / Aisha Ford.
        p. cm.
    ISBN 0-446-53182-0
    1. African American television producers and directors—Fiction. 2. Women television producers and directors—Fiction. 3. African American women—Fiction. 4. Office politics—Fiction. 5. Talk shows—Fiction. I. Title.
    PS3556.O687F58 2004
    813'.6—dc22   2004005808

Book design by Giorgetta Bell McRee

Flippin' the Script

Chapter One

Dry cleaning—sent. Grocery list—complete. Phone calls—returned.

Sabrina Bradley glanced at the clock in the corner of her computer screen. Noon already.

Great. Now that Miss Darci's errands are done, maybe I can actually tackle some of my official work responsibilities. But can someone please tell me why an assistant to the assistant producer at America's most watched daily talk show is nothing more than an errand girl for the host?

Her stomach growled again, but Sabrina didn't relish the idea of walking past her boss's office to head to the cafeteria, or even to the vending machine. Each time Darci saw her, it seemed that she found an additional task for Sabrina to do—something totally unrelated to work.

"And if Darci asks me to rake her leaves again, I'm quitting, I really am," she grumbled.

The second taping of the day wouldn't happen for another two hours, so Sabrina decided to hide in her cubicle, where she would be safe from Darci's endless string of requests. Out of sight, out of mind, as her granny always said.

Sabrina pulled a compact out of her purse and gave her face a quick once-over. Despite the perpetual shimmer on her nose and forehead, her deep brown skin was holding up well under the day's stress level. Nothing a little loose powder couldn't fix. So far. Maybe all those deep breaths *were* helping ward off Darci-related pimples.

But her hair was another story. Her shoulder-length bob was in need of a relaxer touch-up, and soon. If only she could slip away from Darci's watchful eyes long enough to get an afternoon appointment at the salon.

The phone rang, and Sabrina picked up. "Hello?"

"Sabrina. I need you to call my housekeeping service and let them know I need them to come in Friday morning. The caterer is coming at two, and I don't want them all running around the house at the same time.

"Also, can you check with the caterer and remind them that they forgot to bring me a sample of the vegetarian steak? I can't serve something at a dinner party if I haven't tasted it."

What a surprise. There went any chance of that hair appointment. Sabrina barely suppressed a groan. "Hello, Darci. You do realize that in between completing your personal errands, I'm not having much luck doing the work I was hired to do? Maris asked me to type the schedule for the next four days of taping, and I'm running behind."

"So . . . let Maris figure it out. She's the producer and that's part of her job. Why is she pushing it off on you?"

Never mind the fact that I am Maris's assistant, not yours. A better question would be: Why are you pushing your work off on me?

Sabrina cleared her throat, narrowly keeping the words from leaving her mouth. "Darci, this show, *your* show, revolves around a tight schedule. I know you would hate to come in tomorrow and find that I never got the chance to finish it."

Her statement was met with a deep sigh. "Fine. I'll make the calls myself. Please tell me you sent out my dry cleaning. I can't host the party without that dress."

"I did manage that."

"Good. Thanks so much." A click sounded, indicating the end of the call.

Darci's thank-you sounded far from sincere, but at least she had gotten off the phone.

"I'll be glad when this party is over." Darci herself had barely done a thing to get it off the ground. From mailing invitations to giving directions to Darci's house, Sabrina had been designated as the one to do most of the work. Darci knew better than to ask Maris, and she didn't trust most of the other employees to get the job done right. So the task fell to Sabrina.

"And I'm not even invited." Frustrated, Sabrina crumpled a blank sheet of paper and tossed it into the trash. "Not that I wanted to go . . . but she could have at least *asked*."

The phone rang again, and Sabrina steeled herself for more demands from the terror in the corner office. "Hello?" she said, hoping to mask the irritation she felt.

"It's me." The voice on the other end of the line commanded her full attention.

Eric. The realization ignited a spark in her temper. Sabrina didn't know whether to return the greeting or hang up the phone.

Her emotions leaned in the direction of yelling at him, and she struggled to rein in the myriad of feelings that seemed to be playing tug-of-war inside her. A wordless silence passed as Sabrina closed her eyes. *Lord, help me not to blow up at this man.*

Her moment of indecision apparently had no effect on Eric. Without missing a beat, he continued as though their relationship were the same as it had been two months ago.

"I hate to bother you at work, but I just thought I'd check and see if you'd had any luck with the sale."

Sabrina tried to focus on his words, but now that the initial wave of anger had begun to fade, the sound of his voice was too great a distraction. She hadn't realized how much she missed talking to him once, twice, numerous times every day.

"Sabrina? I really do kind of need my share of the money. I mean, if you're still . . . willing to share."

The ring. He's calling about the ring, she realized. The hope that had crept back into her heart at the sound of his voice deflated. After two months, he actually had the nerve to call and ask about the ring.

Shortly after the breakup, Eric had asked her to return the engagement ring. Still too shaken even to think about parting with the piece of jewelry she'd worn for the past two years, Sabrina had flatly refused.

Normally, she wouldn't have been so stubborn, but in a moment of anger, Sabrina informed Eric that she had no intention of giving it back. "It's the least I deserve for putting everything on hold for you all this time," she snapped.

Then Eric launched into a diatribe about how he needed the money. Being a freelance writer wasn't easy. He didn't have a regular salary, and now that he was working on the revisions to his novel, the value of the ring could very well tide him over while he wrote a blockbuster book.

In a fleeting moment of independent-woman-of-the-new-millennium bravado, Sabrina had extended an olive branch.

"Fine. *I'll* sell the ring and split the money with you."

"Thanks, Sabrina, I appreciate that. When I sell the book, you'll be first in the acknowledgments."

"Oh, wow. Thank you, Eric." Sabrina had ushered him out the front door and fumed while he walked to his car.

4

Last week I was the love of his life, and now I'm reduced to the end-less list of names in the acknowledgments, she thought.

Even that was an empty promise. How many people had given Eric some kind of financial support when funds got tight? They were all on his fictitious list of people to mention in the book. They ranged from his landlord, who, after a great deal of prodding, gave Eric a break now and then on the rent, to the cashier at his favorite deli, who gave him the employee discount if her boss wasn't looking.

"Sabrina? Are you listening?" Eric's persistent voice pulled her back to the present.

"I'm here. And, no, the ring hasn't sold yet." She didn't tell him that she hadn't had the heart even to take it to a jeweler.

Nestled between folds of velvet, it now resided on her dresser in its original box, untouched since the breakup, but not forgotten.

"Oh." He was clearly disappointed. "No interest at all? Not even a nibble?"

"Um. Well. No." That was the truth, and yet it wasn't. In all honesty, she had no desire to part with the ring.

"Okay. You haven't tried, have you?" Eric, as usual, homed in on the reason behind her reticence.

He did possess an aptitude for understanding people, and that was what attracted so many to him. Sabrina had no doubt that if he would apply this talent to his writing rather than using it to manipulate others, he *would* write and sell a block-buster novel. He had talent; there was no way to deny that.

"Sabrina, this has been hard for both of us, but we need to move on. I don't think keeping the ring is good for you. What can it represent besides a broken engagement? Trust me, you'll feel much better if you just sell it."

"I'll feel better? Or are you really talking about your bank ac-count?"

"That, too. But at least I'm being honest about it." Eric's tone shifted gears from strong and steadfast to gentle and persuasive. "I need the money; you need the closure. Sell the ring, Sabrina. Please."

She mentally rebelled against his suggestion but kept her thoughts to herself. He was right, of course. The ring did her no good and caused more pain than happiness. But it still meant something—and even though that something was bittersweet, she wasn't willing to part with it so easily.

Eric was wrong to believe that she could walk away from the ring as easily as he had walked away from her.

She was saved from further debate when Maris Russell, her friend and coworker, breezed into her cubicle carrying a giant latte in one hand, two deli bags in the other, and a magazine clamped between her lips. The strap on the gigantic piece of luggage she called a purse had slid down from her shoulder and now hung from her wrist.

"Mmmfff . . . ," Maris mumbled with a frantic gesture for help.

Still holding the phone, Sabrina jumped up and relieved Maris of the coffee and deli bags.

"Look, Eric, Maris just walked in my office, and I have work to do. I'll talk to you later."

Sabrina could hear Eric voicing his last protests as she returned the phone to the cradle.

"Hung up on him, huh?" Maris said, grinning. "Serves him right."

Sabrina shrugged. Hanging up on people, even people who made her angry, wasn't her style. She cast a glance to the Bible that lay almost totally buried under assorted paperwork in the far corner of her desk. How long had it been since she'd even attempted a quiet time? At least three or four days . . .

Figures. I'm always on a short fuse if I haven't had any spiritual food. Lord, forgive me and show me how to keep my appointments with You.

Sabrina sighed in mild frustration. She had no problem making allowances for work, but increasingly it seemed as if Jesus got the short end of the stick when it came to communing with Him.

Tomorrow I'll make sure I get my devotion time in. No, tonight. And maybe this week she would finally make it to Bible study night at church . . . if she didn't have to work overtime.

Sabrina nodded as she made the mental note, and looked up to find Maris giving her a curious look. "Girl, don't even say it. I saw you glance at that Bible and then you got that introspective look." She shook her head and sat down in an empty chair.

"Don't even say what?"

Maris put her hands on her hips. "Don't start beating yourself up about how you hung up on him. Are you trying to tell me that Jesus won't even let you have the satisfaction of slamming a phone down in somebody's ear once in a while?"

Sabrina grinned. "You sure you really want me to answer that? Because I don't want you complaining that I'm giving you a sermon against your will."

Maris exhaled and chuckled. "Forget it. I already have my answer. Guess you have to go to church and repent big-time on Sunday." Maris's eyes sparkled with unvoiced laughter, but Sabrina knew her friend wasn't being vicious.

"Actually, I've already repented. Admitting I'm wrong is hard, but if I wait too long, then it's harder to let go of it. My goal is to repent as soon as I realize I've done wrong. Sometimes I mess up, but I'm working at it."

Maris gave Sabrina a cease-and-desist look. "Okay. Whatever works for you. I'm not a mean person, but I know when to lay down the law and show people how they can and can't treat me.

But you can't even do that." She laughed. "Girl, I think Jesus has even more rules than Darci. Now, I call *that* a miracle."

Sabrina thought of a million rebuttals to Maris's statement but decided to hold her tongue. The good thing was that Maris now felt comfortable asking questions about the Bible. And she could kick herself for hanging up on Eric. All she had *really* accomplished was exposing Maris to a chink in her self-control. Weren't Christians supposed to lead by example instead of ramming the gospel down people's throats?

Some example I'm being this morning. Sabrina felt mildly disgusted but tried to find a positive thought. *Okay, the next time something challenging happens, I am going to be a better witness.*

Changing the subject, Sabrina focused on Maris's bounty. "My, my . . . are we hungry this afternoon?"

Maris shook her head. "Here I am trying to be nice and get you lunch and you make fun of me. If you won't be nice, I'm not going to share." Reaching inside the bag, she pulled out two sandwiches. "Tuna or turkey?"

Sabrina shrugged. "Doesn't matter. You pick first."

"You can have tuna," Maris said, holding out the sandwich. "I didn't get you any coffee, because I know you're trying to quit."

"Thanks so much." Sabrina didn't even try to sound as if she meant it. "Quit, my foot. I'll have to run out after the second taping and get a cappuccino or something. Besides, I'm just trying to cut back, not give up caffeine altogether."

Maris gave her a knowing look. "How many cups did you have this morning?"

"No cups. I don't do plain old cups of coffee anymore. I had a double mocha latte. And a shot of espresso."

Maris arched an eyebrow.

"I overslept," Sabrina admitted. "And I had a hard time waking up."

"Looks like you met your java quota for the day. I did get those jalapeño chips you like. And a yogurt."

Sabrina chuckled. "Yogurt? When do I ever eat yogurt?"

A mischievous glint danced in Maris's eyes. "I'm guessing you didn't watch *The Daily Dose* yesterday. Don't you know that every woman over the age of twelve needs to consume more calcium?"

Sabrina bit into her sandwich. "Is it a crime to go ten minutes without discussing work? I'm trying to salvage the rest of the day and I'd like to *pretend The Daily Dose* doesn't exist until my lunch break is officially over."

Maris nodded and gave her a sympathetic look. "Sorry. Rough morning?"

"You could say that—except I've not done any real work. I've been doing Darci's chores that she doesn't have time for. And her dinner party is wearing me out. I'm doing everything and she's doing nothing."

Maris swallowed and nodded. "Sabrina, you are just too nice. Honey, if she had the nerve to ask me to do all that running around, I would laugh in her face. That's what you should have done."

"The thought has crossed my mind, but I can't afford to make her that angry at me. I need this job. She wouldn't dare fire you, because you are invaluable to the show. I don't have that luxury. At least not yet . . ." Sabrina shrugged.

"But one of these days, when I know my job is secure, she's going to walk in here and hand me a grocery list and I'm going to just . . . just . . ." Sabrina stopped abruptly. Her thoughts hadn't been very Christlike, and she refused to let a few careless words undo all the time she'd spent witnessing to Maris.

"Just what?" Maris prodded. "Just run to the nearest supermarket?"

"No. I'll just . . . hand it back to her." That scenario wasn't nearly as satisfying as some of the others that she had envisioned, but it would have to do. Sabrina folded her hands in her lap, trying to rein in those last renegade thoughts.

Maris chuckled. "Sabrina, what has gotten into you? These little assertive outbursts of yours worry me sometimes." Maris quirked an eyebrow, and a serious expression came over her face. "I guess you didn't read your Bible today."

Sabrina rolled her eyes. "Oh, be quiet."

"Speaking of Darci," said Maris, "you need to read this." She reached for the magazine she'd brought in with her. "Look on page fifty-four."

Sabrina flipped to the page and was greeted with a full-color glossy photo of a smiling Darci on the set of *The Daily Dose.* With a groan, she closed it. "I told you, no work until after lunch."

Maris shook her head. "Too late. You need to see it now."

"Hmm . . . sounds important. Just let me finish eating." Sabrina laid the sandwich aside and moved on to the yogurt. Popping the lid off the container, she stirred the contents and took a bite. The first bite was okay, but the taste went downhill afterward. "What flavor is this stuff?"

Maris sipped her latte and shrugged. "Cherry cheesecake, I think."

Shaking her head, Sabrina put the container aside and reached for the magazine again. "Nope. I think it's called 'fake cream cheese and artificial sweetener with a hint of red flavoring.' You know, that generic red taste they put in stuff that's supposed to taste like fruit."

Maris laughed. "Yeah. In Popsicles and red soda."

"And now in yogurt."

"Maris?" Darci's yell sliced through the air, silencing the low murmur of voices in the office.

Maris let out a low groan. "She calls."

"Has anyone seen Maris?" Darci sounded on the verge of panic. Though this was not an unusual emotion for her, she did seem a bit more piqued than she would for an average temper outburst.

Maris made eye contact with Sabrina, then took her time standing up. Waving over the cubicle wall, she answered, "I'm here."

"I need you in my office. And Avery, where is Avery?"

"I'll find him," Maris said in a soothing voice.

There was the sound of a door slam; then the buzz of voices in the office resumed.

Maris drained the last of her latte and pointed to the magazine. "I have a feeling she just read the article. You need to see it before she sees you."

Sabrina lifted her eyebrows. "That bad?"

"I think so. Lord help us all when she starts plotting her revenge." Chuckling, she added, "You just might want to pray for us, Sabrina."

"Ahem." Avery Benjamin, producer of *The Daily Dose,* stepped into the cubicle, waving a copy of the magazine. "Have either of you read this?"

Maris hefted her purse onto her shoulder. "I have. Sabrina's reading it now, and judging from the pitch of Darci's screech, I'm certain she's seen it, too."

Avery loosened his tie and rubbed the back of his neck. "It's going to be a long afternoon."

"Maris!" Darci called again, then slammed the door.

"Let's go," said Avery. He and Maris bustled away, leaving Sabrina to read the piece for herself.

Seconds later, Avery rounded the corner, returning to the doorway. "You come in, too, Sabrina. You seem to have a lot of creative ideas lately."

Sabrina blinked. Avery was asking her to sit in on a producer's meeting?

"But, I . . . I haven't . . ." she trailed off, pointing to the magazine.

Avery took her hand and pulled her to her feet. "Then walk slowly and read while you walk." He hurried away, and Sabrina did as she was told.

Skimming the introductory sentences, she quickly got to the heart of the article.

. . . Of course, the public adores her . . . In between her timely reports warning consumers of devious scams and introducing the hottest educational toys, Darci Oliver is on a quest to save the world—and in the process, she will teach its inhabitants to bake a better quiche as they learn how to trompe l'oeil a breathtakingly realistic scene of a Tuscan vineyard on their dining room walls. Certainly, she gives the impression that the world would be a less better place if she didn't exist.

However, I can't help but wonder if Ms. Oliver and her producers have purposely neglected to inform us how her guests are doing six months after she brings them on the talk show *The Daily Dose*. Has her concern for today's busy woman, along with the advice dished out by her endless parade of specialists, really helped anyone after the last hug is given and the credits fade from the screen?

Are their closets still organized? Do they still find time to knit sweaters for the family pet during downtime at their children's soccer games? Has her dating advice helped anyone make it past the first date, or better yet, to the altar? Did her financial advice create a bevy of new millionaires?

Will the art of making a perfect yellow layer cake truly cause peace and harmony in any household?

Don't mistake my questions for dislike. I love the show as much as the next person—it's entertaining, if nothing else. But I think it could be better. I believe Ms. Oliver has overextended herself trying to do a bit of everything—and, in the process, accomplished little . . .

Yikes. Sabrina paused just outside Darci's office, wondering how to make an entrance without drawing too much attention to herself.

The problem of the entrance was solved when Avery swung open the door. "Good, you're here. Have a seat at the table."

Unfortunately, Avery's attempt at making her feel comfortable made her entrance even more conspicuous.

Darci sobbed quietly into one of Avery's monogrammed handkerchiefs.

Sabrina did a double take. Darci knew how to cry?

There really is a first for everything. As quickly as the thought came and went, Sabrina tried to push it away, giving Darci the benefit of the doubt.

So maybe Darci didn't usually show emotion—with the exception of anger and frustration—but anyone in her shoes would feel pretty low right now.

Sabrina sat up straighter, feeling Maris's gaze on her. She had promised herself to handle the next challenge better, and here it was.

Does it have to be so soon, Lord? Please give me the strength not to make a mess of this.

Darci sniffed and eyed Sabrina. "What's she doing here? This is a production meeting. She's just . . . Maris's assistant."

Sabrina had a feeling Darci managed to catch herself before she said "errand girl" or "gopher."

Avery chuckled. "Whether you realize it or not, Darce, Sabrina does more than pick up your dry cleaning and schedule your manicures. She's pretty much the assistant to the assistant producer. But, of course, you were probably too busy to notice."

The tension between Darci and Avery was startling, and Sabrina wondered if she had been the only one to notice. Although he'd used his pet name for Darci, Avery's voice carried an edge that normally wasn't present when he and Darci spoke to each other.

Or maybe I'm reading too much in between the lines, she decided.

Maris spoke up, cutting the silence: "Darci, he's right. Sabrina could probably do my job with her eyes closed." Laughing, she added, "Not that I want her to. At least, not while I'm still here."

Darci didn't respond directly but tossed the handkerchief aside, a stony expression chiseled on her features. "Okay. Let's get down to business. I need a way to prove this article wrong. Despite what this piece of paper says, I *am* dedicated to helping people succeed. How can anyone not see that?"

Maris nodded. "Of course you are, Darci. We just need to spend more time getting that message across."

"Right," said Avery. "So why don't we have Sabrina start contacting people from previous shows so we can do follow-up episodes?" Looking toward Sabrina, he asked, "Can you get me a list of topics we can revisit?"

Sabrina bit her lip. "Actually, Maris and I were discussing this the other day. I did some preliminary calls, but . . ."

Maris picked up where Sabrina paused. "It's not a good idea. We didn't do enough early follow-up, and I don't think it would help our case to bring the guests back. A lot of them are back at square one, looking for a way to get on track again. Apparently, our help wasn't as great as we thought."

Darci jumped up. "What are you saying? I brought in specialists and gave them makeovers. I worked hard on those people. How could they not have benefited?"

Avery sighed. "Darce, they're only human."

"He's right," Sabrina said. "And people are creatures of habit. They say it takes thirty days to develop a new habit. It's unrealistic to expect people to change completely after an hour on the show."

Darci stopped pacing and stared at Sabrina. Sabrina's throat went dry. *Oh, boy. Now what did I say?*

"Habit," Darci repeated, as though she had learned a new word. "Habit." She spun away from Sabrina to face Avery. "Then forget the previous guests. It's water under the bridge, and if I couldn't help them . . . well, let's just move on. I have a plan."

Sabrina glanced at Maris, who gave her a quick grin. Darci was notorious for hatching scatterbrained plots for show ideas and tossing them to the production staff to salvage when things got impossible. But she also had a reputation for developing amazing ideas for programming every once in a while.

"We'll form habits," Darci announced.

No one spoke for several seconds.

Finally, Avery asked, "*We'll* form habits? I don't get it."

Darci sighed impatiently. "Not us, silly. The guests, the viewers. We'll teach *them* how to form habits." She paused dramatically, then continued. "And not just Sabrina's thirty-day habits—these habits will last for months, years . . . even a lifetime."

Not just Sabrina's thirty-day habits, Sabrina thought, resisting the urge to roll her eyes. *Okay, what's wrong with my thirty-day habits?*

Maris tapped her pen against the table, and Sabrina knew that her friend sensed this was one of Darci's grandiose but unrealistic ideas.

"That's a little . . . overly ambitious . . . don't you think?" Sabrina ventured.

"Overly ambitious? In what way?" Darci challenged.

"I mean, as far as time and preparation . . . we don't have enough lead time to get something like that together . . ." Sabrina gave Maris an "I need backup" look but only got a sympathetic glance in return.

"There is no such thing as too much ambition. People who don't have ambition never get anywhere," Darci shot back, dismissing Sabrina's concerns.

Fortunately, Avery came to the rescue. "Darci, let's think on a smaller scale. From now on, let's just do follow-up episodes."

Darci would not be moved. "No. I'm not going to give in to that article and do things on his terms. He said I should have follow-up episodes, but I'm not letting him tell me how to run my show."

Avery leaned back in his chair and shrugged. "Then explain in detail what it is you want to do."

"New Year's resolutions. We'll have a yearlong campaign to help people make and keep them."

Maris laughed. "You're kidding, right? That'd definitely be shooting ourselves in the foot. No one ever keeps New Year's resolutions. We'll look like clowns if we attempt it."

"She's right," Avery said. "And besides, it's the middle of November. We don't have time to get something like that off the ground."

Darci put her hands on her hips. "We can do anything if we put our minds to it. Do I need to remind you of that, Avery? Of all people, you should know this."

Avery shrugged again. "I like your vision, but we'll run ourselves ragged trying to put it together before Christmas."

"Then we'll run ourselves ragged," Darci persisted. "I might not always have the best ideas for the show, but trust me on this, Avery. I can feel it," she said, placing her hands over her heart. "This will be a major success. Please?"

Avery sighed deeply. "Okay. We can give it a shot."

Darci smiled. "Great. We'll work out the details later." She glanced at her watch and headed toward the door.

"Hey, what do you mean, 'we'll work out the details later'? This is your idea," Avery protested.

Darci pointed to the clock. "We tape in a little over an hour. I have an appointment with hair and wardrobe. You all get started and I'll catch up later." With a wave and a laugh, she was gone.

"Ha!" said Maris after Darci was out of earshot. "With Darci, 'we' usually means everybody but her."

"Especially lately," said Avery. "But she's got her heart set on this. I suggest *we* get to work and get some things set in stone before she can do too much damage. I have to admit, the idea does have some merit."

"I guess so," Maris admitted.

"Sabrina, what do you think?" Avery spun his chair around to face her.

"I . . . I guess I'd have to think about it. I never do resolutions myself, so I'm not sure I'll be any help."

"Oh, come on, everyone makes resolutions."

She laughed. "Okay, I have made them in the past. But my good intentions lasted no longer than a couple of months. After four or five years ago, I gave up completely."

"But you told me once that Christians are always changing," Maris cut in. "Wouldn't resolutions be a good way to make sure you follow all the rules?"

Sabrina hesitated for a moment. How should she answer that? She began her response slowly, searching for the correct way to respond. "Well, you're right about having to change. But

I can't fix myself on my own power. I can ask the Lord to help me be different.

"But being a Christian is not some checklist hanging over my head. It's more about developing a relationship with the Lord and making my choices based on what I know will please Him.

"Just like in a friendship or relationship. When you love or know someone well, you don't need a list. You do what makes them happy because you have a mutual relationship." Sabrina paused, wondering if she had stepped over any invisible lines talking about faith at her job. Maris didn't look offended, and Avery was nodding.

Feeling relieved, she cleared her throat. "Still, regardless of my own personal experience with resolutions, I will do my absolute best to help with Darci's idea. Just don't look to me as someone who has actually been successful at using her approach."

"Me, either," said Maris.

"Count me in," said Avery. "I like Sabrina's approach much better. I know you're not ready to make that choice yet, but that's how it really works, Maris." He stood up and stretched. "I'm running out for a bite to eat before the taping. Anyone want to join me?"

Maris stuffed a notebook back in her purse. "I'm getting out of here before somebody pulls out a Bible. About this resolution thing—I promise I'll do some brainstorming, but right now I have to get on the phone and get some confirmations for next week. You two have a good time."

Avery nodded. "My schedule is free until the next taping." He looked at Sabrina. "How about you?"

Sabrina bit her lip. "I just ate, and I have a million things to get done before the taping."

Avery looked disappointed. "That's right, I walked in while you two were finishing lunch. How about tomorrow?"

"Maybe." Sabrina collected her notes and headed for the door. In her haste to get out of the office, she bumped into Avery, who remained in the doorway. Thankfully, she kept a grip on her papers, unlike in one of those absurd scenes in the movies.

Boy meets girl; girl bumps into boy; boy picks up girl's purse and sweeps her off her feet.

Yeah, right, Sabrina thought. *Never in real life.*

Avery did, however, grasp her arms for a moment. "Are you okay?"

"Yeah, I'm fine." Sabrina ignored the woodsy scent of his cologne and composed herself. Feeling her face grow warm, she quickly marched down the hall and back to her workspace.

Good grief. Why did she have to do a clown act in front of her boss? And just after he'd asked for her input on future shows? Not that it mattered . . . Darci would likely shoot down any of Sabrina's ideas. Either that or she would take the idea and finagle it to sound like her own.

"The same way she did with my comment about habits," Sabrina mumbled.

Forget about it. Sabrina forced herself to remain calm. No use getting up in arms about something that really didn't amount to much in the long run.

She hoped to be a producer herself someday and had no desire to get bogged down with petty arguments on the way up.

And, as her mother loved to remind everyone, vengeance belonged to the Lord. No use trying to punish folks on her own.

Safely back at her desk, Sabrina got to work on the day's tasks. She moved at a feverish pace, hoping to make a dent in the long list of duties before the second taping of the day.

Half an hour before the taping, Avery showed up in her cubicle, as he seemed to do so often in recent weeks. "I'm just about to head down to the control room, and I thought you might want to come along," he said.

Sabrina didn't answer right away. Avery was one of those men who could strike up a friendly conversation with anyone, anywhere, and make that person feel as though they had been friends for years in five minutes' time.

That in itself wasn't a bad quality—in fact, it was a good thing. But she knew from experience how easily the lines between friendship and love sometimes blurred. Right now she didn't need an extra worry.

Avery backed away a couple of steps. "Or not. I just thought we could throw around ideas for Darci's resolutions project."

Sabrina nodded, hoping to bide her time, wondering what she should say. Why did something so simple seem so difficult?

For the past three months, she had seen more of Avery on a regular basis than she had over the past three years. Her first thought was that he had finally taken notice of her hard work and had ideas of promoting her.

But after a couple of weeks passed and he made little mention of work, Sabrina realized that his short conversations with her were not formal talks but leaned more toward friendly banter.

When he began, she'd been too preoccupied with planning her wedding to question whether Avery might be taking small steps toward asking her out. During those blissful days, no man even came close to Eric.

Now that her relationship with Eric had come to a definite end, Sabrina had no desire to begin a new romance.

Especially not with Avery. Not that there was anything wrong with him . . . but her emotions had been wrung inside out, and most days it took all of her resolve not to cry or even get angry about Eric.

Besides, she knew very little about Avery. She did know he was a Christian. In fact, they attended the same church. But the membership at their church totaled well over a thousand people, so she rarely even saw him there, let alone spoke with him.

He was smart, well-educated, successful in his business, and handsome. All in all, Avery was a good man. He was also Darci's man. And *that* was enough to keep any woman in her right mind away from him.

Since Avery was her boss, Sabrina couldn't very well tell him to leave her alone or go away—especially now, when he specifically wanted to talk work.

The problem stemmed from worrying whether Darci would read more into their time together than what was actually true. Sabrina had seen other women mysteriously lose their jobs for less.

"Ahem." The sound of Avery softly clearing his throat reminded Sabrina that he was awaiting a response. "If you need some extra time, why don't you meet me there in ten minutes or so?"

Sabrina shook her head and stood up from the desk. "No, that's okay. I'll come now."

Avery looked pleased. "Good. We've got a lot to work out if we're going to get this off the ground for the New Year."

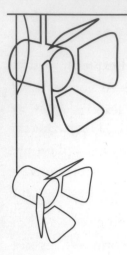

Chapter Two

Avery cleared his throat and made eye contact with each person in the conference room, signaling the beginning of the meeting.

"I apologize for keeping you here this late, but it's been two weeks since we decided to put this line of programming together for the next year. My goal for tonight is to get a progress report and determine what our next steps will be."

Darci yawned. "I know this is an important meeting, but is it possible that I can leave early? Can't someone take notes and fill me in tomorrow morning? I desperately need to get some rest."

Avery suppressed a sigh. True, Darci was one of the hardest-working women he'd ever met. In fact, *The Daily Dose* was his idea, but Darci had been the one who pushed him to bring the concept to life.

In the early days, when he wanted to give up, Darci had been his biggest encourager. He might be the producer of a successful TV show, but Avery knew that a good deal of the credit belonged to Darci—even though she continually seemed to rub him the wrong way in recent months.

Avery looked around the room. Maris, Sabrina, and Vincent

Byrne, the show's director, all wore exhausted expressions. The truth was, the day had been busy for everyone. As good a friend as Darci was, Avery didn't want to let her leave just yet. It wouldn't be fair to the others. Sabrina had already pointed out that this was the third week in a row she'd had to miss Bible study because of work.

He frowned slightly. At least Sabrina had attempted to go. He hadn't attended anything but Sunday morning service for at least five years. Work always found a way to worm into his free time. But Sabrina was busy, too. Maybe he should ask how she made time for extra church functions.

Darci's loud sigh cut into his thoughts and grated on his nerves. She had managed to skip the past two meetings, and Avery knew the rest of the production staff felt that Darci had dropped the ball on this resolution idea.

He could count on one hand the number of days she had worked overtime with everyone else on the project. Even then, she had done little more than criticize the progress they had made, and when she finally left, everyone was relieved.

In a way, the predicament might be funny. Whether she was there or not, morale was slipping.

I'm going to have to talk to her about her attitude at work, he noted. *I can't afford to have good people quit or grow unproductive because she has forgotten the concept of teamwork.*

Hoping to ease the tension in the room, Avery tried to cajole Darci into sticking around for a while longer.

"I ordered takeout and it should be here in ten minutes or so. Why don't you at least stay long enough to have dinner?"

Darci sighed, but when he didn't acquiesce, she gave a hesitant smile. "Well, I hope you got sesame chicken."

Avery grinned, and exhaled in relief.

"Actually, I ordered stir-fried vegetables for you, Darce. I thought you weren't eating meat this week."

Darci sank back into her chair, clearly irritated. "Chicken is not meat, Avery. Not really. And what if it is? Don't I have the right to change my mind?"

Avery laughed and sat down at the table. "Let's get started. Darci, have you checked out the list of experts Sabrina and Maris contacted to coach the viewers in keeping their resolutions?"

"Yes. I have a few more people I'd like to add, but we won't need to schedule them until later in the year, maybe October or November."

"Why don't you give me those names in the morning so I can touch base with them and find out how their schedules are shaping up?" Maris asked.

"I will. Just remind me," said Darci. "And I have another idea. I think it would be good for the viewers to not just listen to expert after expert giving them tips on how to live up to their goals."

Avery noticed that Sabrina and Maris exchanged glances. He felt as wary as they looked. Darci had plenty of great ideas but, in recent months, lacked the enthusiasm to follow up on them. He had taken up the slack on a fair amount of her work, and so had the others. Soon he would have to confront her about it. He didn't look forward to that conversation one bit.

Darci must have picked up on the lack of enthusiasm. "Okay," she said, placing her hands on her hips. "At least let me get my idea out before you all fall asleep from boredom."

"We're listening," Avery said, gesturing for her to continue.

"I want to compile a panel of local people from different backgrounds to share their resolutions with the viewers. They can attend regular accountability meetings and then come on the show once a month and share their victories and their struggles."

"I like that idea," Sabrina was the first to respond. "It adds a human touch."

"Same here," Avery agreed. "We can even follow them around and do short features on each person to show how they are implementing the changes in their lifestyle."

"Exactly," said Darci. "And I want to assure you all that I will personally oversee the process of finding the participants. I'd like some high-profile individuals—maybe a news anchor and someone in public office—but I'd like to add variety. Maybe some housewives, teachers . . . a cashier at a grocery store, and maybe even someone who works here."

Avery felt excited about work for the first time in a long time. This was the old Darci—the Darci who had blockbuster ideas and the commitment to get them done. Moments like this were now few and far between, and lately he even wondered if she had lost her creative edge for good.

"I like it. If you need help getting the word out, talk to the publicity department," he suggested.

"I will."

Before anyone could say more, a knock on the door announced the arrival of dinner.

Avery paid the bill and adjourned the meeting for a quick meal. "I hate to work and eat," he said. "Let's take ten or fifteen to have dinner, and then we'll get back to the meeting. I promise, it won't be a marathon session."

Darci gave him a light kiss on the cheek. Avery blinked in surprise. Given the current state of their relationship, this action was unusually affectionate.

What had gotten into her?

"If you don't mind, I'm going to use my break to run to my office and return some personal phone calls," she whispered. "I'll just be down the hall, so call me when you get started again."

"I will," he said, spearing a piece of shrimp with his fork. As Darci left the room, he noticed Sabrina sitting in the corner, watching him with a curious look on her face. As soon as he caught her staring, she blushed and turned away. Avery grinned. He hadn't seen a woman blush in ages.

Vincent and Maris pored over assorted papers as they ate, oblivious to anything other than what they read. They were classic workaholics—a practice Avery now fought to abandon. And even now he felt the pull of the office drawing him away from what should be time spent developing relationships with the Lord and other people.

Avery had given his all and then some during high school, college, and the first years of the show. Now, at thirty years old, he realized he needed time simply to enjoy life, and constantly focusing on work did not make leisure time easy.

Work was fun and challenging, but a day came when he stepped into his empty house and longed for a family to fill the rooms with laughter and love.

Avery had long assumed that Darci would be the one to fill the role of wife and mother to his children, but time had unraveled the tapestry of that dream.

Maybe he had waited too long. Maybe he had pushed her away too many times when she wanted to talk marriage. Or maybe he'd simply been fooling himself, waiting for her to fully share his convictions and accept his relationship with the Lord.

At any rate, it probably wouldn't ever happen. And now he was starting from square one. He had no real friendships with any other women except for Maris, and she was married. Then there was Sabrina. She'd been with the company since the beginning, but only recently had he taken the time to get to know her.

She seemed nice but guarded. Someone had mentioned that she was engaged. Judging from the look on her face whenever she saw him coming, she wasn't too thrilled with the idea of being his friend. But he didn't know where else to begin. He needed someone to talk to, and she seemed like a good choice.

At least she shared his faith; they attended the same church. Other than that, he had learned little else about her during the three years she had worked here. But he longed to discover more. Something about her intrigued him, and he wanted to find out what that something was.

After a few moments of debating whether he should join Vincent and Maris, Avery decided against it. He could talk about work any time. Instead, he pulled up a chair next to Sabrina, who sipped a bottle of water.

"Aren't you hungry?" he asked, noticing she hadn't fixed anything for herself.

"I had a late lunch," she explained, shaking her head. She shifted away from him slightly, giving the impression that she didn't want to talk.

Avery nodded, feeling awkward. "Look, I'm sorry you had to miss church. I'll make sure you get out of here on time next week."

"Thanks," she said coolly.

Avery felt helpless as his attempts at making conversation ran out of gas. Should he just get up and walk away?

Almost as though she had heard his unspoken question, Sabrina turned toward him and spoke quietly.

"Do you have a minute?"

"Sure." He waited, trying not to look too surprised.

After a deep breath, she began: "I've been debating about how to say this without sounding rude or ungrateful."

Avery leaned closer, his interest piqued by her statement.

Sabrina put the bottle of water aside and folded her hands together. "It's simple actually, and probably a silly worry on my part, but I feel . . . well, uncomfortable sometimes when you single me out to talk. I don't mind if it's about work, but most of the time, I get the feeling that you want to . . . just talk."

Avery shrugged, feeling confused. "I understand what you're saying, but I'm not sure why we can't talk to each other. I thought we could be friends. What's wrong with that?"

Sabrina seemed surprised by his admission. "I have nothing against being friends, but to be honest, your attempt at friendship could place me in a difficult situation with Darci."

Now he felt clearly puzzled. "But how?"

Sabrina stared at him in disbelief. "You're kidding. You know how she can be, how she gets in her moods and—" She stopped mid-sentence, looking embarrassed. "I really don't mean to be disrespectful, because I love my job, and I don't want to say anything to jeopardize it. Really, I just think . . ." She didn't finish the sentence and looked over his shoulder at some distant point in the room.

Avery patted her shoulder, hoping to make her feel comfortable enough to express herself. "It's okay. Go ahead and tell me what you're feeling."

She shook her head. "Maybe I should quit while I'm ahead. I think I've said too much."

"Really. I want to hear." Avery wondered whether he sounded as if he was pleading. Even so, he didn't care. For some reason, it didn't make him feel any less a man to let Sabrina see his emotions.

She took a deep breath, then continued. "Okay. I'll get to my point. Darci is highly possessive of you, and I've seen other women here lose their jobs for seemingly innocent things—sometimes for reasons that don't fully make sense.

"But the one thing they had in common is that they were attracted to you—or Darci thought they were. I don't mind being friends with you, but I can't put myself in a precarious situation."

"Sabrina, Darci can't keep me from having friends. And I promise I wouldn't let her fire you because of it."

"Really." It was more a statement than a question, and the incredulous look on her face suggested she felt otherwise.

"Really," he answered, feeling confused. "Why do I get the feeling you don't believe me?"

Sabrina kept eye contact with him. "Why I am so special?"

"What?"

"You certainly sounded chivalrous when you said you'd protect my job, but why didn't you do the same for those other women? Why do I get the special treatment?"

Avery felt as though the wind had been knocked out of him. Sabrina was right. He had let Darci fire those women without getting a decent explanation as to why they had to be let go.

But Darci could be so unbearable when she got her mind set on something that she couldn't have. It was much easier to let her have her way so her mood would return to normal—although "normal" didn't necessarily mean pleasant.

"Okay, I stand corrected," he told Sabrina. "But you have my word. I won't let her do that to you."

She lifted an eyebrow.

"Or anyone else. I promise to keep a closer eye on the employee situation around here. Now will you be my friend?"

"Why do you need a friend all of a sudden?" Sabrina leaned a bit closer. "Put yourself in my shoes. Forget about the job situation. Wouldn't you find it a little odd that an engaged man suddenly needs a female friend? What does Darci think? Isn't she a good enough friend?" She shook her head. "I just don't understand where this is going. I feel like I'm unwillingly being placed in the middle of something, and I don't like the feeling."

Avery took a deep breath. "What if I told you that Darci and I are not engaged?"

Again his words were met with an expression of disbelief. She gave him a wry grin. "That's funny, because it doesn't look that way."

"Actually, we never were. It's been implied, and most people, myself included, assumed that we would eventually get married."

Sabrina gave him a look that suggested she didn't quite believe him.

He wanted to explain, but time didn't permit. Instead, he went for the condensed version. "Okay. Without going into details, about six months ago, I realized that marrying Darci was not what the Lord wanted for my future."

"And . . . I'm just curious. Does Darci know this?" She held up a hand before he could reply. "Because, from the way she's been acting, I'd say you forgot to tell her."

Avery felt like a kid getting reprimanded by his teacher. "Yes. And no. Our relationship has been . . . unusual. Since we were never formally engaged—I never got down on one knee and proposed or gave her a ring—it's a little hard to break things off. The boundaries are a little blurry."

"Of course. Take, for example, the kiss she gave you a few minutes ago." Sabrina still didn't seem totally convinced. "I guess I'd put that in the category of a 'blurred boundary.'"

"You're right. I probably shouldn't have let that happen, but she's actually been pretty annoyed with me lately. I didn't expect or want that kind of affection from her, but it would hurt her feelings if I pushed her away from me with an audience watching."

Sabrina blushed again, and Avery realized she thought his comment about the "audience" was a reference to her. "I didn't mean you. I just—"

"I'm back," Darci announced from the doorway. "But it looks like this has turned into a social event instead of a meeting." Her voice was crisp and measured. "What in the world are you two talking about all huddled in the corner with your heads so close? Juicy gossip?" She arched an eyebrow and crossed her arms.

Sabrina moved away and gave him an "I told you so" look.

"No gossip, Darce. Just talking." Avery inwardly winced at having chosen this pivotal moment to use his nickname for Darci. All his explaining to Sabrina probably didn't seem very credible right now.

Avery didn't miss the once-over look Darci gave Sabrina, but he felt helpless to address her actions. Despite the failed relationship, she was the host of the show and his longtime friend. He owed her the respect of not reprimanding her in front of others.

"It's late, Avery," Maris said. "My husband is going to be disappointed if I don't get home before nine."

"Yeah, you're right." Avery loosened his tie and tugged at his collar. "And it's eight thirty now. You know what? Let's go home now and finish this sometime tomorrow when we can all grab fifteen minutes or so."

"Oh, great. You mean I stayed this long for nothing?" Darci groaned. "Good night." She turned and left before Avery could apologize for the delay.

"I guess that's it, then," he told the remainder of the group. "I'll lock up after everyone is out."

Vincent was the first to leave, and Maris and Sabrina left together, just ahead of Avery.

As the three of them silently walked through the parking lot, Avery hoped for a moment to clear the air with Sabrina, since Darci's interruption had understandably been less than reassuring to her concerns. Maris reached her car first, and Avery waited to be sure her car started and she drove off safely before jogging over to Sabrina.

By the time he reached her, she was already in her car.

"So can we be friends?" Avery asked hopefully. "I know, I need to define my relationship with Darci better, but I would like to get to know you better."

Sabrina didn't answer for several moments. Finally, she answered. "You've been honest with me, so I'll be honest with you. I was engaged for almost two years, but a couple of months ago, my fiancé called the whole thing off. I will be your friend, if that's all you're asking. But I'm not ready for anything else."

Avery knew it wouldn't be polite to show his pleasure at the expense of Sabrina's obvious pain. He fought to keep his emotions under control and said, "I'm sorry about your breakup. I know a little about how that feels. And it looks like we both need a friend, so that's what we'll be. Friends."

"And I think it's best if you don't seek me out for any 'friendly' discussions until Darci is clear about the state of things between you two. Don't you agree?"

Avery sighed. "Yeah. I guess I do. Consider it done."

Sabrina smiled, and he could read the relief on her face. "Well, it's late." She turned the key in the ignition and started her car. "I'll see you tomorrow."

"Right." Avery backed away from the car and watched as she pulled out of the parking lot. He smiled, feeling a sense of satisfaction.

She was perhaps overly adamant about the "only friends" part of the deal, but he could agree to that. At least, for now.

Avery felt energized to spend some time on his knees when he got home. Although he didn't know exactly how to pursue a relationship with Sabrina, he had no doubt the Lord would have answers.

Chapter Three

Sabrina awoke to the high-pitched tune of her cell phone. Eyes still closed, she stretched out her hand, fumbling for it on the bedside table. It wasn't there.

Sabrina sat up and strained to hear where the sound originated. *My purse,* she realized, jumping out of bed. *I left it in my purse.*

Now, where was the purse? Sabrina grabbed her glasses and glanced around the room. It hung on the closet door.

As she sprinted the distance across the room to retrieve the bag, the phone went silent.

"Oh, thanks for being so patient," she mumbled. "It's only a quarter till six in the morning. Does anyone answer before ten or fifteen rings at this hour?"

As she checked the display screen, Sabrina was relieved she'd missed the call.

"Eric," she said. Her thoughts returned to the ring. It was still in her jewelry box, and she still hadn't gotten around to placing the ad in the paper.

Or should I take it to a jewelry store? she wondered.

One thing was for sure: she didn't want to talk to Eric until she'd done one of the two.

Sabrina marched over to the dresser and dropped the velvet box into her purse. On her lunch hour, she'd dash over to the mall and see if a jeweler would be interested in it.

Her alarm for work wouldn't go off for another forty-five minutes, and she was determined to get a few more minutes of sleep.

Just as she climbed back under the covers, her home phone rang. She didn't have to look at the caller ID to know that Eric was still trying to reach her.

Feeling a bit guilty, she turned on the answering machine and gave herself a few more hours of reprieve. One thing was for sure: she needed to get the ball rolling with the resale, and soon. Knowing Eric, he'd be knocking on her door tonight, wanting answers.

Surprisingly, she slept like a baby until the alarm clock trumpeted the six-thirty wake-up call.

Though she had slept well, Sabrina awoke feeling groggier than usual. The predawn call from Eric must have thrown her body clock for a loop.

For the second time that morning, Sabrina stumbled out of bed, this time headed to the kitchen. Waking up would definitely require some assistance, preferably in the form of caffeine.

Sabrina microwaved a cup of instant espresso and downed that while she waited for her special blend of premium beans to brew.

As the stream of liquid dripped into the pot, she leaned over the coffeemaker and inhaled deeply.

The aroma, coupled with the instant jolt of the espresso, was soothing and energizing. She poured a big mug of it and carried it back to her room to sip while she got ready for work. Already feeling better, she relaxed under the hot stream of water in the shower until the temperature grew cooler. She emerged from the shower fully awake and ready to take on the world.

She slid open the closet door, wondering what she should wear. The dress code at the studio was pretty relaxed, but today didn't feel like a shirt-and-slacks kind of day. A flash of turquoise at the far left of the closet caught her eye.

Sabrina smiled and pulled out the elegant pantsuit and held it up. It was one of her favorites but had somehow been forgotten after its last trip to the cleaners.

It didn't matter. It was now pressed and ready to go. As she carried the outfit to the other side of the room and laid it across the bed, Sabrina contemplated hairstyles.

Up . . . down . . . curling iron . . . flat iron? What should I do?

Sabrina returned to the bathroom mirror to apply makeup. As the minutes passed, she became increasingly aware that this morning's preparations for work were much more in-depth than usual, but she tried to push that train of thought aside.

But the thought wouldn't go away. With a sigh of frustration, she put down the eyeliner and stared at her reflection. The Sabrina in the mirror didn't say a word but seemed to know that all this extra fuss was for the benefit of a certain man at work.

Sabrina shook her head. "It's not about Avery—really," she announced to the Mirror Sabrina.

Mirror Sabrina didn't look convinced. In fact, Mirror Sabrina wanted to lean forward and make sure she had enough mascara on. She wanted to put on another coat of lipstick and swipe her forehead with pressed powder.

"I can't help it if I want to look really good once in a while," Sabrina said, still trying to throw Mirror Sabrina off the trail.

Mirror Sabrina didn't buy the explanation.

"Okay," Sabrina admitted to her reflection. "So I want to look good. And maybe it has a tiny bit to do with the attention Avery has paid to me."

Mirror Sabrina seemed to be hiding a smirk.

"Well, wouldn't you do the same thing?" Sabrina challenged.

Mirror Sabrina didn't argue with that. She seemed to say, "How about a little more eye shadow?"

Moments later, Sabrina pulled her hair up into a French roll, then headed back into her bedroom, anxious to be away from the gaze of Mirror Sabrina.

As she walked, she considered what Maris would say if she'd seen Sabrina talking to her reflection in the mirror.

Moments later, she stepped into the turquoise pants only to find they were a little snug.

After another minute of alternating between sucking in and fighting with the zipper, Sabrina tossed the pants back on the bed and headed to the closet again.

Unbelievable. Rifling through the clothes, Sabrina fumed over the loss of the beautiful pantsuit. *I can't believe they shrunk my pants. I should march right in that cleaners and demand my money back.*

Finally, she selected a long wool skirt and the matching jacket. The jacket seemed a little more fitted than she remembered, but she reasoned that it would be more comfortable after she'd had it on for a few minutes.

The skirt was a different story. Unlike with the pants, she at least managed to button the waistband, but she might as well have left it undone.

Observing her reflection in the mirror, Sabrina wondered which was worse: not being able to get the pants on or standing in front of the mirror, staring at the way her hips and thighs were fighting with the seams in this skirt. Not to mention the skin on her waist that wanted to bulge over the top of the skirt.

The worst part was, she couldn't blame *this* on the cleaners. Heaving a sigh—after she unbuttoned the waistband—Sabrina stepped out of the skirt and tossed it on the bed as well.

All the excitement over getting dressed up had melted away. What good did it do to get dressed up if nothing would fit?

Feeling apprehensive, she pulled her trusty pair of jeans off the top shelf and prayed while she pulled them over her hips.

They fit . . . pretty much. *Thank you, Lord.*

While she rummaged in her closet for a sweater long enough to cover her hips, Sabrina compiled a list of foods she would swear off until the turquoise pants fit again. Pizza . . . ice cream . . . cheesecake . . . All were a definite no-no for the next few weeks. *Won't this be fun?*

Just thinking about the word "diet" cast a gloom over the rest of a day that had seemed so bright and full of promise only twenty minutes earlier.

Grabbing her purse, Sabrina faced the mirror one last time for a once-over. Despite the bumps and potholes along the path to getting dressed this morning, she felt she looked good.

"And that's what matters, right?" she said to Mirror Sabrina. Feeling defiant, Sabrina placed her hands on her hips. "I feel good about myself. I really do." *And I sound like yesterday's guest on* The Daily Dose.

Mirror Sabrina's gaze landed on the hips, where Sabrina's hands rested—hips that were bigger than they had been a few weeks earlier.

"Okay. Point well taken. I look good; I feel good, but don't worry. I'm going on the diet for the sake of the sixty-nine dollars I spent on those pants."

Mirror Sabrina seemed satisfied at this, and Sabrina left on that note.

Since she had a few minutes to spare before she was required to be at work, Sabrina made a pit stop at her favorite coffee shop and got a tall mocha for the road . . . and for dealing with Darci.

Hopefully, Maris would be too busy to notice the giant cup. Ever since Sabrina had admitted that an excess of coffee sometimes made her jittery, Maris had been after her to give up the habit. But Sabrina wasn't ready for anything that drastic—yet.

Darci pulled into the busy parking lot, sandwiched between Sabrina's sensible white sedan and Avery's black SUV. Lately, the mere sight of Sabrina made her cringe. The same went for Avery.

Well, sort of, she conceded.

Sabrina moved at a snail's pace, searching for an empty space. Darci rolled her eyes as she watched Sabrina tip her head back and take another sip from a familiar paper cup. Darci shook her head. Sabrina was positively *addicted* to caffeine.

Too bad it didn't make her drive any faster. Or better. Darci slammed on her brakes as Sabrina pulled to a sudden stop and her reverse lights clicked on. "C'mon, you weren't paying attention and you missed the space. So keep going." She briefly considered making her feelings known with her horn, but she thought better of it.

After all, Avery was right behind her. The man was courteous to a fault when he got behind the wheel, and he had never hidden the fact that he felt she was too impatient a driver—especially when it came to using the horn. And she needed him to be in a good mood this morning.

With that in mind, Darci reluctantly pulled her car into reverse and gave Sabrina enough room to get into the space. But as soon as soon she was able, Darci maneuvered her tiny green coupe into her personal space. She watched as Avery pulled into the space next to hers, and applied another coat of lipstick as she waited for him to walk over and say good morning.

They'd shared the first few moments of each workday in this manner for years. He'd open her door, say hello, maybe give her a hug; then they'd walk inside, discussing work. What had once been a romantic start to her day had shifted to a comfortable routine.

She had once seen Avery as the one true love of her life. Now he increasingly struck her as a clingy, overgrown boy who tended to worry too much over what was right and wrong, and she had pushed him away a bit to pursue other, more exciting relationships. It had hurt him, and he had even come up with some nonsense a few weeks ago about his not being able to continue a relationship with her. But the fact that he hadn't changed the morning routine made her feel good. She always knew where she stood with Avery: first.

Despite his silly ramblings about the Bible and breaking up, she would be able to regain his full attention when she needed him. He might not be the most exciting man right now, but one day he'd be the type of guy she could settle down with. He was good-looking, chivalrous, and just plain old . . . *good.*

Goodness knows, there was definitely a shortage of good men around, so it would prove well for her to keep one on the back burner until she'd had all her fun.

Darci put her lipstick away, wondering what was taking Avery so long to get over here. He wasn't in his car. She glanced around the parking lot and saw no sign of him. *Surely he didn't go inside without me.*

Darci turned around just in time to watch Sabrina disappear inside the building—along with Avery. It was too late to be sure, but Darci almost thought it looked as though Avery had patted Sabrina's shoulder. And they were chatting and laughing about something. And standing awfully close together—too close for a producer and a . . . whatever it was that Sabrina did around here.

Darci scrambled to get her purse and paperwork together and hurried out of the car. The ground was a little slippery, and she tottered more than once as she hustled toward the front door. As she skidded inside, she felt another wave of irritation as the elevator door closed. Too late for her to see who was inside.

The security guard at the front door looked up and gave her a smile. "I guess you slept late this morning, Ms. Oliver. You just missed Mr. Benjamin by a few seconds."

Darci caught the faint smirk on his face and pasted on a smile. He knew. She had lost her grip. She cleared her throat in an effort to regain her composure. "Thank you for the information, Mr. . . ." She paused, leaning in closer to read the name on his badge. "Mr. Lincoln." She winked and gave him one of her flirty smiles. "And you have a nice day."

Security Officer Lincoln seemed flustered by this sudden attention and stumbled over his words. "Thank . . . thank you, Ms. Oliver. And you have a nice day, too."

"I will," she said, continuing down the hallway to the elevator. Silently she added, *Because you won't be here tomorrow.*

On the way up to the third floor, Darci debated how best to handle the Mr. Lincoln problem. Normally, if she needed to get rid of someone, she'd go to Avery and let him take care of things.

But she couldn't face Avery right now. Her emotions were still shifting back and forth between anger and annoyance, and she'd have a hard time keeping him from figuring out that she was upset about him and Sabrina.

Her solution presented itself when the elevator stopped at her floor. Jim Cooper, head of personnel, stood at the coffee station, stirring cream into his cup.

"Jim, you are just the man I needed to see." She moved to a corner of the coffee lounge and sat down, gesturing for Jim to follow.

Darci put on her most concerned, tentative expression, then spoke. "You know, Jim, I really hate to bring this up, but considering some of the security issues we've had lately, I feel like I need to say this."

She paused and waited for Jim to ask her to continue.

Predictably, he spoke up. "Darci, if you have a security problem, there's no reason in the world you should try to push it under the rug. Now, what's wrong?"

She lowered her voice conspiratorially. "Today was the third time I've walked in and caught that guard downstairs . . . Lincoln, I think, asleep." She looked down at her hands. "I know it must sound petty, but with some of the mail we've gotten from disgruntled viewers . . . I don't know."

Jim jumped right up. "I'll take care of this immediately; don't worry about it."

Darci nodded soberly and reached for his hand. "Oh, and, Jim, could you do this . . . quietly? I don't want to embarrass the poor man. I think he has a crush on me, and . . . that makes me a little nervous as well."

Jim held up a hand, signaling for her to stop talking. "I'll leave your name out of this, and blame the cut on . . . budget or something."

Darci stood. "That would be wonderful."

Jim took his coffee and hurried to the elevator while Darci

walked to her office. The day had gotten off to a bumpy start, but so far, she hadn't met a problem she couldn't fix.

Darci passed Avery's office and pretended to ignore his wave. Their offices were adjacent, and both were completely walled in with glass. Both she and Avery had wall-length blinds on the dividing walls for privacy, but she couldn't remember the last time either of them had actually closed them.

Avery was on the phone, pacing the floor in his office, but he tapped on the glass and waved again. Darci gave him a tight smile and decided she couldn't spend the next few hours looking at the man who had completely embarrassed her this morning. It was time to show him how lonely it felt to be ignored by an old friend.

She closed the blinds.

Chapter Four

Darci had her blinds closed.

Avery glanced at the window again and wondered what in the world she could be up to.

And knowing Darci, something was definitely up. First the little huddle with Jim, and now the barrier between their offices. Not a good sign

But what could he do? Knocking on her door could end in one of two scenarios. Either she'd make a scene and refuse to speak to him, or she'd let him in. The first option wasn't very appealing, but the second definitely made him nervous. It was apparent that Darci didn't really understand—or didn't *want* to understand—that their romance was over. So, if she did let him in her office, he might run the risk of giving her the wrong impression of his feelings for her.

Avery stood, walked to his door, and closed it. Sometimes, doing nothing was more productive than taking action.

"Hey, guess what I just overheard." Maris Russell stepped into Sabrina's cubicle and lowered her voice to a suitable level.

Sabrina looked up from the stack of papers on her desk. "Does it have anything to do with this ridiculous survey Darci passed out this morning?"

"Survey?" Maris peered down and took a closer look at the paper. "No . . . I don't think so. Unfortunately, I got in late and haven't checked my mailbox yet. Give me the details in a nut-shell."

Sabrina blew out a weary sigh. "Basically, Darci would like for all employees to fill out this sheet, listing our main goals for the coming year. Then, two lucky folks will get to spend the next twelve months trying to keep these resolutions on *The Daily Dose* while all of America watches."

Maris resisted the urge to roll her eyes. "Is there a deadline for getting this paper back to the queen?"

"Tomorrow morning." Sabrina gave Maris a look of disbelief. "Why in the world would I want to tell *her* anything about my personal life?"

Maris held up a hand. "You don't have to convince me. In fact, I'll probably just . . . *forget* to turn mine in on time."

Sabrina laughed and pushed the paper aside. "Good one. And I think mine will accidentally get lost under the mountain of paperwork on my desk."

Maris couldn't control the giggles that erupted as she watched Sabrina make quotation marks with her fingers as she said the word "lost." When she finally regained her composure, Sabrina's face held a look of expectation.

"So, tell me what you just overheard."

"Oh, yes, that." Maris loved being the first to report office goings-on. She pulled an empty chair closer to the desk and made sure she was good and comfortable before she began. In all her years of disseminating news of workplace happenings, she'd learned that dramatic pauses and a slow release of information made for a rapt audience. After taking a deep breath, and checking to make certain Sabrina seemed impatient to hear the news, she began.

"Jim fired the front-desk guy. The unofficial word is, he was sleeping on the job when Darci came in this morning. And it wasn't the first time."

"And the official word?"

Maris shrugged. "Budget cuts."

Sabrina leaned back in her chair, looking worried. "Whoa. I think she's on the warpath."

"Isn't that a given? The question is, what's the real reason this time?"

"I have no idea. And I'm not sure I'd like to know. That would involve thinking like Darci—and I know I wouldn't want to experience her thought patterns."

Sabrina frowned and shook her head. "You know, Darci came in right after Avery and me this morning. And the guard was wide awake when I saw him. Can anyone else corroborate the sleeping-on-the-job accusation?"

Maris rolled her eyes. "I doubt it. Better yet, there are probably ten or fifteen people who could prove the man was awake. But why risk it?" She stood up and moved toward the cubicle entrance. "Nobody else wants their job to get sucked under the quicksand of 'budget cuts.'"

Sabrina nodded. "I take it you're heading back to your office?"

"Yeah. Things are tense this morning, and I'd hate for Darci to walk in and find I'm not there. But maybe I'll catch you for lunch?"

"Sure, if you don't mind tagging along while I make a run to

45

the mall. Eric called again this morning, and I've got to do something definitive with the ring before I can talk to him. I'm going to take the ring back to the jeweler at the Galleria where he bought it and see if they have an 'Oops, we made a mistake' return program." Sabrina flashed a quick grin.

Maris considered for a moment. She'd like nothing better than to get out of the office for a while, but Darci's attitude might make such a lunch break impossible. When Darci was in a bad mood, it gave her pleasure to see other people unhappy. Darci was a walking personification of the old cliché "Misery loves company."

"I'm not sure it's such a good idea for me to leave the dungeon for that long—at least not today, considering the state of things—but I'll see what I can do," she told Sabrina.

"Okay. Then I'll give you a heads-up call about fifteen minutes before I'm ready to go," Sabrina promised.

"Deal." Maris waved good-bye and headed down the corridor to her own workspace. She loved this job, but sometimes the drama was too much even for her. A sweeping glance of the floor revealed that everyone was bracing for something.

The newer employees huddled in small clusters, whispering and gesturing. Those who had seen it all before were now hunched over their desks, hoping to look busy and escape being noticed.

Darci had her office blinds closed, effectively shutting herself off from the rest of the world, while Avery, on the other hand, sat in his own office, looking somewhat bewildered.

As she settled in behind her desk and surveyed the territory once more, Maris wondered if Darci even realized how her mood swings negatively affected the quality of work.

Watching everyone struggle to get ready for the worst reminded Maris of the time she and her husband had vacationed in Louisiana, only to be stranded as a hurricane blew in and battered the coast.

Seasoned locals had scurried back and forth, battening down the hatches, while tourists huddled together, wringing their hands and hoping for an escape.

"I am getting too old for all this stress," Maris grumbled as she flipped through a notepad of phone calls she'd missed. She wished it were already time for lunch, so she could chat with Sabrina right now.

Maris chuckled inwardly as she thought about how Sabrina usually seemed to remain steady under the impending doom of Hurricane Darci. Sure, the kid got flustered sometimes, but nine times out of ten, she held firm and let the winds blow around her.

Of course, she did practically have the Bible glued to her hand. Almost every time Maris stepped into Sabrina's cubicle, the girl was trying to read a verse here and there. And not a week passed without Sabrina inviting her to church at least once.

Maris tossed the papers aside, feeling too distracted to concentrate on working. Maybe Sabrina's Bible was part of the reason that she could hold it together when Darci went on a rampage. She was forever telling Maris about how Jesus could give peace that couldn't be found anywhere else in the world.

And while he wasn't quite as persistent as Sabrina, Avery was the same way. Sometimes he gave in to Darci's whining and complaining and let her have her way, but more often than not, when Avery put his foot down, he had the last word. Huff and puff as she might, Darci and her antics didn't sway him—especially in recent months.

Perhaps he and Sabrina really *did* have something—some kind of inner peace, or strength, that allowed them to weather the storm that raged so often in the office.

In a flash of recognition, Maris's memory replayed part of her last conversation with Sabrina. " . . . Darci came in right after Avery and me . . ."

Since when had there been an "Avery and me"?

Of course Avery had been paying a bit of attention to Sabrina as of late, but Sabrina was an attractive woman. Lots of men in the office had tried to get her attention and failed. But what were Avery's intentions? Were they spending time together simply because they shared the same faith, or was this the beginning of an office romance?

The very phrase "office romance" made Maris shudder. Who needed that kind of drama? Whenever two people started dating right in front of their coworkers, it became an open invitation for everyone and their mama to put in their two cents' worth. The romance was doomed before it began, and when it ended, everyone had an opinion about *why.*

Of course, with Darci being Avery's ex-girlfriend, the situation became a high school chemistry project gone horribly wrong. The kind that turned purple, bubbled over, exploded, singed the teacher's toupee, and set off the school fire alarm.

Maris instantly understood the reason for the impending storm this morning. And she knew she had to warn Sabrina. Because she doubted the Bible could shield Sabrina or Avery from what Darci would do if she wasn't truly ready to call it quits with Avery.

"But, really, Sabrina, the two of you should know better."

Sabrina picked at her salad and eyed Maris's turkey-and-cheese sandwich. Why did she have to pick today to start a diet? And why was Maris sitting here giving her a speech about why she and Avery shouldn't even consider a relationship? For some reason,

Sabrina had mistakenly assumed that Maris would be happy. Instead, it was almost as though Maris had taken Darci's side.

"Come on . . ." Maris lowered her voice to a whisper and made a face. "An office romance?"

Sabrina sat up straighter, unwilling to let Maris ruin any more of her day. "It's not a romance. At least not yet."

"So you're not dating?"

Sabrina sighed deeply and pushed her fork through her salad. Maybe she and Avery weren't really dating, but she knew that Maris wouldn't understand. For someone who was such a good friend, Maris could get downright stubborn when it came to proving a point.

"We're not anything. That's the point. We've barely just started talking," Sabrina answered.

Maris stared at Sabrina for several moments, and Sabrina stared back, willing herself not to break eye contact first.

"Fine." Maris shrugged and returned her attention to her sandwich. "You're an adult. So you know the risks that come from dating someone from work. Especially when you have a boss like Darci."

"I'm aware of all of that," Sabrina said, hoping that Maris would just drop the matter.

Maris seemed satisfied with Sabrina's answer. "So let's change that subject. I interviewed an assistant for Darci today, and I think we'll hire her. She's in her early sixties, kind of motherly, easygoing . . ."

"You mean a pushover," Sabrina cut in. "Kind of like me?" She quirked an eyebrow.

"Actually, no. Maybe she gives that impression on the outside, but underneath, I think she's got some gumption. She's mature enough to do what she needs to in order to get along with Darci—without letting the woman run roughshod over her."

"She sounds like my dream come true. Now maybe I can actually get my real work done, since it seems we've hired a lady-in-waiting for Darci."

Maris laughed. "And, for the record, I never called you a pushover. But I do think you probably take that 'turning the other cheek' part of the Bible too literally. Maybe you could learn something from her."

Sabrina stood and lifted her tray from the table. "I'll admit that I've probably taken too much abuse from Darci, but I'm working on it. It's a delicate balance, especially since she is my boss."

"And it'll get even more delicate if you start dating her ex-boyfriend," Maris supplied.

Sabrina sighed deeply. "Thanks for telling me something I don't know."

Maris chuckled softly. "Oh, I know that you *know* this. I just hope you *understand.*"

"Well, I've got fifteen minutes of break left," said Sabrina. "Do you want to walk down to the jeweler's with me so I can do something about this ring?"

"Why not? I'm in no rush to get back to the dungeon. And besides, I want to stop by that new boutique and see what's on sale."

"Hey, this isn't a shopping spree. We have work to get back to. And I need to get this ring out of my possession before Eric calls me again."

"You should know by now that you can't take Maris to a mall and not let her at least do a little window shopping. But if you don't have time, we can split up."

"Never mind. I think we can do both if we walk fast. Besides, I wanted to check out that boutique, too. There's something intriguing about a store that has chairs for customers in the display window."

"No kidding," Maris agreed. "I just wonder how many real people get mistaken for mannequins."

"True. I heard they hired real models to pretend to be mannequins for the grand opening."

Ten minutes later, the ring no longer burning a hole in Sabrina's conscience, she and Maris got a chance to investigate the new boutique. Just looking at the price tags was enough to put Sabrina's checking account in jeopardy, so she opted just to look. Besides, she was now two thousand dollars richer after selling the ring back to the jeweler. Maybe it was time for a little post-engagement shopping spree.

Maris, on the other hand, found three dresses she wanted to try on, and promptly retreated into the depths of the fitting room.

While she waited, Sabrina took a seat in one of the posh armchairs in the front display window and did a little people watching. Most of the people in the mall at this time of day appeared to be housewives, pushing babies in strollers and constantly reaching for the hands of adventurous, wandering toddlers.

There also seemed to be a steady stream of college-aged men and women, lugging shopping bags that bore the brands of the latest "in" retailers. Then there was a smattering of folks in career attire, probably sneaking a little time away from the office, much like Sabrina and Maris.

Feeling a little bored, and somewhat self-conscious at the prospect of being on display for all the passersby to stare at, Sabrina selected a magazine from the nearby coffee table and flipped through the pages.

Looking at photo after photo of fashion models helped strengthen Sabrina's resolve to stay on her diet, but the prices for the ensembles also reminded her that should she ever be a perfect size four, she wouldn't have the money to buy high fashion.

Sabrina put the book aside and tried to ignore the smell of the warm chocolate and vanilla wafting over from the cookie shop across the hall.

Resting her chin in her hand, she did some thinking. *If I start a savings account now, maybe I can actually buy some cute clothes for summer. Skinny clothes, at that.*

She closed her eyes and could picture herself—new clothes, new figure, and cute shoes—walking on the streets of the Central West End, checking out a trendy art gallery. Avery would be there, too . . .

Avery? Sabrina opened her eyes. Who gave him an invitation to be in her daydream?

And who is that woman staring at me from the other side of the window? Better yet, why is Eric standing next to her?

Sabrina forced herself to keep her jaw from dropping while the woman rushed around the glass, Eric reluctantly following behind.

Laughing, the woman apologized for staring at Sabrina. "You were sitting so still, I couldn't tell if you were real or fake."

Sabrina found a small measure of comfort in the fact that the woman hadn't written her off as not svelte enough to be a mannequin. But even that quickly evaporated when Eric introduced her as his new girlfriend, Sharon.

"Oh." Sharon's lips formed a little o shape as her eyes grew wide. "So you're Sabrina. Eric still talks about you a lot."

Sabrina felt her upper lip bead with sweat. There were pills for headaches, for allergies, even pills for motion sickness. So why hadn't someone ever invented mortification pills?

Or at least a portable "melt" button. One could carry it around and push it when the only way to escape a tough situation would be to melt into a puddle on the floor. Like right now.

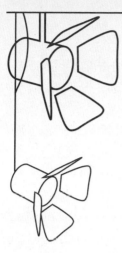

Chapter Five

Three hours later, Sabrina sat at her desk, trying to focus on her work. Unfortunately, the scene at the mall with Eric and his new girlfriend kept replaying in her memory.

Actually, the encounter hadn't lasted for more than a couple of minutes, but it had felt more like hours. Embarrassing, excruciating hours.

"Why couldn't I think of something clever and indifferent to say?" she mumbled. "I should have at least found some way to mention Avery. But, no . . . I had to stand there smiling and nodding and feeling tongue-tied. Why did I let him do that to me?"

Sabrina bit her lip, willing herself to remain quiet. Goodness knows, she didn't want the whole office knowing how she felt.

She closed her eyes and tried to remember some of the deep-breathing exercises one of the newest fitness gurus had demonstrated on Darci's show last week. After a couple of rounds of rhythmic inhalation and exhalation, the tension faded. But only a tiny bit.

An insistent burning worked its spindly fingers across the surface of her eyes. The sensation was all too familiar and even more humiliating. If she'd had more warning, she would have rushed to the ladies' room before anyone could notice and hidden in one of the stalls, dabbing her face with wet paper towels. But this time it was too late. The telltale streams were already rushing down her cheekbones.

Sabrina hunched over her desk, shielding her face with her hands, suppressing the urge to hiccup like a two-year-old and keeping her mouth open to silence the threat of audible sniffles. There was an art to crying silently.

As much as she hated to admit it, seeing Eric with Sharon had hurt. Deeply. And part of the reason was because he had replaced her first. Why was it so easy for men to move on and find someone new? Part of her had held out hope that Eric—quirky and idiosyncratic as he was—would come back. Knowing that he had no plans to do so made Sabrina feel like the thirty-something single woman's version of the last kid picked in dodgeball. Unwanted. Inept. And ugly.

Of course, feeling ugly didn't count in dodgeball, but in these circumstances, looks were a big part of the big picture. Sabrina couldn't help but wonder if Eric really found Sharon more attractive.

Maris, having been in the same position more than once before she'd gotten married, had given Sabrina the obligatory consolation speech on the ride back to the office.

Sabrina knew The Speech well, having given this same pep talk to many of her own girlfriends plenty of times. It consisted of phrases like "Of course you look better than she does," and "Didn't you notice that he couldn't keep his eyes off you?" and "I'll bet he's sorry now. You can see it in his eyes."

The Speech almost always alluded to the fact that Ms. New Girlfriend held a *striking* resemblance to the dumpee but couldn't really hold a candle to the original.

This part of the talk had never settled well with Sabrina, since it sometimes threw the dumpee into a tailspin of distress as she pondered whether she herself looked better than the woman the guy had dated before she met him. And so on and so forth. According to this reasoning, every man, no matter how old, was looking for a woman who reminded him of his first crush from kindergarten.

The one who gave The Speech never neglected to begin to vocalize several unflattering thoughts about Ms. New Girlfriend and then back away from them—taking care to leave the actual sentence unfinished, yet casting no shadow of doubt about what she could have said had she not chosen to take the high road.

All in all, notwithstanding the absurdity at the very core of The Speech, Maris had done her duty and done it well. But Sabrina had been unable to draw any solace from her friend's well-meaning words.

Instead, she had knowingly allowed a three-minute event to ruin her day. It seemed that by the time she got over one hurdle concerning the confrontation, another, larger obstacle appeared from nowhere, mocking her.

Sabrina's current impediment was her memory of the smug look on Sharon's face. *What has he told her about me? Did he make me out to be a total witch? What did that smirk mean?*

A surge of frustration welled up inside Sabrina until she felt she would burst.

"And why is it that he can replace me so quickly and not feel . . . anything?" she grumbled. Feeling defiant, she crumpled up a sheet of paper and tossed it toward the trash can.

Her missile went off course and ended up knocking a precariously stacked pile of neglected papers off the corner of her desk, to the floor.

Sabrina groaned aloud. "Wonderful." She quickly wiped

away remaining signs of any tears and bent down to retrieve the papers.

As she reshuffled the sheets into a new pile, she noticed Darci's memo about the resolutions program. Attached to the letter explaining how Darci wanted to feature an employee from the office on the show through the coming year was another blank sheet, on which Darci invited people to list their hopes and goals for the new year.

Sabrina rolled her eyes. Despite her earlier gung ho attitude about helping people make new habits in order to keep their resolutions, the idea seemed ludicrous.

"Besides, it was my idea," she grumbled. "I can't believe she's actually taking the credit for my suggestion."

Sabrina glanced at the paper again. "And it was a good idea. Why did I just sit there and say nothing while she pretended she was the mastermind behind this?"

Sabrina's cell phone rang, interrupting her thoughts. She glanced at the caller ID display and was surprised and irked to find that Eric was trying to reach her. Opting not to answer it, Sabrina turned off the phone, silencing the nonstop digital tune. Besides, Darci really frowned on anyone taking personal calls at work.

Almost as if on cue, Darci's new secretary, Sunny—what an oxymoron for anyone working under Queen Darci—poked her head inside Sabrina's cubicle.

"Sorry for interrupting you, Ms. Bradley, but Ms. Oliver wants to know when you'll have her interview notes done for tomorrow's taping."

Sabrina tried to remain calm. This was a new thrill of Darci's. Instead of researching the questions she should ask her guests, Darci had taken to asking Sabrina to take over this pesky little detail. Quite honestly, the work fascinated Sabrina. But it also took a good deal of extra time—time she didn't really have.

"Could you tell Darci that I'm running a bit behind with those? But I should have them done in an hour."

"Will do. I'll be back in an hour and a half." Sunny gave Sabrina a wink and a grin, then exited the cubicle.

Sabrina shook her head. Sunny was obviously excited to be working here. Apparently, she hadn't yet seen one of Darci's tantrums. The poor thing still had a spring in her step.

Sabrina would take pains to be extra nice to her, to sort of balance out the woman's exposure to Darci.

The thought was both laughable and sobering. Was it possible that Sabrina worked under the meanest boss in the universe?

"I need a promotion," she blurted. "Or maybe a new job altogether." Sabrina covered her mouth with her hands, hoping that no one had overheard. It wouldn't do for folks to know that she was dissatisfied; otherwise, sharks would begin fighting to best her at the responsibilities she did have—and, in the process, take her job.

But her feelings on the matter were firm. She did need a promotion. Within the year. Or else.

"Or else what?" she murmured.

She already knew the answer. *Or else I'll quit. Move on. Start over. Get a change of scenery.*

Sabrina found Darci's resolution paper and wrote on the first line: *Get a promotion at work.*

I can't even believe I'm doing this. But even if resolutions were impossible to keep, she'd heard that it never hurt to write down specific goals. In fact, keeping a written log of what you wanted to accomplish was supposed to help you achieve them faster—as opposed to never.

And Lord knows I could use some improvement. Sabrina nibbled the corner of her pinkie fingernail and tried to decide what else she should list. After a few moments, she decided that it wouldn't hurt to get more involved in church. It would give her an opportunity to grow personally and develop new friendships.

Opening a savings account would give her the chance to save money for new clothes. Skinny clothes. Clothes from the new boutique. Sabrina scrawled, *Open a savings account.* As an afterthought, she went back and added, *And keep it open.* She'd had savings accounts in the past but always ended up raiding her stash for frivolous spending. But not this time. She'd save religiously and have something to show for it by the end of next year.

With a sigh, she added *Cut down on coffee* to the list. That went without saying. Except that she'd been saying she wanted to quit for a long time without actually doing much. But writing it down would help her to remember it.

After a few more minutes of deliberation, Sabrina decided that getting a hobby—and sticking with it—would be another goal. She'd tried in the past: tennis, sewing, writing bad poetry, painting—you name it, she'd tried it. But honestly, she needed something to help her unwind after work, and a hobby would fit the bill nicely. Only this time, she'd find something she really loved doing, so it wouldn't seem like a chore.

Sabrina perused her list and felt a surge of accomplishment. Of course, it only consisted of five items, but five was better than none.

She was about to put the list in her purse when she caught a glimpse of her raggedy fingernails. She needed a manicure. Only it would be hard to manicure nails that weren't even there. With a sigh, she added *Stop biting nails* to the sheet. Might as well be honest.

She'd always had a problem with biting her nails, but in recent weeks the problem had gotten worse—"recent" meaning "post-Eric" and "post–engagement ring." Maybe she had kept her nails in better shape because she wanted her hands to be a nice-looking showcase for the ring.

And while she was being honest with herself, Sabrina added losing that extra ten pounds to the list. Regardless of how much money she saved, she wouldn't be able to get into the boutique sizes until she buckled down and started eating more healthily.

Maybe the next time she saw Eric, he would be the one feeling sad.

With a groan, Sabrina shook her head. She needed to get over Eric and get over him now. For that matter, this whole relationship thing was beginning to wear on her nerves. Twice in love and twice dumped by the object of her affections was not a good track record. Maybe she was addicted to falling in love. And if so, she would be doomed to the same cycle of finding love and losing it . . . over and over and over . . .

With a flourish, Sabrina added one final item to her list: DO NOT FALL IN LOVE!

Maybe in a couple of years she could reconsider. But for now she had to devote herself to becoming a church-involved, savings-account-having, no-coffee-drinking, hobby-loving, slimmed-down sister with a perfect manicure and a great promotion.

Between accomplishing all that and managing her ever-expanding list of duties at work, Sabrina didn't even have time for love.

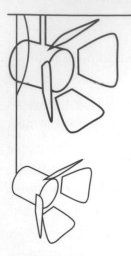

Chapter Six

Sabrina awoke early the next morning in order to get in a half hour on the treadmill.

While she walked, Sabrina reflected on her list of resolutions. Already she was feeling motivated. She hadn't had any coffee since yesterday morning. Last night's dinner had been spinach salad and baked chicken. And tonight she planned to give some thought to choosing a hobby. The rest would come later, because she didn't want to get burned out trying to do it all at once.

But to make sure she stayed on track, Sabrina decided she would keep the list on her refrigerator.

A few moments later, she changed her mind. The refrigerator was too . . . public. Too many eyes could see it there. She didn't mind her friends knowing that she was making changes, but she didn't exactly want them to think she was desperate. And she didn't want anyone to think she was participating in Darci's resolutions program.

Sabrina's list was about making lifestyle changes in order to live a more fulfilling life, whereas Darci's plan was about proving the critics wrong and making herself look good.

Besides, what if a delivery person or a repairman had to come in her kitchen? She certainly didn't want them knowing all her business.

Instead, she would put the list on the wall in her walk-in closet. The only person who would ever venture in there would be Maris, and Sabrina didn't care if Maris saw it.

After half an hour of walking, Sabrina stepped off the treadmill, feeling triumphant. She located her briefcase so she could find the sheet of paper and pin it to the wall before the exercise-induced endorphins wore off.

Five minutes into the search, Sabrina felt herself battling a case of grouchiness. Where was that paper? Why couldn't she find it now, while she was feeling excited about it?

Maybe it was in her purse. But after rummaging through her purse and the oversized carryall she used to hold the overflow that wouldn't fit into her purse, the paper still remained unfound.

Sabrina sat cross-legged on her bed, mentally retracing her steps at the office. Her cubicle wasn't that big, so the paper couldn't have gotten far.

She closed her eyes and concentrated. After finishing the list, she'd focused on finishing Darci's interview questions. Then what?

Let's see . . . I set the list on the corner of the desk . . . finished sorting through that pile of papers I knocked over . . . made sure Darci's interview questions were in order . . . Maris called and asked me to come to her office and look over some notes from the afternoon meeting . . . and since Sunny hadn't come to my office for the notes, I dropped them off at Darci's office on my way to see Maris . . . Maris and I sat at her desk and made adjustments to the taping schedule for next week . . . and then I went back to my office . . .

Sabrina trailed off as a niggling sense of foreboding settled in the pit of her stomach. She should have left Maris's office, gone back to her cubicle, put the list in her purse or briefcase, and then gone home.

She could retrace her footsteps up to the point she left the office. But no matter how much she tried, she couldn't remember putting that list in her purse. To make matters worse, she didn't even remember seeing the list on the corner of the desk, where it should have been. That corner was clear. In fact, the only papers she remembered seeing were the miscellaneous sheets from that massive stack she had sorted through earlier in the day.

And since the list wasn't in her purse, briefcase, or carryall, that meant one of three things: (1) The paper was in the leftover stack. (2) Someone had swiped it from her cubicle while she was meeting with Maris. (3) Sabrina had hand-delivered her innermost hopes and aspirations to the dragon lady herself.

Option 1 was the most appealing but, in Sabrina's opinion, pretty unlikely. And while option 2 would be embarrassing, option 3 was a nightmare come true. And she was pretty certain that the list had met with option 3.

Sabrina's endorphins shriveled up and fizzled away like a helium balloon that had been poked with a straight pin.

If Maris were here, she'd tell Sabrina not to get worked up over something she wasn't sure had happened. Then she'd say, "Imagine the worst and try to find the bright side."

The bright side. Ha! No way would there be a bright side. Sabrina's stomach turned over, and she woldered if she might lose her healthy bran-muffin-and-green-tea breakfast.

As Sabrina hurried to the bathroom, she decided she had indeed found the bright side.

She had lost her appetite. Had anyone ever lost ten pounds from sheer humiliation?

Darci paced the length of her office, reading the paper again and again. She could hardly contain her curiosity. Had Sabrina meant for her to see this list?

Of course she had hand-delivered it to her office. But it had been mixed in with the interview notes. Darci surmised that it meant one of two things: (1) Sabrina really wanted to be chosen for the resolutions program and had decided to better her chances of getting picked by giving her list directly to Darci rather than putting it in the collection box designated for the applications. (2) Sabrina had written the list, never intended for Darci to see it, but *accidentally* mixed it in with the interview notes.

Given Sabrina's personality, option 1 was an obvious departure from the norm. At least, Sabrina's norm.

Option 2 was definitely more delicious. Darci couldn't believe her luck. To think of all the time she had wasted being jealous of the way Avery was starting to look at Sabrina. The solution had literally fallen right into her hands.

She pushed the intercom button to speak to her secretary. "Sunny, when Sabrina Bradley gets in, would you ask her to come to my office?"

"Certainly, Ms. Oliver. Is there anything else I can do for you?"

Darci smiled. Her life was getting better by the moment. Not only had she finally found a way to bring Sabrina down a notch, but this new secretary was working out perfectly. She did as she was told, quickly and without complaints—even when Darci knew she was being a teensy bit unreasonable.

Darci pushed the intercom button once again. "Thanks, Sunny, but nothing else for the moment. And please, call me Darci."

"Will do, Darci."

Avery kept his office blinds open so he could see when Sabrina arrived. She had to pass his office on her route from the elevator to her cubicle, so there was no way he would miss her.

He had wanted to ask her to dinner yesterday, but he'd spent most of the morning wrestling with his own nervousness. By the time he saw Sabrina, she had just returned from her lunch break and she seemed a bit preoccupied.

To make matters more difficult, Darci had cloistered herself in her office until late that evening, and Avery had braced for one of her tantrums all day. Fortunately, the tantrum never materialized. In fact, she had emerged from her office late last night just before he went home, and she seemed quite calm and sedate.

In fact, it was quite unsettling. Her good mood had carried over to this morning, and Avery couldn't shake the mental image of Darci as a lioness on the prowl. Despite her claims that she thought her new secretary was more capable than anyone else in the entire office, Avery was certain Darci was up to something else—he just had to figure out what.

Sabrina stepped off the elevator at five minutes to seven, and Avery jumped out of his chair to meet her in the hallway.

"Sabrina, hi."

She stopped and blinked, as if she hadn't seen him. "Hi." She gave him a smile that seemed a little forced, but Avery decided to forge ahead with small talk nonetheless. The only problem was, his mind had gone completely blank.

What should I say next? he wondered. Now that he had her full attention, why couldn't he come up with something really clever and charming?

But he didn't have her full attention. She was actually gazing in the direction of Darci's office. After a few moments, he cleared his throat, and Sabrina shook her head and looked him in the eye. "I'm really sorry, Avery, but I must have zoned out. Do you mind. . . . repeating . . . what you just said?"

Avery felt his neck and face grow warm. He hadn't said anything before, so what was he supposed to say now? He shook his head and cleared his throat again. "Actually, I didn't . . . ah, I was clearing my throat."

Sabrina leaned closer, looking concerned. "Oh, do you have a cold?"

Avery cleared his throat again and shrugged. "I'm not really sure . . . maybe I'm coming down with something." *I think it's an acute case of too-nervous-too-ask-for-a-date-itis,* he added silently.

And in all honesty, he had been fighting some congestion and a slight sore throat the past couple of days. And at the moment, the room seemed about fifty degrees too hot. So maybe a fever had clouded his ability to think normally.

Sabrina nodded. "Yeah, there does seem to be a bug going around. You should get some rest and take your vitamins."

"Right. I'll do that." He noted that Sabrina's attention was focused on Darci's office again.

If he hurried, there was still just enough time to ask her out before she got bored and headed to her cubicle. Avery took a deep breath and summoned every ounce of courage in his body. "There was one thing I wanted to ask—"

"Oh, there you are, Ms. Bradley." Sunny Harris came running over. "Ms. Oliver wants to see you in her office as soon as possible. She said she has something very important to discuss." That said, Sunny retreated as quickly as she had appeared.

Avery watched as Sabrina grew three shades paler. For a moment, he wondered if she might faint. He gently took hold of her shoulder in case she needed steadying.

"Are you okay?" he asked, moving a bit closer to her and extending his arm to wrap around her shoulders.

For a few seconds, she seemed to lean into him for support, but then she recoiled and pulled away. "I'm fine. I just—I have a lot to get done today. Please, if you'll excuse me . . ." Without a look back, she turned and fled down the hallway toward her cubicle.

Avery was left alone in front of his office, feeling much like he had when he realized that Veronica Mills had stood him up for the prom.

He turned and faced Darci's office, wondering what in the world had just happened. He fully expected to see Darci standing in front of her windows, giving him one of her disapproving looks.

Instead, he found Sunny staring at him. Avery drew himself up to his full height and met her gaze. There was no reason for him to feel as flustered as he now felt. He was the boss around here, not Darci, not Sunny, and not even Sabrina, who apparently wanted nothing to do with him.

Sunny didn't flinch but instead winked and stepped inside Darci's office.

Great. No wonder Darci loved the woman so much. She had found her own private secret agent in the form of a secretary. Someone to be her eyes and ears to hear and see what no one would do or say in close proximity to Darci.

He'd have to watch himself around this Sunny. There was no telling what kind of spin she would put on the truth.

Sabrina didn't stop moving until she reached the ladies' room. She gave the room a quick once-over to make sure that no one else was around, then locked herself in the biggest stall.

What was she going to do? There was no mistaking the fact that Darci had the list. Why else would she call for a sudden, private meeting this early in the morning?

Sabrina stood in the stall for a few minutes, trying to decide what to do. She could fake illness and duck out before Darci saw her. Since a bug was going around, it would be perfectly feasible that Sabrina had taken ill and had to go home.

This train of thought brought back the memory of the encounter she'd just had with Avery. What was wrong with him this morning?

Granted, he did say he wasn't feeling well, but was it absolutely necessary for him to stop her in view of the entire floor and Darci just to ask . . . ? Sabrina remembered that he hadn't gotten the chance to ask her anything. Sunny had interrupted, and Sabrina took off before he could say anything else. Well, technically, she hadn't run away until after she'd felt a little woozy and Avery reached out to help her keep her balance.

Great. Now he probably thinks I'm some kind of frail thing who goes around swooning and fainting like women did in the Victorian age.

And anyone else who was looking probably thought I was brazenly flirting with the man.

"But I wasn't," Sabrina said, even though no one could hear her. In fact, she was anti-flirting for the time being. Flirting led to dating, dating led to love, and love led to getting dumped. She was not allowing herself to fall in love right now. Not for at least a year.

If Maris were here, she would help Sabrina figure out a plan to escape Darci. But no, today had to be the one day Maris had taken off in two months. Sabrina could not call this early in the morning and wake up Maris with a problem of this proportion.

Sabrina covered her face with her hands. With the exception of actually inspiring her to do a workout this morning, the list had done nothing but create trouble for her. Maybe she should just toss the thing.

That is, when she actually gained possession of it. Which brought her back to the meeting with Darci. She didn't feel comfortable with telling a lie and hiding out at home—although she was beginning to feel rather ill.

But God hasn't given me a spirit of fear. One of her favorite scriptures came rushing to her memory. God didn't want her to feel afraid; instead, He'd given her a spirit of power, love, and a sound mind.

But right now I don't feel power or love, Lord. This is way too much for me to handle. Sabrina closed her eyes and prayed silently, asking the Lord to take away the fear and help her to handle the situation in a way that would be pleasing to Jesus.

When she finished the prayer, she still felt a little shaky. But she knew that her prayer had been heard. And now she had to exercise her faith and believe that God would take care of the rest of the jitters she still felt. And hiding in the ladies' room all day would not be an exercise in faith.

Taking a deep breath, she unlocked the door, gathered her purse and coat, and stepped out of the stall. It was time for the meeting.

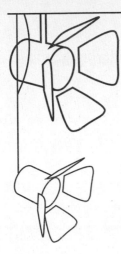

Chapter Seven

Won't you sit down?" Darci gestured to the empty chair on the opposite side of the desk.

Sabrina did as she was told, crossed her hands in her lap, and tried her best to appear both pleasant and bold.

"Could I have Sunny bring you something—coffee, tea, Danish?"

Sabrina shook her head. "No, thanks."

Darci chuckled and opened a file folder on her desk. "That's right. I forgot that you were cutting out coffee . . . and the Danish would not help you in your quest to lose those ten pounds." The smile vanished from Darci's face as she locked gazes with Sabrina.

Now there was no question concerning the whereabouts of the list. Sabrina unfolded, then folded her hands, wishing she knew how to end the uncomfortable silence. *Should I simply ask for her to return it to me?*

"I assume you already know that I have your list of resolutions," said Darci.

All Sabrina could do was nod.

"At first, it struck me as rather odd that you would have even turned in one of these sheets." Darci shrugged. "I realize that I asked everyone in the office to fill out an application—even Avery has one—but I didn't really expect anyone on the production team to be interested. I figured you all would be too busy actually working on the shows.

"So then I put two and two together and came to the conclusion that this was your own personal list and you hadn't really meant for me to get it. But I did. Call it fate if you wish—since I know you seem to lean to the religious side."

Darci put up her hands as in surrender. "Now, I know you probably would like nothing more than for me to just give this back to you and pretend that it never happened. I have a better idea."

Darci paused for several moments, and Sabrina simply waited. As the seconds ticked by, Sabrina mentally recited, *God has not given me a spirit of fear,* over and over again.

"You see, Sabrina, I think we can help each other." Darci arched her eyebrows. "I need the critics to realize that I do make a lasting impact on people's lives. You, on the other hand, need . . . several things. I see you want to manage your money better, stop biting your nails, stop drinking coffee, lose ten pounds . . . and stay away from love.

"Now, if you'll agree to be on my panel of ordinary people, I can provide professional support to help you reach these goals. What do you think?"

Sabrina hesitated. Was this the worst Darci could dream up? It was almost laughable. Of course there was no way she wanted to participate in this panel—no matter how many coaches Darci could produce—but she had to break the news gently. "Thanks for the offer, but I think I can handle this on my own. I appreciate your willingness to help and everything, but I'll have to pass on this opport—"

"It also says right here that you want a promotion at work." Darci dangled the paper in the air. "Sabrina, I never said that your participating on the panel would come without adequate compensation.

"Now, I happen to be able to get you this promotion you've been dreaming about. So it seems that each of us has something the other one wants." Darci paused and stared Sabrina in the eye.

"Now, I think life would be a lot more pleasant for both of us if we just made a little trade. Don't you think?"

Sabrina opened her mouth to refuse but then thought better of it. Given that Darci was the mastermind behind this plan, getting out of it probably wasn't as simple as it sounded.

Sabrina decided to probe for more details. "I'm not sure I understand exactly what you're offering me."

Darci sighed and looked at Sabrina as though Sabrina were five years old. "What I'm saying, Sabrina, is this: You sign on as part of my panel of ordinary people trying to keep your resolutions. In return for your participation, I will give you a raise and promotion at the end of the year." Darci did one of her talk show host dramatic pauses, then continued.

"Instead of being Sabrina the errand girl, you'll have the title of co-assistant producer. You and Maris will equally share assistant producer responsibilities."

"Does Maris know about this?"

Darci shook her head. "No. And she won't find out until everyone else does—the day you get promoted. This deal is strictly confidential—between you and me only."

"But I'm not sure I understand. If Maris and I share the assistant producer job, won't that mean less work and possibly a cut in pay for her?"

"Not necessarily." Darci leaned closer and lowered her voice. "Honestly, Avery is feeling a little burned out from his duties as producer. He does way too much work anyway, but he's a hands-on kind of guy.

"He wants to cut back, but he's too much of a perfectionist to delegate his duties to anyone else. For his own health and well-being, I've decided to start giving some of his work to Maris. I'll have you work more closely with Maris over the coming year, and then you'll be able to learn how to do what she's currently doing. By the time it's over, Avery will have less work, and you and Maris will be running the production team. Avery will still have the final say, of course, but he'll be the producer almost in name only."

A flurry of butterflies took flight in Sabrina's stomach. There always had to be a catch. "But getting a promotion is on my list of resolutions. Won't the audience find that a little contrived?"

Darci shrugged, looking impatient. "Who cares? If everything goes as planned, it'll look perfectly natural and be a seamless transition. The audience will just be happy for you. And they'll feel encouraged—in an 'If she can do it, I can, too' kind of way."

Sabrina sat thinking. In all honesty, it didn't sound that horrible. So what if the entire country knew she bit her nails and needed to lose ten pounds? And if Darci thought people wanted to watch her find a hobby and balance her checkbook, Sabrina could deal with that.

The only part that made her feel truly uncomfortable was the last resolution on the list: *Don't fall in love.* The entire country did not need to know that. But if Darci was in a bargaining mood, then perhaps it would be possible to scratch that one from the list.

Darci cut into her thoughts. "You understand, of course, that I will need extreme commitment from you. I expect you to actually keep your resolutions."

"And if I don't?"

"The deal is off."

Sabrina sighed. Another catch.

Darci spoke before Sabrina could voice her reservations about such a deal. "Come on, Sabrina. It's not like you resolved to climb Mount Everest or learn a new language. These are simple resolutions. I know you can do it. In fact, I'll throw in a ten-thousand-dollar bonus for you."

Sabrina had been ready to walk out of the office until Darci mentioned the bonus. She could do a lot with ten thousand dollars. "So is everyone from the employee panel getting this kind of monetary deal?"

"No, just you."

"Why me?"

"Because I trust you. This whole thing was your idea in the first place, really. And you know how much I need to prove to the critics that I can help change people's lives. I know you have the strength and willpower to carry out these resolutions, so you'll make me look good."

"What if I want to change one of my resolutions?"

Darci's gaze narrowed. "Which one?"

"The last one?"

Darci consulted the list, although Sabrina had a feeling Darci had the thing memorized. "Hmmm . . . 'Don't fall in love.'" Darci put the paper on the desk and stared at Sabrina. "I don't think so. In fact, that's one of the best ones. It'll add an extra zing to things. No one will be able to resist wondering why a person wouldn't want to fall in love. And people will keep tuning in to see if you can live up to it. It's your best resolution, and I can't afford to throw it out. It's a sure-fire ratings boost. Better than any reality show out there."

"So what happens, if, hypothetically, I *did* fall in love?"

"If you fall in love or break any of the resolutions, you can kiss the ten grand good-bye."

"And our promotion deal?"

"I never heard of it."

"What if I say no to the whole deal right now?"

Darci put her forefinger to her chin and looked off into the distance. "There are a couple of really bright interns in the department this year . . . I think both of them could be good candidates for promotion. It would only take Maris a year or so to fully train them to be independent in their jobs."

"I see." Sabrina could read between the lines. If she said no to this whole thing, her job was in jeopardy. If she said yes and messed up, then her job was *still* in jeopardy—and no ten grand.

And since the agreement was a secret, Darci held all the cards. If Sabrina ever tried to publicize this deal, then Darci would deny, deny, deny. Great. Just great.

Darci tilted her head to the side and stared at Sabrina for a moment.

"So, what do you think? In my opinion, it's a win-win situation for both of us." She shrugged. "I mean, it *will* be if you say yes."

Sabrina gazed at the floor and silently sorted through her feelings.

What am I supposed to do? No matter how much I dislike Darci, I really can't afford to lose my job right now. And what would it really hurt to humor her and keep my resolutions? She's right. It seems like a win-win situation. I get ten thousand dollars and a promotion . . . and she gets seen in a positive light by her viewing audience and the critics.

Sabrina looked at Darci. "Okay."

"Okay?" Darci arched an eyebrow. "Okay, what?"

"Okay, I'll do it."

Darci grinned. Sabrina tried to remember if she had ever seen the woman look this pleasant—aside from the time she spent in front of cameras, hosting the show. "Sabrina, I can assure you that you've made the right choice." She stretched out her hand. "Let's shake on it."

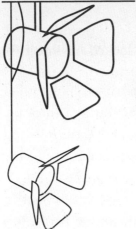

Chapter Eight

No way. Go back and tell her right now that you've changed your mind." Maris shook her head and tried once again to make Sabrina reconsider.

"I can't. I already told her I would do it. And besides, it sounds like fun."

Maris lowered her voice in case someone nearby might overhear. "Look, Sabrina, this is not the kind of thing I'd expect you to do. You don't even make New Year's resolutions. So why in the world would you just jump up and volunteer to be a guinea pig for *The Daily Dose*? I mean, two days ago, you told me that you felt sorry for the people who had to be a part of this program."

Sabrina merely shrugged. "I guess I changed my mind."

Maris sighed deeply. There had to be something Sabrina was holding back. "Come on, girl. Tell me what's going on. What's the *real* reason you're doing this?"

Sabrina looked at the floor, and Maris relaxed. She had finally gotten to the bottom of this. All she had to do was wait for Sabrina to open up.

Several moments ticked by, and still Sabrina said nothing.

"Sabrina? Please tell me what's going on. Maybe I can talk to Darci and help you get out of it."

Sabrina looked up from the floor, a determined look on her face. "I know I said it sounded silly at first, but . . . there are some things I'd like to change in my life. The way I see it, being a part of the program will help add some accountability to my life. That way, I know I'll get everything accomplished."

"I don't believe you." As soon as the words left her mouth, Maris wanted to take them back. She was being too harsh, but she had to put her foot down sometime. There was no way she was going to sit back and watch Sabrina march right into Darci's hands like this.

Sabrina stood, and Maris could see the hurt in her friend's eyes. "If you don't believe me, that's fine. But I really have changed my mind. I was hoping you'd be a little more supportive, but if you can't, that's fine."

"Sabrina, I didn't mean to be . . ."

"Unfair," Sabrina supplied. "Or did you mean to say 'controlling'? All of this time, I thought you were on my side, but it looks like you only approve of what I do if it's something you think I should do."

"That's not true and you know it."

"Then what *is* the truth?"

Maris stood so she could be eye to eye with Sabrina. "I think this is one of your scatterbrained schemes to tell people about Jesus."

Sabrina looked confused. "What are you talking about?"

"Don't play silly with me. You're my friend and I think you have a good head on your shoulders, but sometimes you get a little . . ." Maris paused, searching for the right words. "You lose sight of what really matters because you're trying so hard to prove to people that they need religion. Face it, Sabrina. We don't all need to go to church every Sunday. We don't need to read the Bible every single day."

"We all have sinned and fallen short of the glory of God."

Maris inhaled deeply and counted to ten before she spoke. "See, that's what I mean. You're a lot of fun, and you could be even more fun if you didn't have to go around quoting Bible verses and making people feel like they're something less than special if they don't share your beliefs."

Sabrina stepped back. "Is that what you really think? Are you saying that I come here every day with the intent to make you feel like less of a person because you don't share my beliefs?"

Maris stopped to consider. "I don't know. Maybe it's not intentional on your part, but I'm beginning to wonder. You never give up. Frankly, I'm getting tired of you waving your Bible in my face every day. I'm a nice, decent person and I treat people the way I want to be treated. I think that makes me just as good as you are."

"Fine." Sabrina put her hands up in a surrendering gesture. "I won't 'wave the Bible' in your face again. But the Bible is a part of who I am, so this may just mean that you and I won't be able to talk to each other about anything that isn't work-related."

Maris shook her head. This was getting out of hand. All she had wanted to do was find out the real reason Sabrina decided to be on the show. Now things had gotten to the point that her friendship with Sabrina was in real danger.

"That's not what I want, and I don't think you want that, either. All I'm trying to say is . . . if you get on *The Daily Dose* spouting all of the same platitudes you give me every day, Darci will freak out. You'll make yourself look ridiculous on national television and you might even lose your job."

Sabrina smiled a tight smile. "I can assure you that televangelism is *not* my purpose for going on the show. So you can put your worries aside."

Maris didn't like the tinge of sarcasm that laced Sabrina's voice, but she decided not to push the matter further. "That's good. I hope you're telling the truth."

Sabrina sighed. "You know what? I'm getting really tired of working in a place where it seems like my job is always in jeopardy. I'm actually pretty confused, because I don't think this is what God wants for me." Without waiting for a reply, Sabrina left the room.

Maris watched her friend leave. There was no point in saying anything more to Sabrina right now. But she wished the girl would learn to stop trying to equate everything with God. If there was a God, Maris doubted He would really care about every facet of every person's life.

Sabrina prayed for the strangest things—like a good parking space at the grocery store or a good deal on a new washing machine. If God existed, Maris had a feeling He couldn't be bothered with such trivial requests from people all over the world, every day.

Regardless of the God issue, there was something fishy about Sabrina's decision. Maris intended to get to the bottom of it, one way or another.

"Are you busy?"

Avery glanced up from his paperwork and found Darci standing in his doorway. Her voice had thrown him for a loop. Normally, she barked out orders in sharp tones, but on occasion she did choose to speak in a soft, soothing manner.

Even so, as he put his papers aside and waved Darci into his office, Avery couldn't help but wish Sabrina had been the one at his door. Thinking of Sabrina, Avery made a mental note to check in on her later this afternoon to see how she was doing. He remembered she hadn't looked too well after their brief talk this morning.

Darci didn't waste any time. She sat right down and clasped her hands together in her lap. It was the Darci gesture for "I have news to tell."

Avery decided to get the ball rolling. "What's going on?"

"I've been looking through the employee applications for the resolutions program, and I think I've made my decision."

Avery shrugged. "That's great. Why don't you give me more detail when we have the next production meeting with Sabrina and Maris and Vincent?"

Darci looked crestfallen. "Oh, I guess I could do that. I just thought . . . hoped . . . that maybe . . ." She trailed off.

Avery didn't know what to do. Darci knew he wanted to cut back on his workload, so why was she bringing him something so trivial? Surely she knew that he trusted her to make simple decisions such as this. She'd been making choices like this for years, and he'd never really had an issue with what she wanted to do.

After all, she was bound to have her finger on the pulse of what was important, since she was the host of the show. His work was more behind the scenes.

When he didn't say anything more, Darci stood up. "Never mind. I guess I got a little excited and wanted to share with someone. Sorry."

Avery felt guilty. Darci was an innovative woman, and he didn't want to stifle her creativity. Besides, the resolutions program was unknown territory. He waved her back inside the office. "You know what? I would like to hear who you've picked.

But not here." Avery leaned back in his chair and stretched. He had been sitting at the desk all day and needed a change of scenery. "Have you had lunch yet?"

Darci nodded. "But if you want to get a bite to eat, I'll just tag along."

"Great." Avery grabbed his jacket and followed Darci out of his office. After telling his secretary to forward any calls to his cell phone, he headed down the hallway, where Darci was waiting for the elevator. "Where do you suggest we go?" he asked. "I'm in the mood for soup and a sandwich."

"I'm in the mood for a bagel, peace and quiet, and no autographs," Darci said flatly.

Avery well understood Darci's need for privacy, but it usually complicated simple matters such as finding a place to eat lunch. She was a nationally recognized figure, and while people were used to seeing her around town, there were always a few people who couldn't resist asking for autographs.

And if, by chance, people had the good sense not to interrupt a meal, they generally stared, which was almost worse. At least an autograph was quick. Staring was usually quite protracted.

Avery glanced at his watch. It was nearly two in the afternoon, so the lunch rush in most places would have abated by now. He suggested to Darci they head to a local bakery chain store and find a table in a corner.

"I guess I'll have to make do with that," she said. "If only this elevator door would open, we could be on our way."

As soon as she finished her sentence, the bell rang, indicating that the elevator was about to reach their floor. Moments later, the door opened and they stepped inside. Before the door closed, a woman shouted, "Hold the door, please!"

Avery quickly pushed the door back open and ignored the sour look on Darci's face. She had never liked being in elevators with other people—she claimed it hampered her ability to have a private conversation with anyone. Avery felt it didn't matter. The ride only lasted a few seconds, so anything pressing could surely be put on hold for such a short period of time.

Darci would have pretended not to hear, but Avery couldn't do that in good conscience. Especially since the elevators seemed to be running so slowly today. Who knew how long the poor woman would have had to wait for the next car to reach their floor?

Seconds later, a slightly breathless Sabrina stepped inside. Her eyes widened for a brief moment, and she took a step back. "Oh," she said. She grabbed the door just before it shut. "I'll just take the next one. I don't want to . . . interrupt."

Avery shook his head. Actually, he was glad to see her. She looked only slightly better than she had that morning, and he wondered if she was coming down with something. "No, it's fine. We're not discussing anything earth-shattering. Darci's telling me about the latest developments in the resolutions program."

For the second time that day, Avery watched Sabrina grow pale. She pushed the door fully open and stepped back into the hallway.

"Wait, where are you going?" he asked.

Sabrina didn't answer him directly but hurried away, mumbling something about having left some papers in her office.

"That was odd," he said, thinking out loud.

Darci didn't answer. There was an unreadable expression in her eyes, but before he had the chance to analyze what it might be, she shifted away from him and became engrossed in looking at the buttons that indicated the floor numbers.

Avery remembered his suspicions about Darci from the previous day, when she had buried herself in her office. She was up to something, but what?

Sabrina got off the elevator and kept walking straight to her office cubicle. Once there, she put on her coat, grabbed her purse, and headed right back to the elevator. It was just two thirty, but she felt as if she'd been at work for forty hours straight. Her head hurt, her stomach felt queasy, and she had been on the verge of tears since her argument with Maris.

I can't take this right now. I'm going home.

Once she was in her car and headed back to her house, she left a voice mail message telling Maris that she felt sick and had left for the day.

Avery prayed over his meal, then waited for Darci to tell him her news about the program.

"I've picked my two employees for the panel of ordinary people."

Avery wanted to ask, "Is that it?" but he thought better of it. Obviously, Darci figured this was important enough to call an impromptu meeting, so he decided to exercise patience and go the distance with her.

He smiled. "Apparently, this decision is pretty important, so I'm all ears—so long as you don't try to make me a member of the panel."

She laughed. "No, that's not it. I'm just really excited. I want to make sure I have your approval."

Avery nodded and waited for her to continue.

"Okay. The first person I picked is George Blake, in the advertising department. He wants to do the usual resolutions-type things: go to the gym more often, spend more quality time with his family, take a vacation, read more books—stuff like that.

"I picked him because he's a guy, so hopefully, male viewers will be able to identify with him. And women watching him can help their husbands or boyfriends stay focused on their goals."

"Sounds good," said Avery. "Who else did you pick?"

Darci hesitated before speaking. "Well, this one is probably going to surprise you—it surprised me at first. But I picked Sabrina."

Avery put down his sandwich. "Sabrina? She said she doesn't even *make* resolutions."

Darci frowned. "She said that?"

"At one of our production meetings when we first started working on the resolutions series."

Darci shrugged. "Maybe she changed her mind."

Avery pressed for more details. "This really doesn't seem like her. How did you get her to do it?"

Darci blinked, a blank look on her face.

Aha! Avery thought. *Now I'm getting to the bottom of Darci's strange behavior.* "Did you ask her to do this, or did she actually volunteer for it?"

Darci shook her head. "I didn't . . . she wanted to. She filled out one of the applications and personally delivered it to my office."

"Sabrina?"

"Yes, Sabrina," she snapped. "Why do you keep asking the same questions over and over again. It almost feels like you don't believe me."

Avery studied Darci's face. She was clearly agitated. Her frown lines were working overtime, and the lines of her jaw had hardened. Her brown eyes flashed with indignation. Avery briefly remembered the days when he had found Darci's flashing eyes attractive. Now those same sparks caused him to brace himself for an argument.

He chose his words carefully and spoke slowly. "I never said that I don't believe you. I was basically thinking out loud that Sabrina doesn't seem like the type to want to be in the spotlight."

"Well, maybe you have the wrong opinion of her. Besides, Avery, all women crave attention—even if only a little. They dream about being in the spotlight and having the money that goes along with it. Unfortunately, not everyone can have that luxury. But I see that desire in Sabrina, so I'm doing my best to help give her fifteen minutes of fame."

Avery greatly doubted the authenticity of Darci's little speech—especially the part about Sabrina wanting fame and fortune—but he decided not to make an issue of it. At least, not right now. He knew when to pick his battles.

"So you picked Sabrina. Good for you and for her. Is there anything else?"

Avery tried to shake his growing irritation. Lately, it seemed that Darci spent an increasing amount of time pointing out the imperfections of other women. It seemed nothing more than thinly disguised backbiting, and he couldn't stand to listen to it.

Suddenly, he longed to be back in his office, surrounded by work, with Darci at a reasonable distance.

Unfortunately, Darci wasn't finished. She pulled a sheet of paper from her purse and handed it to him. "I picked Sabrina because I think a large percentage of women viewers will find that they can identify with her resolutions."

Avery took the sheet and glanced over it. "That's great. I hope so. Are we ready to get back to the office?"

Darci's lips formed a pout. "You didn't read it. Not really. At least take a look at the last one."

Avery looked. It knocked the wind out of him. What woman didn't want to fall in love? Never mind "woman"; what *person* didn't want to fall in love? Did that mean that Sabrina honestly wanted nothing to do with him?

He pushed aside his empty soup bowl and placed Sabrina's list in front of him. Taking great care not to let Darci see that the list had surprised him, he read through the other items. They all seemed pretty normal and matter-of-fact. So why was the last one so drastic?

"Amazing, isn't it?" Darci broke into his thoughts. "What person wouldn't want to fall in love?"

Avery suppressed a shudder at the thought of him and Darci having a similar thought. "I wonder why," he finally said.

Darci shrugged. "I've heard around the office that her fiancé dumped her. It probably has something to do with that."

Avery looked at the paper once again. "I suggest you cut that resolution before the show begins. She obviously doesn't mean it, and it'll be embarrassing for her if she changes her mind in a couple of months."

Darci shook her head. "No way. That's the most sensational part of her list. Viewers will tune in to see the woman who doesn't want to be in love. Besides, how do you know she doesn't mean it? Did she tell you that?"

Darci eyed him carefully, and Avery felt slightly uncomfortable under her intense scrutiny. Despite the fact that their romantic relationship was over, she still knew him better than most people did. At one time that had been nice, but now he found himself wishing she couldn't read him so easily. He would have to choose his words carefully.

"No, she hasn't mentioned any of this to me. And even though I find the angle about her not wanting to fall in love interesting, we may be setting up Sabrina for something she can't finish. I just don't want her to feel too much pressure."

Darci murmured sympathetically. "Point taken, Avery. Taking on too many resolutions at once is a mistake a lot of people make, and we'll explore that as well. We all need to change, but we need to find the balance between too much transformation and not enough. Don't worry about Sabrina. She'll be fine."

Avery hoped Darci was being sincere. But just to be sure, he would keep tabs on Sabrina himself to make sure the pressure didn't become overwhelming. If he decided the situation was too stressful, he would find a way out for her.

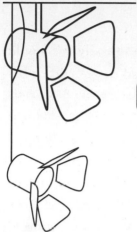

Chapter Nine

And last but not least, I'd like to introduce the final member of our panel. She's one of my own production staff, and she's got a pretty ambitious list of resolutions . . ."

Sabrina felt her upper lip bead with nervous sweat, and she waited until the camera cut back to Darci before she wiped the perspiration away.

Today was December 28, and the taping of the first New Year's resolutions show was in full swing.

Darci droned on and on with a longish introduction, then paused while the crew rolled a prerecorded segment of Sabrina reading her list of resolutions.

The four-minute piece had been recorded last week, just before Christmas, and Sabrina had already lost two pounds since then, so she hoped her face looked thinner today than it looked on that tape.

While she watched, she fought the urge to roll her eyes. The whole segment had been scripted and directed by Darci, and it consisted of Sabrina running around, demonstrating why she needed to make resolutions.

First Sabrina had to flash her raggedy fingernails in front of the cameras, and Darci brought in a gigantic coffee cup for Sabrina to set on her desk. Then Sabrina had to pretend to balance her checkbook—and look anguished at the fact that she had overspent.

Darci had wanted to film Sabrina at the mall trying to squeeze into a pair of too-small jeans, but Sabrina had put her foot down and flatly refused. Darci might hold her job by the throat, but she had to maintain a tiny sliver of dignity. There was no way she would give Darci the satisfaction of knowing what size pants she wore—or couldn't wear, to be more exact.

When Darci got perturbed about it, even Avery had stepped in to voice his disapproval. "We're not making some cheesy infomercial, Darce. Let's not go there," he'd said, shaking his head.

The same went for the scene in which Darci had wanted Sabrina to fling a dozen roses across the room and grumble, "Who needs a boyfriend, anyway?"

Avery said it would look absolutely ridiculous, and he wouldn't allow it on the show. "I want to stay a step ahead of the competition," he said.

They reached a compromise by having Sabrina read the rest of her resolutions aloud and end the list by saying, "Darci, please help me get my life organized!" Darci did her best to help "direct" that segment by standing off to the side and continually saying, "Try to look more frazzled, Sabrina."

When the tape ended, Sabrina breathed a sigh of relief. Granted, the other nine members of the panel had similar segments, but Sabrina couldn't help feeling that hers seemed more . . . demeaning.

"So, Sabrina, which resolution would you like to start with?"

Sabrina focused her attention back on Darci and did her best to look and sound intelligent. After all, she was on national television.

"Well, Darci, I'm not really sure. I guess that's why I'm here. I want to know what the experts think."

Darci broke into one of her friendliest smiles. "And that's why we have the experts here." She stared into the eye of the camera and addressed the viewers.

"Throughout the coming year we'll be checking in on our brave resolutioners twice a month. I'll be calling in nationally known experts, who will guide them through this process.

"In the beginning stages, the experts will help everyone get started, and as time progresses, our focus will shift to helping them get through the rough spots. And finally, we'll focus on how to make sure they maintain the goals they've reached."

Sabrina listened patiently as Darci continued with her closing statements. In about five minutes, she could get off the set and head back to her office, where real work awaited her.

These next few days were bound to be extremely busy, since Darci wanted to air five resolutions shows the first week of the year. Since the next four shows consisted of the experts helping the resolution-makers get started, Sabrina only had to appear in one of the next four episodes. And that show didn't tape until tomorrow afternoon.

As soon as the director yelled "Cut!" Sabrina hurried back to the elevator so she could return to her own office. While she waited for the elevator car to arrive, Maris emerged from the producer's booth and asked Sabrina to hold the door for her.

They stepped onto the elevator and rode in silence. Sabrina didn't really know what to say. Maris had apologized for her reaction to the news that Sabrina would appear on *The Daily Dose,* but since that time their friendship had been strained.

Maris held the position that she felt Sabrina wasn't telling her everything about her decision, and Sabrina was between a rock and a hard place because Maris was correct. But of course, she couldn't tell Maris that she was right, because that would be in violation of her agreement with Darci.

"I need to go to your church with you this Sunday," Maris said from her corner of the elevator.

Sabrina blinked in surprise. Maris wanted to go to church with her? Why the sudden change?

Before she could say anything, Maris chuckled. "I see your wheels spinning, and I have to warn you that it's not what you think. Your preaching hasn't won me over. We just need to take a camera crew and follow you around for a bit to see what you're doing to 'get more involved.'"

Sabrina nodded, recognizing the phrase from her list of resolutions. Somehow, she hadn't even considered the possibility that she would be filmed in church. But then again, Miss Hands-on Darci would come up with something like that.

Great. This opened a whole new can of worms, and she would have to take extra time to call the church office and make sure it would be okay to drag a film crew with her on Sunday. The last thing she wanted to be accused of was distracting the other worshippers. And certainly, some parishioners and church staff would have concerns about how they were being portrayed.

Sabrina voiced her concerns to Maris, who listened sympathetically.

"Since Darci's too busy to actually go with the crew and film these segments, I'll give you a little leeway. Maybe we don't actually have to come to a church service. Your list doesn't say 'go to church more'; it says you want to get more involved.

"It might not be necessary to film a Sunday morning service. But is it possible that you could just go to the church one afternoon and ask if they have any programs you could join? Maybe some community service–type thing?"

Sabrina nodded. "Actually, I think we do have a volunteer

committee meeting coming up soon. I'll call the office and see what I can find out."

The door opened, and they stepped out into the hallway. "What are you doing for lunch?" Maris asked.

Sabrina grinned. "I think I'm skipping lunch."

Maris frowned. "That's not healthy. Please don't tell me it's because of the resolutions."

Sabrina shrugged. "Yes and no. I did say on national television that I need to lose ten pounds, so the diet issue does have some bearing on my decision. But I also have a ton of work to do, and actually having to be on the show really put a crimp in my workday. So I'm skipping lunch to cut calories and save time."

Maris shook her head. "You'll have enough of that in about three days. Trust me; I've done it. You won't get much extra work done, because you won't be alert enough. By five thirty, you'll be so hungry that you'll devour anything and everything in sight."

Sabrina sighed. "Okay. I give. I'm already getting pretty hungry. What did you have in mind?"

"Deli sandwich? I'll order out so you can still catch up on your work. Maybe we can both put aside our to-do lists for half an hour and chat like we used to."

"Sounds good to me. But maybe not a half hour. I'm seriously going to be working some major overtime to get everything done. What about a fifteen-minute lunch in your office?"

"Deal. I'll put the call in now. Turkey on wheat, mustard, no mayo?" asked Maris.

"And strawberry yogurt."

Maris made a *tsk-tsk*ing sound. "You sure about that yogurt?"

"Yes, I'm sure. Just make sure it's low-calorie."

"Will do."

Maris hurried off toward her office. Sabrina walked down the hallway to her own cubicle and reached her desk just as the phone began ringing.

Sabrina picked up on the second ring. "Hello?"

"Sabrina, why did you rush off so quickly after the taping? I need to see you in my office."

Sabrina suppressed a groan. Why did it seem that Darci couldn't let ten minutes pass without pestering her?

"I'm on my way," she said. Darci didn't bother to answer. The line went silent, and Sabrina heard nothing but dial tone.

She sat down and rested her forehead on the desk for a few seconds. There was no use running down to Darci's office if she couldn't compose herself first.

She closed her eyes and prayed silently: *Lord, please help me. She's being very demanding, and I feel dangerously close to losing my temper. Show me how I can get along with her so I don't lose my job.*

"Taking a nap?" Avery's voice sounded from the doorway.

Sabrina sat up quickly. How embarrassing. Of course she wasn't sleeping, but still . . . "No, I was just taking a little prayer break."

Avery smiled. "I do that myself. And I'm sorry for interrupting."

Sabrina shook her head. "No, I'm supposed to be on my way to see Darci, so you interrupted at a good time."

"On your way to see Darci," Avery repeated. "Seems like you've been doing a lot of that lately. Have I missed something?"

Sabrina stood. "Not really. She's just . . . well, we talk about the show."

"The show?"

"Well, we talk about my part of the show. About the resolutions."

"I see," he said slowly. The look on Avery's face disagreed with his words.

Sabrina felt guilty. Could she really keep this deal a secret for an entire year?

"So what do you talk about? I'm just curious, since you two have these meetings without the rest of the production crew around."

"Not much, really. She gives me pep talks."

"Pep talks?"

"Yeah. You know, she tries to encourage me to focus on my goals."

Avery grinned. "So Darci keeps calling you to her office to encourage you to keep your resolutions."

Sabrina took a deep breath. Avery didn't seem to be buying her explanation. "You do realize how important it is for her to prove to the critics that her show really helps people, right?"

"Of course."

"And since I work here, she just wants to go the extra mile to make sure that I . . ." Sabrina trailed off, searching for the correct choice of words.

A knowing look spread over Avery's face. "Ah. I see. Since you work here, it's especially important to her that you succeed."

"Exactly."

Avery appeared to be holding back laughter. "Interesting. Just let me know if her pep talks get to be overwhelming. I'll talk to her and let her know that too much encouragement can be just as harmful as none at all."

"I will." Sabrina took a step toward the doorway, but Avery didn't move. "Was there something you wanted?"

He hesitated for a moment. "Actually, there was. I have tickets to *Fiddler on the Roof* tonight, and I was wondering if you wanted to come with me."

Now it was Sabrina's turn to hesitate. Going to a play would be a nice, relaxing way to end the day—if she ever got all her work done. But what would Darci have to say about this?

Avery held up a hand. "Let me guess. You're thinking about resolution number eight."

" 'Number eight'?" she repeated.

"Otherwise known as 'Do not fall in love.' "

She laughed. "Guilty."

He held a finger to his chin. "Now, the way I see it, coming to see *Fiddler* with me wouldn't necessarily be breaking your resolution."

"You don't think so?"

Avery shook his head. "I'm just asking you to come to dinner with me and be my guest at this play. Nowhere in that invitation did I ask you to fall in love with me."

Sabrina felt her face grow warm. Did he think she was being too presumptuous? Was this his way of letting her know that he saw her as a friend only and nothing more?

"So? Should I take your silence as a yes or a no?" Avery asked.

"I guess . . . yes?" What could it hurt? As long as she didn't fall in love, Darci couldn't hold it against her. And Avery had just made it pretty clear that he didn't have romance in mind.

A loud *thump* sounded in the corridor outside the cubicle. Avery and Sabrina hurried out to see what the commotion was about.

Sunny was on her knees, surrounded by several shoe boxes. Most of the boxes were open, and many shoes lay haphazardly on the floor.

Sunny was frantically stuffing the escaped shoes back into their proper boxes.

Avery and Sabrina spoke at the same time.

"What happened?"

"Are you okay?"

Sunny flushed a deep pink. "I'm fine. I just got back from the mall. Darci sent me out to find a pair of shoes to match her taupe suit . . . I guess I was moving too fast and I tripped over my own feet."

"Let me help you carry those," said Sabrina. "I'm on my way to see her, too."

Sunny gushed thank-you's as Sabrina helped her sort through the boxes. Avery, however, merely stood and watched.

Sabrina could well imagine the woman's distressed state of mind. She herself had been sent on similar errands, and generally there was a looming time deadline involved.

Since Sunny had arrived, Sabrina's participation in Darci's emergency shopping errands had steadily decreased, and though she was relieved, Sabrina knew that the brunt of the work had fallen to Sunny.

"I'll carry half of these for you," she offered.

"Oh, thanks so much," Sunny said. "I always was clumsy, and I just hope Ms. Oliver won't be upset that I'm late. Oh, dear . . . I just hope none of the shoes are scuffed. I have to return the ones she doesn't want." Sunny's face clouded over, and she headed for Darci's office with great speed.

Sabrina started to follow her, but Avery cleared his throat. "Did you forget about me?"

"I did. But not intentionally."

"Is it okay if I pick you up at six thirty?"

"Perfect."

Sabrina turned to go to Darci's office, but Avery stopped her again. "Do you remember hearing the elevator open?"

Sabrina had no idea what he was talking about. "What?"

Avery tilted his head to the side. "I don't remember hearing the bell that sounds when the elevator opens."

As if on cue, the bell sounded and the elevator door opened. A maintenance man emerged and walked through the lobby area and passed by Sabrina and Avery.

"It looks like the copier is on the blink again," said Sabrina.

Avery shook his head. "And I don't remember hearing Sunny walk by, either."

Sabrina frowned. What was he getting at?

"There are two ways to get to Darci's office from the elevator. The quickest route would be to walk down this corridor and pass by your cubicle. But I don't remember hearing the elevator door open, and I don't remember Sunny walking past your cubicle."

Sabrina laughed and rolled her eyes. Did Avery have secret ambitions to be a detective? "It could be because you had your back to the corridor and you were a couple of feet inside the cube."

"But you didn't. You were facing me. So did you see her walk by?"

Sabrina tried to remember. She could remember every bit of her conversation with Avery, down to his mannerisms and gestures, but she couldn't recall seeing Sunny walk past.

Of course, that might have had something to do with the fact that she had been too preoccupied with determining whether Avery was romantically interested in her. But the last thing she wanted to do was admit that to him. He would probably laugh.

She shrugged. "I'm really sorry, but I don't remember."

Avery shook his head. "It just doesn't add up. If Sunny were really coming back from the mall in a rush, we would have heard the elevator door open; then in a matter of seconds, she should have rushed by the door."

"So what are you saying?"

"I'm not really sure. I hate to say it, but it almost seems like she was already on the other side, listening. And then maybe she dropped the shoe boxes and used the story about being in a hurry to cover up the fact that she was eavesdropping."

Sabrina laughed. The woman didn't look a day younger than fifty-five, and with her short stature and old-fashioned style of dress, she came across as more of a grandmother than an office-gossip hound. Avery was clearly making too much of nothing. She voiced her thoughts aloud.

His lips formed a tight line while he listened, but he didn't interrupt. When Sabrina finished talking, he nodded. "You're probably right. I guess I've just had this suspicion that Darci's been up to something a little . . . well, I've just had this feeling that she's not being totally honest with me about something.

"And it seems like every time I turn around, Sunny is some-where in the vicinity. I tried to put two and two together and I guess I deduced that Darci was using Sunny as an office spy or something."

Sabrina patted Avery on the arm. "Nice try, but I think you're way off. She may be Darci's new errand slave, but I don't think Sunny has devious capabilities. Yes, she may be interested in finding out what's going on around the office, but I think everyone's been guilty of that at some point."

"You're right." He winked. "I was probably so engrossed in getting you to come see *Fiddler* with me that she could have danced in a circle around me and I wouldn't have noticed."

They both laughed, but were interrupted when Darci came barreling down the corridor. "Sabrina, I believe I asked you to come to my office a good fifteen minutes ago. And now you're wasting my time, holding five pairs of shoes that I need to try on."

"I'm sorry. I was on my way—"

"And Avery is just standing around spewing mindless

chitchat." Darci glared at him. "Come on, Sabrina. The first rule of moving up on the corporate ladder is to get away from people who only come to work to socialize."

Darci turned on her heel and marched toward her office. Sabrina had no choice but to follow. She turned and waved good-bye to Avery. He didn't appear too upset by Darci's outburst, and he pointed to his watch and mouthed, "Six thirty."

Sabrina smiled and nodded her head to let him know that she hadn't forgotten. Despite the smile she pasted on, her stomach was a jumble of butterflies. There was no misreading the subtext in Darci's statement about climbing the corporate ladder. She clearly wasn't pleased that Sabrina was talking to Avery. So what would she say if she knew about Avery's plans for the evening?

Sabrina paused outside Darci's office and prayed that Avery's suspicions about Sunny weren't correct. And after tonight, she would have to stay as far away from Avery as she could.

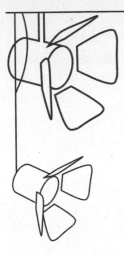

Chapter Ten

The following Saturday morning, Sabrina awoke to the sound of the phone ringing. A glance at the alarm clock revealed the time: 7:34.

Sabrina knew only one person who called at such inconvenient hours.

She grabbed the cordless phone and didn't waste time with a polite hello. "Eric, call back later or don't call at all. Some people are trying to sleep. Come on, it's my day off."

The line was silent, and Sabrina smiled in satisfaction.

"It's me, Avery."

Sabrina sat straight up. "Avery?"

"Yep."

"Oh. Well, obviously, I thought you were someone else."

"I kind of figured."

"Yeah, well . . . sorry about that. I don't normally answer the phone like that."

"I know. But I think I will call you back later, since you do have a point. It is your day off, and it was rude of me to call so early. I've been getting up early for so many years that seven feels like sleeping in to me."

99

"Well, you might as well go ahead and finish what you started. I'm awake now."

"You sure you don't mind?"

Sabrina shook her head even though she knew he couldn't see her. "No, it's okay. In fact, if you hang up now, I'll be in suspense wondering what it was you wanted."

"Really?" She could hear laughter in his voice. "So would it be safe to say that I would occupy your thoughts even when we're not together?"

"Okay, Avery. Don't push it. I'm still entertaining thoughts of hanging up."

"I had a great time with you at *Fiddler.*"

Sabrina waited for him to say more, but he didn't. To fill the silence, she said, "I had a good time, too."

"So I guess I'm a little curious as to why you've been avoiding me at work. I was thinking you were upset with me."

"No . . . that's not it. But I'm sure you've noticed that I spend a lot of time under the watchful eye of Darci."

"So?"

"So? You're kidding me, right? Didn't you see the way she fussed at me for chatting with you in the hallway the other day when I was supposed to be bringing her the shoes?"

"Yeah. But Darci's all bark and no bite."

"No bite?" Sabrina wasn't convinced. "You're sure about that?"

He chuckled. "Well, maybe a little bite. Like when a puppy nips you. Little teeth, no big gashes."

"Hmm."

" 'Hmm,' what?"

"Hmm . . . If what Darci does is like a puppy nipping someone, I'd hate to see a full-grown dog bite."

He let out a full-bodied laugh, and Sabrina could picture him leaning his head back, thoroughly enjoying the joke. "So you're scared to talk to me when Darci's around?"

" 'Scared' is such a . . . cowardly word."

"Okay. Strike the word 'scared' from the record. What's the deal?"

"I'll just say that after that incident in the hallway, she gave me the third degree about whether or not I was falling in love with you. She told me I would be disappointed with myself if I couldn't keep my resolutions."

"What did you tell her?"

"I didn't tell her anything."

"So you are falling in love with me?"

"No. And I intend to keep every one of my resolutions, no matter how much you try to sabotage me."

"I promise I'm not trying to sabotage you. But I would love to know more about why in the world you picked not falling in love as one of your resolutions. Does it have something to do with the Eric you thought was calling you on the phone?"

"Well, maybe I would consider telling you, but I just don't think it would be wise for us to just stand around talking anymore."

"Then we won't do that again. But that doesn't mean I can't talk to you when we're not at work. And I don't think it means that we can't spend time together."

Sabrina was silent. This sounded like something that could potentially make her lose her deal with Darci. That is, *if* Darci found out.

"Sabrina? You still there?"

"I'm still here. But I'm having internal conflict because this is starting to sound awfully underhanded and secretive."

He sighed. "I agree with you and I disagree with you. I want to spend time with you, but we seem to have the obstacle of Darci and this silly resolution standing in the way of things."

"Exactly. And I am not going to break my resolution."

"You already said that."

"I just want to make sure you know that I mean it."

"I understand. Believe me, I do. But I don't think you necessarily don't want to ever fall in love again."

"I never said that. It's just one of my resolutions for the next twelve months."

"In my opinion, you've just been incredibly hurt by your ex-fiancé, and you want to save yourself from the possibility of another failed relationship—for at least one year."

Sabrina didn't answer. In a sense, he was correct. At least, that had been her original purpose. But she hadn't really ever planned *not* to fall in love. That had only become a reality once Darci got hold of the list.

"Sabrina? Are you still there?"

"I'm here."

"I'm guessing I overstepped my bounds when I stated my opinion. Please don't be upset with me."

"I'll try not to be. But I'm running out of patience. Did you really interrupt my sleep just to grill me about my resolution?"

"No. I actually called to find out what you're doing later today."

"I'm pretty booked. I have to go to a volunteer committee meeting at church at ten o'clock. After that, I have to go to the craft store to find a hobby. And after that, I have to go and work out with Maris. In case you weren't paying attention at yesterday's taping, my fitness expert told me that joining a gym and having an accountability partner would help me stay committed to my exercise plan."

"I guess I wasn't really paying that much attention. If you

think about it, those so-called experts pretty much spout the same clichés and catchphrases over and over again. If you've heard one, you've heard them all."

"Don't tell Darci that you feel that way."

"She already knows I think so, and she agrees. But we bring them on for the viewers." Avery paused, then shifted back to the original topic. "What are you doing after the gym?"

"After that, I think I'll be too tired to do anything but sit down and catch up on my reading or maybe try my new hobby."

"How about I come to the volunteer meeting with you?"

"Why?"

"Why not? I could probably use some volunteer time myself. Maybe we can even volunteer in the same department."

"I don't know if that's a good idea . . ."

"You think Darci will flip out."

"Pretty much."

"Or maybe not. She knows we both go to the same church, and if she wants to keep an eye on things, she can always come. But she won't do that because she's not into 'the religion thing,' as she refers to it. So, the way I look at it, she won't have any reason to be upset."

Sabrina sighed. He had obviously made up his mind, so there was no use in trying to convince him otherwise. Besides, she didn't exactly hate the idea of spending a couple of hours with Avery. Even if it was only a church committee meeting in the middle of a Saturday afternoon.

"Okay. I'll see you at the meeting. Maris will be there, and so will a camera crew."

"If you're worried about Darci coming, don't. Weekends are her leisure time, and she rarely sticks her nose into work issues."

"I never said I was worried about Darci."

"I could hear it in your voice."

Sabrina smiled and shook her head. There was no use arguing with him. Right now all she wanted to do was go back to sleep.

"Good-bye, Avery."

"Good-bye, Sabrina."

Darci arrived at the church before Sabrina and Maris and the crew.

She sat in the parking lot and tapped her fingers against the steering wheel while she waited. She glanced at the clock: 9:25. The meeting didn't start until ten, but the crew needed a half hour to get set up.

Darci turned up the heat another notch and fought off a wave of shivers. Three inches of overnight snow hadn't made for the best driving conditions, and the temperature had to be around five or six degrees. Darci hated Midwest winters. They seemed to be either very mild or very cold, but never in between.

Was it really necessary to drag her body out of a warm bed this early on a Saturday morning just to keep tabs on Sabrina? At a church, no less.

After considering for several moments, she decided that this was indeed important. For the past three months, almost as long as the resolutions program had been in the works, Avery had been increasingly distant to her but more and more talkative to Sabrina.

What was going on? Avery wouldn't talk to her long enough to let her broach the subject, and Sabrina kept feigning innocence.

The other day, she couldn't believe the nerve of that girl. First Sabrina had the nerve not to come to her office when she was first asked. And then Sunny came and reported that she had seen Avery and Sabrina just standing around chatting.

Darci made a mental note to give Sunny a small bonus. For someone with a decidedly matronly image, that woman certainly got around, and she always seemed to have her finger on the pulse of what was going on in the office. And somehow, she always got her work done.

A car pulled into the lot, interrupting her thoughts. Darci glanced over and noted with some surprise that it was Avery's car. So he and Sabrina had resorted to sneaking around behind her back at *church*!

Darci opened her door and knocked on his passenger-side window. Instead of unlocking the door, he rolled down the window a few inches. "Yeah?"

Darci held back her irritation long enough to put on what she hoped was a sweet smile. Like Sabrina's. "Can I come in? My heat's not working well and I'm freezing."

Avery didn't look too pleased, but he did unlock the door. "If you were that cold, you could have just gone inside, you know."

Darci couldn't believe him. "Why? I'm not here for a life transformation; I'm here to get some work done. I don't want to be in there any longer than I have to."

Avery nodded. "So work is what's gotten you out of bed before two in the afternoon on a Saturday."

"Yes. I want to make sure they get some good shots for the show."

"I see." Avery quirked an eyebrow, and she could tell by his emerging grin that he didn't quite believe her.

"And I wanted to give Sabrina some moral support."

"Oh. Well, that's certainly commendable. You really seem to have taken an interest in her lately."

So have you, she thought. She almost spoke the words aloud, but then thought better of it. What was that old saying, about catching flies with honey instead of vinegar?

"So what brings you here?"

He stared straight ahead. "I was interested in seeing what type of volunteer positions they have open."

"Really? Just like that? All of a sudden?" Now it was her turn not to believe him. "Imagine that. On the same day we come to film Sabrina at the meeting." She shook her head. "What a small world."

Avery turned his key in the ignition and shut off the car. "I think I'm going to go in. And just for your information, Sabrina and I do go to the same church. Not that you'd know, since you seem to spend more time putting down religion instead of actually coming with me."

Darci swallowed. She'd gone too far and made him angry. He was opening his car door when an idea hit her. "You know, I've been thinking about that."

He turned to face her. "About what?"

She shrugged and tried to look timid while she searched for the right words. "About the whole . . . religion thing."

He didn't move, so she continued.

"I mean, it's been on my mind lately, and I'm wondering if . . . maybe someone's trying to get my attention."

"Someone, as in God?"

Darci widened her eyes. "Is that what you think? God's talking to me?"

He inhaled loudly, and Darci wondered if she'd taken the ruse too far. If there was one thing Avery hated, it was for people to make light of God.

"I thought you didn't believe in God."

Good. He was still in a listening mood, but she had to make

her move fast or he would get frustrated. "I did, too. But now I'm not so sure."

"Well, you know how I feel."

Darci nodded. "Of course I do. And I guess I'm asking you to help . . . help me learn?" As soon as she said the words, she wished she could take them back. Either he would see straight through her ruse or he would believe her, which would mean a lot of time listening to him ramble on and on about the Bible.

Then she thought of Sabrina's apparent hold on Avery. He'd made it clear that the woman he would marry needed to be religious, so maybe the girl was onto something.

"You want to learn about the Bible?" he repeated.

Darci nodded, noting that he seemed pleased. Now she was on the right track.

"I'm glad to hear that. Give me a chance to check with the pastor on some things and I'll get back to you on Monday."

Darci wanted to roll her eyes. He could never resist anyone who asked him a question about God. But she didn't understand why he had to check with his pastor. And why would he wait until Monday? Why couldn't he just come over tonight or tomorrow and talk to her? Maybe they could even have dinner afterward.

She felt as though the situation had slipped her control again. She reached out and grabbed his arm.

He nearly hit his head on the ceiling of the car trying to wriggle free of her grasp.

Oops. She'd overdone it again. She quickly let go of his arm and giggled nervously. "Sorry if I scared you. I was just wondering if . . . well, I was hoping that . . ." She trailed off, hoping he would take the hint and offer to spend some time with her this evening.

But he didn't say anything. Instead, he sat silently with an expectant look on his face.

Darci steeled her nerves and reached for the ace up her sleeve. Desperate times called for desperate measures. "I was hoping I could come to church with you tomorrow."

The words hurt even as she said them. This meant no sleeping late for an entire weekend.

Avery seemed very surprised. She'd caught him off guard. No way would he refuse her now. And if she played her cards right, they might be able to spend the entire day together.

"You want to come to church tomorrow?" That look of disbelief returned to his face.

Was it her imagination, or was Avery repeating everything she said, like a parrot? Darci pushed her irritation aside for the moment. "Yes, I'd really like to give it a try."

He didn't say anything for a long time but instead kept nodding his head.

"So? What time will you pick me up?"

"Pick you up?"

Couldn't he come up with an original sentence and stop repeating everything she said?

"Yes." Darci made a point of enunciating each word slowly, as though she were giving directions to one of the absentminded interns in the production department. "What time will you pick me up?"

He was looking out the window now. Sabrina had just pulled into the lot. Avery nearly fell out of the car trying to get out and say hello to her.

"Hey!" Darci had no choice but to yell to get his attention.

He stopped in his tracks, turned, and looked at her.

"What about tomorrow?"

"Oh, church starts at ten. Why don't you just meet me here?"

Darci wanted to protest, but Sabrina was watching now. It would be far too damaging if Sabrina saw her get all upset over Avery's refusal to pick her up in the morning.

"All right. I'll see you at ten," she told Avery. Without another glance at either of them, Darci marched into the church. That whole exchange had been rockier than she'd expected, but it didn't matter. She would find a way to get back in Avery's good graces. Starting with this church thing.

What in the world had gotten into Darci? Avery watched as she swept past him and into the church. Maybe that was the best place for her to be. Hopefully, some holiness would rub off on her by osmosis.

Hopefully.

Sabrina gave him a curious look. "Earlier this morning you were pretty sure Darci wouldn't show up. What'd you do, talk her up?"

He could tell by the glint in her eye that she wasn't upset.

Avery shrugged. "I have no idea. This is really unlike her."

"Not in my opinion. I told you she's keeping me under her watchful eye."

Just then the camera crew pulled up in a van, with Maris right behind them in her gray sedan.

Maris got right out and headed toward Sabrina and Avery. "Is that the queen's vehicle I spy?" she asked, pointing to Darci's car.

Avery nodded.

Maris made a face. "That's wonderful. I was really looking forward to escaping her today. I guess I'll stay out here as long as I can just to be out of her immediate presence." She turned her attention to Sabrina. "Any idea why she takes such an interest in your resolutions segments?"

Sabrina shrugged, then said, "It's way too cold to stand out here speculating. I don't care if Darci's inside. I'm going in to get warm before the meeting."

As Sabrina walked away, Maris nudged Avery. "Did you see that? She's giving half answers. Not exactly a lie, I'll bet, but not the full truth, either."

Finally, someone who suspected what he suspected. "But why do you think Sabrina feels like she has to keep something from us? Don't you think she trusts us?"

"I know she trusts me. My only guess is that she has some specific reason to keep us in the dark. I do know that she will resort to answers like that whenever she's feeling like she needs to avoid telling the exact truth. So, yes, something's up."

Avery didn't know what to say. He almost got the feeling that Sabrina and Darci were involved in a plot together. But Sabrina seemed incapable of Darci's level of plotting. And why would she?

"You think Darci's blackmailing her or something?" he mused aloud.

Maris laughed. "No way. Who could get anything on Sabrina? No offense, but she's the squarest square I've ever met." She rubbed her hands together and blew on them. "But she's right about one thing. It's way too cold to stand out here. I might as well go in now. No sense in putting it off any longer."

The chilly air was becoming increasingly difficult to withstand. After a few moments, Avery followed Maris's lead and went inside.

The crew was busily arranging cameras and lights while parishioners filed in for the meeting. Avery wanted to sit next to

Sabrina, but he thought better of it and took a seat in the back row.

During the course of the meeting, Avery had a hard time concentrating. He was supposed to be listening to descriptions and explanations of all the available volunteer positions, but instead his thoughts bounced back and forth between Darci and Sabrina.

Was Sabrina truly involved in some plot with Darci? It seemed highly unlikely. But why else would Sabrina be so gung ho about the whole resolutions plan?

And why in the world, after so many years, was Darci having some type of religious conviction? He told himself that he shouldn't be upset that she seemed to want some kind of change in her life, but he was hard-pressed to believe that she was actually sincere.

When the meeting ended, Avery worked his way through the crowd to find Sabrina. Darci was holed up in a far corner of the room, engrossed in what looked to be a highly dramatic cell phone conversation. By the looks of things, she wouldn't be bothering him any time soon.

Sabrina was busy talking with Maris, so he stationed himself at the coffee-and-pastry table to wait until he could speak with her alone.

A few minutes later, one of the crew members called Maris over to ask a few questions, so Avery quickly went and stood next to Sabrina.

"Krispy Kreme?" he said, offering her a doughnut.

She eyed the proffered pastry with a skeptical gaze. "I really shouldn't, but I left the house in a rush and forgot my healthy, tasteless, fiber-fortified . . . thing."

"Thing?"

"The package claims that it's some kind of bar or muffin . . . but I've seen bricks that weigh less." She rolled her eyes and grinned as she reached for the glazed doughnut. "Thanks."

"My pleasure." Avery swallowed the last of his own doughnut, then asked, "Did you decide where you want to volunteer?"

"I think I'm going to help with Sunday school. Kids are always a lot of fun."

"So you can mark that resolution off the list."

"I have to stick with it, you know. So I can't ever really check anything off the list. But I can note when I've met my goals, so, yes, I would consider this a goal met."

"So now the search for the hobby begins?"

Sabrina gave him a curious look. "I guess. So how about you?"

"Me?"

"Yeah. I thought you were here because you wanted to try being a volunteer. What did you decide?"

Avery's throat went dry. After all the commotion with Darci, he'd totally zoned out during the meeting and forgotten all about signing up for a position. He grinned sheepishly. "I know you'll have a hard time believing this, but I really didn't pay that much attention during the meeting. I guess I'll have to come to the next one."

Sabrina gave him a wry smile. "Did your inability to focus have anything to do with Darci?"

Avery didn't answer right away. Was it his imagination, or was there a spark of jealousy in Sabrina's words? Although the idea that Sabrina might be feeling pangs of jealousy pleased him, he decided to answer as honestly as he could. "Yes and no. She wants to come to church with me. That's never been really high on her list of priorities, and it did surprise me."

Sabrina's eyes widened. "I see. So she's coming tomorrow?"

Avery nodded. "So she says. We'll see."

Sabrina nodded but didn't say anything. An awkward silence set in, and when Darci came bustling over a few moments later, Avery was almost glad for her interruption.

"Sabrina, I hear that you're joining a gym today," she said, getting right to her point.

"Yeah. Maris is going to introduce me to her trainer tonight."

Darci nodded approvingly. "Good, good. Nothing like a personal trainer to really target those saddlebags and love handles."

Avery watched as Darci swept Sabrina with a once-over gaze. Sabrina blinked twice, then, almost defiantly, took another bite of her doughnut.

Darci sniffed. "Pastry. I never touch the stuff. But then again, I suppose that those of us who live their lives off camera have the luxury of carrying around ten or so extra pounds." She looked at her watch. "Well, I've got to run. See you in the morning, Avery. And, Sabrina, I'd like to meet with you sometime Monday to track how you're doing with your resolutions. Hopefully, you'll be back on track with your diet by then."

"I'll be there," said Sabrina. Avery noted that she sounded terse. And why shouldn't she?

He wished he could have cut Darci off and said something to negate her biting remarks, but he didn't know if he'd be making things better or worse for Sabrina. And it was too late now, since Darci had already stalked away.

Avery looked down at Sabrina, who was wrapping the rest of the doughnut in her napkin. Should he say something or just keep quiet? In his experience, women always tended to get a little antsy when men started making weight-related comments. Not that he saw anything wrong with Sabrina's figure. But she apparently did, given her resolution to lose ten pounds. And now Darci was making sure Sabrina wouldn't forget it.

He sighed and decided to try to remedy the situation. "You know, I think you look fine. If you want a doughnut, you should go ahead and eat it."

A long silence ensued, and Sabrina seemed to be staring at some point beyond his head rather than actually looking at him. This was the point at which other women had nearly bitten his head off for what they assumed were left-handed compliments. No amount of explaining on his part had been able to convince them otherwise. But moments later, to his surprise and utter relief, she smiled.

"Thanks for the vote of confidence, but she's right. I won't reach my goal if I can't exercise a little self-control. And if I can't keep my resolutions, I don't—" She stopped mid-sentence, her eyes wide.

"You don't what?" he prodded, hoping she would feel comfortable enough to confide in him.

She shook her head. "If I don't keep my resolutions, I won't be happy with myself. Bottom line." She looked at her watch. "Which reminds me, I need to get a move on if I'm going to make any headway with this hobby search."

"Let me come with you," he blurted out.

"You want to tag along while I find a hobby?"

"Why not? I'll do my best to offer my advice. I've had a lot of hobbies, so I can tell you what's worth trying."

"Really. Like what?"

"Rock climbing, hiking, racquetball, biking. Stuff like that."

Sabrina laughed and shook her head. "If that's your idea of a hobby, I can tell you right now, you won't enjoy my search. I was thinking more along the lines of something I can do at home. Stuff like knitting or calligraphy or decoupage."

Now it was Avery's turn to laugh. He hadn't exactly envisioned spending a day at the craft supply store, but he'd brave it if it meant he got to spend a few more hours with Sabrina. "All right. Let's go shopping for yarn and knitting needles."

"Really? You don't mind?"

"Hey, I'm a man who's not afraid to admit that I watch HGTV."

"Really." She had her hands on her hips, and her tone was somewhere between disbelieving and impressed.

"Sometimes." He paused. "I might stop and watch for a few seconds while I'm channel surfing."

"That's what I thought. I didn't really picture you as the type to sit around learning how to reupholster sofas and turn old door frames into desks."

"Then I take it you have more than just a passing interest in that kind of thing," he said.

"It's fun to watch, but I don't see myself doing it every day. We might say that my hobby is watching other people do crafts."

He laughed heartily and reached for her hand. "Then let's hit the stores so we can make you an active participant."

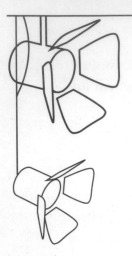

Chapter Eleven

Sabrina walked into church the next morning feeling more than a little apprehension. Darci was due to make an appearance, and Sabrina couldn't shake a growing sense of dread.

This meant another few hours under Darci's microscope of scrutiny, and Sabrina didn't know if she could take it. She tried to reason that it was a good thing that Darci wanted to come to the service, but she had a feeling that Darci's sudden interest had more to do with Avery than with finding the Lord.

She wondered if Avery even realized that Darci had upped her efforts to get him back. During their trip to the craft supply store, he had stayed away from the subject, and Sabrina decided it was best not to mention it. Instead, he had seemed truly intent on helping her find a new hobby.

They'd gone up and down every aisle of the store and perused many different craft kits. After she'd picked up several skeins of yarn, some knitting needles, and a how-to book, he'd suggested they go see a movie.

Sabrina declined, reminding him that she had to meet Maris at the gym.

"How about dinner, then?" he asked. "We could get a quick bite to eat and you could still make it to the gym in time."

"Wouldn't that be classified as a date?"

He shrugged. "Maybe."

"Maybe?"

"Okay, yes."

Sabrina shook her head. "I can't. Remember my resolutions?"

Avery sighed. "Sabrina, I promise you that going on a date is not falling in love."

He was right—in a way. But going on repeated dates could very well lead to love. And Darci had made it clear that there could be no love in Sabrina's future for the next eleven months. If there was even a hint that Sabrina might be falling for someone, the deal would be off.

In the back of her mind, she wondered if true love would be more valuable than her deal with Darci. But was Avery really looking for love, or was he simply looking for a temporary relationship to help him feel better? There was a very fine line between dating and just spending time together with no strings attached.

But was Avery mature enough to keep things strictly friendly?

Although he seemed to be sincere in his wishes to spend time with her, it didn't take a rocket scientist to realize that he and Darci had an extensive history as a couple. For reasons not fully clear to Sabrina, Avery and Darci were no longer romantically involved, but that didn't mean they wouldn't ever get back together.

Common sense told her to be wary. Her experience with Eric had proved that promises didn't mean that much. How long had it taken him to find Sharon after he'd broken their engagement?

After a few moments of consideration, she decided to decline Avery's invitation.

"I think I'll just go home and get ready to meet Maris."

Avery looked disappointed. "Because you think it's a date?"

"Because going out to dinner would be defeating the purpose of my workout."

"All right. Then maybe another day."

Sabrina shrugged. "We'll see."

They parted ways, and Sabrina spent the rest of the evening wondering whether she should have said yes to his invitation.

At the gym, Maris had refused to discuss the issue, saying that Sabrina was making a huge mistake even to consider getting in a semiromantic relationship with the boss.

Instead, Maris seemed more interested in grilling Sabrina about the resolutions program. To be more specific, Maris was convinced there was some hidden reason why Sabrina wanted to be involved in the show.

Of course, she was right, but Sabrina couldn't very well let Maris in on the details of her deal with Darci. So she tried to keep the conversation centered on the workout.

As Sabrina made her way to a seat inside the church sanctuary, she could tell that the workout had been fruitful. Her whole body ached, and some muscles felt as though they would snap in half at any moment.

Sabrina eased herself into the seat and made a silent promise that she would go home and soak in hot water for at least an hour. She couldn't imagine having to hobble around the office Monday feeling like this.

With around ten minutes to go until the service began, Sabrina sat and watched people arrive and get situated. Some folks clustered in good-sized groups, chatting and laughing with friends.

Others sat in groups of two or three, and their tone was more somber. They either talked in hushed tones or prayed, earnest expressions on their faces, and eyes closed to the rest of the world.

Then there were those who walked in and stopped to have

brief conversations with almost everyone in their path. They seemed to know everyone in the building, and everyone seemed to know them. A number of other people arrived and went right to their seats without saying anything to anyone.

These were the people Sabrina related to most. After attending this church for over two years, she hadn't really made an effort to get to know anyone. It was simply too easy to arrive for service and leave as soon as it was over.

Given her past church experiences, Sabrina had adopted a new policy for church attendance. Simply put, her goal was to get in and get out. It was quick and painless and presented less of an opportunity to get hurt.

Her grandmother, a woman who'd spent nearly every day of her life in church, wouldn't approve, but Sabrina's mom thought it was a wise choice.

Get in and get out. Listen to the sermon and leave. Don't give anyone a chance to hurt you.

This morning as she watched those around her, Sabrina couldn't help feeling a pang of regret. There were probably fewer than ten people in the entire building who actually knew her by name. A larger number probably recognized her face, because she knew the faces of quite a few people.

Sabrina wondered if she had made a mistake in closing herself off from church-based friendships. She'd made a point of engrossing herself in work to get ahead on the job, and look where that had gotten her.

Maris was fun just to hang out with, but when the conversation took on a religious tone, she clammed up and even got upset. Avery was a nice guy, but she didn't know him that well. And Darci—well, Darci was just Darci. At a time like this, she felt as though she could really use someone to talk to.

Scanning the crowd, she noted that Avery and Darci were

nowhere to be seen. She wondered if Darci had talked Avery into spending the day with her instead of going to church.

"Is that okay?"

Sabrina snapped out of her reverie and noticed a woman standing in the aisle next to her. The questioning look on her face alerted Sabrina to the fact that she was awaiting an answer.

"I'm sorry?" she apologized. "I guess I wasn't listening "

The woman looked annoyed. "I said, is this seat taken?" She pointed to the seat next to Sabrina.

Sabrina looked at the chair. "I don't think so." She shifted slightly in her seat and allowed the woman to pass by. Sabrina looked farther down the row of chairs and noted that the woman could have taken her pick of the remaining ten or twelve empty chairs. *Why in the world did she have to sit right next to me?*

Sabrina turned away from her and continued her search for Avery and Darci. Moments later, the two made their entrance. Together. They were impossible to miss.

Avery was tall and handsome, and Darci was slender and attractive. Physically they were well matched. Emotionally and spiritually they were seemingly worlds apart, but perhaps Darci was sincere about changing.

Sabrina's spirits sank. There went her friendship with Avery.

"So what's your name?"

Sabrina turned abruptly and found the woman staring at her again. *Why can't she leave me alone?*

"I'm Sabrina," she said, more out of obligation than genuine kindness.

"Sabrina, what a pretty name. It's nice to meet you." The woman hesitated.

"And what's your name?" Sabrina didn't really care what her name was, but it would be rude not to ask.

"I'm Jasmine."

"Jasmine," Sabrina repeated. "That's a pretty name, too."

Jasmine smiled. "My mom named me after her favorite flower."

Sabrina nodded and fought the urge to turn around and see where Avery and Darci were sitting. But that would be extremely rude. She took a deep breath and willed herself to contribute to the conversation that Jasmine seemed so intent on having.

"So is this your first time visiting here?" Sabrina asked.

Jasmine blinked and shook her head. "No . . . I've been going here for about two years."

Sabrina felt silly. But then again, how was she supposed to know? There were literally thousands of people in this church, and she wasn't exactly on the attendance committee.

"Oh, I'm really sorry. I guess I just hadn't seen you before," Sabrina explained.

Jasmine laughed. "Don't worry. I'm used to that. I guess I'm one of those people who just tends to blend into the woodwork."

Sabrina nodded and stole a glance in the direction where she'd last seen Avery and Darci. They were sitting down now, and Darci was chatting away, Avery's full attention focused on her and no one else.

"I know how you feel—about blending into the background," she told Jasmine. "I feel like that all the time here."

Jasmine grinned and lowered her voice. "Do you want to know a secret?"

Sabrina didn't know what to say. Did she really want to hear a secret from a complete stranger?

Jasmine didn't seem to notice that the conversation had lulled. She leaned closer to Sabrina and said, "Actually, I've been trying to blend in. I never sit in the same area; I never stop and introduce myself to anyone." She shrugged. "In fact, I just come for the sermon and leave as soon as it's over."

Sabrina nodded. "I do that, too—come and leave as quickly as I can."

"I woke up this morning and just felt like doing something different," Jasmine said. "I've had some bad experiences with churches and I figured that things would be easier if I didn't make any friends here."

"That way, no one could do anything to hurt you," Sabrina added. "Same here."

The two women sat silently for several moments.

"But I really think it's time I met some people here," Jasmine said. "The people I work with don't really share my same beliefs, so it gets a little difficult to just hang out with them. I live in a condo complex and my neighbors all work long hours, so I don't see them."

Sabrina nodded. She knew the feeling.

"Honestly, I've been feeling lonely for the past few weeks, and this morning when I woke up, I decided I might as well take a chance and meet some people here. It was either that or sit around and feel sorry for myself."

Before Sabrina could say anything else, the worship leader began the first song. She forced herself to focus on singing the songs instead of thinking about Avery, Darci, or even Jasmine.

Usually, praise and worship was her favorite part of the church service, but today she couldn't shake a feeling of sadness.

Suddenly, the events of the past few months seemed too tough to bear. The breakup with Eric, her troubles with Darci, the distance between herself and Maris, and now her growing attraction to Avery . . . The issues settled on her shoulders like a pile of weights.

Grateful to be in the seat closest to the aisle, Sabrina escaped to the bathroom before the tears started falling. Thankfully, no one was around, so she allowed herself a couple of minutes to pull herself together.

When the tears subsided, she took a look in the mirror. The telltale streaks of ruined mascara gave her away. She hurriedly ran some cool water on a paper towel and did her best to correct the damage.

While she wiped her face, the door swung open, and Mrs. Mallory, one of the ushers, walked in. Sabrina recognized her because she was one of the few people who had been persistent in talking to her on a weekly basis. At the very least, they always said hello to each other, but most of the time Mrs. Mallory succeeded in drawing a two- or three-minute conversation from Sabrina.

As soon as Mrs. Mallory saw Sabrina, she rushed to her side.

The diminutive woman was at least a foot shorter than Sabrina, but her presence was warm and comforting. "Sabrina, dear, what is the matter?"

Sabrina just shook her head, feeling overwhelmed and embarrassed. If she tried to talk, she knew she would burst into tears again.

Mrs. Mallory didn't pry. Instead, she closed her eyes and started praying. She asked the Lord to comfort Sabrina and to give her peace and courage in whatever trials she was facing.

Sabrina felt instantly better. She knew her problems were still waiting for her outside the door of the ladies' room, but knowing that God cared about her was comforting.

"Thank you, Mrs. Mallory," she said.

"Call me Erma, honey." Mrs. Mallory patted Sabrina on the arm.

"I really wish I could tell you about why I was upset, but . . ." Sabrina trailed off. So much of what weighed on her mind had to be kept a secret, and the rest—the rest might seem petty to someone who wasn't in her shoes.

Erma shook her head. "Tell it to God, Sabrina. He'll listen and He'll fix it."

Sabrina nodded in agreement. Erma was right. How many days had passed since she'd really sat down to read her Bible and pray? Work had been so hectic, Sabrina could barely remember the last day she'd had more than five minutes just to sit still, let alone study her Bible.

"Thank you so much for taking the time to pray. I probably should get back into the service," Sabrina said.

"I'll see you later," said Erma. "And don't forget. Take everything that's worrying you to the Lord."

"I will." Sabrina left the restroom and headed back inside the sanctuary. The sermon was just about to begin as she slid into the seat next to Jasmine.

While she listened to the sermon, Sabrina felt a peace wash over her. When church ended, Jasmine stopped her before she could leave.

"Hey, it's almost noon. Do you want to go and get a sandwich or something?" She grinned. "I'm a little rusty at making new friends, so this may sound incredibly cheesy, but I figured we can sit and talk for a while."

"You know, that sounds like a good idea. I guess I'm kind of out of practice at making friends, too, but that sounds fun."

Jasmine glanced at her watch. "There's a new deli around the corner. How about I meet you there in ten minutes?"

Jasmine gave Sabrina directions and left in order to get a table before the place got too crowded.

Out in the foyer, Sabrina saw Erma, who gave her an encouraging smile. Seconds later she ran into Avery and Darci.

Wonderful.

Darci smiled cloyingly. "Sabrina, it's so nice to see you again."

Sabrina bit back the customary "You, too," because she wasn't overly thrilled to see Darci. Instead she asked if Darci had enjoyed the service.

Darci gave Sabrina a flat look. "It was . . . nice, I guess."

"Nice." Sabrina looked at Avery.

He appeared to be nonplussed. "Darci had car trouble this morning, so she rode with me. We're heading out to get a bite to eat, and I wondered if you wanted to join us."

"Thanks, but no thanks," Sabrina told them. Meeting Jasmine had been a small miracle in more ways than one. "I actually made plans to meet someone for lunch." She looked at her watch. "And if I don't leave now, I'll be late."

Avery gave her a questioning look, while Darci appeared to be relieved.

"That's too bad." Avery didn't appear to be in any hurry to end the conversation.

"I guess I'll see you two in the morning," Sabrina said, trying not to let any hint of jealousy creep into her voice.

"Bye, Sabrina," Darci said. "And don't overdo lunch." She leaned closer and spoke in a stage whisper. "Those ten pounds won't go away on their own."

Sabrina resisted the urge to roll her eyes. "Thanks for the advice. I'll keep that in mind."

Before either of them could say another word, Sabrina escaped to the great outdoors. She was looking forward to lunch with Jasmine, but she would have to make sure the time didn't get away from her.

That scheduled soak in the tub was going to involve some serious prayer time.

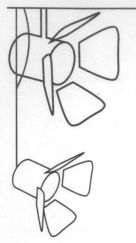

Chapter Twelve

I can't believe this. I'm really amazed." Maris handed the magazine to Avery. "This week's issue of *Celebrity Journal* has a two-page article about the resolutions program. After only a month—just two resolutions features—it looks like we've got a hit on our hands."

No sooner had Avery gotten hold of the book than Vincent wanted to see it. Avery handed it to him. He had never been able to understand all the fuss about celebrity gossip magazines anyway. He didn't really care which movie star had a new girlfriend and which pop singer had a wild night on the town.

Vincent nodded. "The ratings are up, and the numbers don't lie. And the viewer phone and mail feedback confirms it. Definitely a hit."

"Let me see that magazine, Avery," said Darci. "If all this is true, then I suggest we double our resolutions programming. Instead of just doing one show every two weeks, let's do one a week."

Avery glanced at Sabrina, who sat quietly.

"What do you think, Sabrina?"

"What difference does it make?" Darci said. "If it's good for business, we'll do it."

"Hey, check it out," Vince exclaimed. "They did a poll of people out in malls and grocery stores, and Sabrina was voted 'favorite resolutioner.'"

"What?" said Darci. "Hand it to me," she demanded.

Vincent ignored her and kept reading, "It says they like her because they think she's down to earth. She's the top pick to keep her resolutions."

"Way to go, Sabrina," Maris said.

Sabrina grinned. "I hope I can live up to their expectations."

Vince went on. "She's the new sweetheart of daytime television. Here's a quote: 'Those polled overwhelmingly chose Sabrina as their favorite because she's easy to identify with.' But . . ." He paused dramatically and waited to make sure he had everyone's attention. "They're worried that she's digging a hole with the 'not falling in love' thing. They think she won't be able to keep it."

Darci grabbed the magazine. "Well, they don't have to worry. Sabrina's not going to fail. Will you?"

Sabrina sighed. "I've got it under control."

Even as Sabrina spoke, Avery saw uncertainty in her eyes. She seemed so doggedly determined to be perfect at keeping her resolutions, and he felt certain that if she didn't give herself some room for adjustment, she was setting herself up for ultimate failure.

I wish she would let me talk to her about it.

But the last time he'd really been able just to talk to Sabrina had been over three weeks ago—that Saturday afternoon he'd helped her look for a hobby.

Ever since then he hadn't been able to spend time with her alone. At work she seemed to go out of her way not to be with him one-on-one. Outside work, she said she was too busy just to hang out with him.

Between helping in the children's ministry at church, working out every day, attending financial planning classes, and doing her regular duties at work, Sabrina's resolutions were beginning to take over her life.

Darci had been coming to church with him every Sunday, and Sabrina seemed to shrink even further away from him.

Avery felt as if Sabrina was being stretched too thin, and now it appeared that Darci was ready to exploit her even more.

Avery cleared his throat. "Before we jump on this resolutions bandwagon, I'd like more details. We won't schedule any additional shows until I can see some written outlines of what we'll accomplish with two more episodes per month."

Darci looked up from the magazine, her mouth agape. "What did you just say?"

Avery sighed. Why did Darci always have to be so difficult when other people were around?

"I said, I'd like to see a written proposal on my desk that will outline exactly what will happen on those two extra shows."

"You haven't done that for years, Avery. Come on, this is my show, and I know what works. This resolutions thing is hot, and if we wait too long, it'll fizzle out."

Avery met her gaze. She was obviously perturbed. And maybe he had been too harsh. He'd pretty much handed over complete content control to Darci a couple of years ago. In a sense, he was asking her to take a step down.

Should he back off and let Darci have her way? A glance at Sabrina told him he was on the right track. The faintest trace of dark circles had taken form under her eyes, and her shoulders drooped as she sat at the table. She looked as if she might fall asleep any minute.

He fixed his gaze on Darci, who silently challenged him with her eyes.

"Then don't waste time. Get that proposal to me before things have time to fizzle out."

Darci didn't say anything but turned and stalked out of the conference room.

Maris, Vincent, and Sabrina hurriedly gathered up their papers and followed shortly afterward.

"I guess this meeting's over," Avery said to the empty room. "I think I need a vacation."

Sabrina left the meeting and headed straight to her cubicle. Darci was waiting there, sitting at Sabrina's desk.

"Did we have a meeting scheduled? I must have forgotten."

"I just scheduled it," Darci announced. "But don't worry, it'll be brief."

"Okay." Sabrina sank into the spare chair at the end of the desk.

Darci folded her hands in her lap and spoke slowly. "Look, I don't know what you've done to Avery, but whatever it is— stop."

Sabrina didn't know what to say. She had practically been running from Avery for the past few weeks. How could Darci accuse her of doing anything to him? "I'm not sure I understand."

"I think you understand a lot more than you let on." She tossed the copy of *Celebrity Journal* at Sabrina. "Do you notice anything unusual about this article?"

Sabrina gave the feature the once-over but didn't find anything exceptionally strange. But it was a little jarring to see a large photo of her own face smiling up from the glossy page.

She looked at Darci and shrugged. Darci snatched the book away.

"Don't lie to me, Sabrina. I can read you like a book." Darci crossed her arms over her chest and rolled her eyes.

Sabrina felt bewildered. What exactly did Darci want her to say? Feeling annoyed, she put her hands up in the air. "Well, maybe you need to go back to school and learn *how* to read. I'm not lying to you. Why don't *you* tell *me* what's wrong with the article?"

"It's about my show and there's no picture of me! All they did was talk about you and the resolutions," she hissed.

Pointing her finger at Sabrina, she continued. "You're trying to take over my show, and I won't let you. You're trying to make Avery be on your side, and I will do everything I can to stop you. Even if it means you don't work here any longer."

Sabrina felt her pulse speed up. Her mouth went dry, and she felt the beginning of a tension headache. She was about to lose her job.

Darci stopped abruptly and seemed to struggle to regain her composure. "Now, I'm going to ask you a question."

Sabrina didn't really want to answer any questions right now. If she was about to get fired, then why didn't Darci just get on with it?

Lord, please help me. She's attacking me for no reason, she prayed silently.

"Are you in love with Avery?"

"What? No . . ." Sabrina shook her head. Three weeks ago she'd been dangerously close to falling for him, but Darci had stepped in and put an end to their time together.

"Are you dating him?" Darci pressed even further.

"No."

Darci paused, then spoke up again. "Has he kissed you?"

Sabrina couldn't hold back the laughter, even as Darci scowled angrily. The tone of this conversation had gone from menacing to downright ridiculous in less than sixty seconds.

That question didn't even deserve an answer, but Sabrina knew that if she didn't reply, Darci would assume the worst. Not that kissing Avery would be a worst-case scenario . . .

Sabrina pulled herself together and put on a straight face. "No, Darci, I have not kissed Avery."

Darci appeared to be relieved. "Well." She stood up. "I guess that's that."

That's what? Sabrina thought. How could the woman walk in here, threaten her job, then ask if she had kissed the boss, all in a matter of minutes?

"Well, Darci, if you don't have any further pressing questions, I have work to do." Sabrina stood and gestured toward the hall. "We have a taping this afternoon, so I'll see you then."

Sabrina felt intensely happy to be showing Darci the door for a change. Darci didn't look at all happy, but she must have run out of things to say. For once, it appeared that Darci was actually speechless.

Sabrina watched as Darci left the cubicle, then sat down to tackle her daily duties. Ten seconds later, she was interrupted by a rap on the wall.

"Sabrina, I'm sorry to interrupt you, but . . ." Sunny stood in the hall, holding out a small slip of paper. "While you all were in the production meeting, I was passing by your cube and the phone on your desk just kept ringing and ringing." Sunny shrugged. "Well, in my house, I can't stand to let it just keep going like that, so I hope you don't mind. I stopped and answered it."

Sunny slipped on her reading glasses as she spoke. "He was a very mannerable-sounding young man. His name was . . ." She referred to the paper again. "Oh, yes. Eric. Said he's your fiancé."

Sabrina reached for the paper, shaking her head. "Ex-fiancé, actually, but he never seems to completely go away. Every time

I train my brain to stop thinking about him, he calls or we end up running into each other somewhere."

Sunny murmured sympathetically. "I know exactly how you feel. I had a falling-out with my friend Olivia once after she stole my recipe for apple pie and beat me at a baking contest. The harder I tried to avoid her, the more she popped up."

"So what did you do?"

"Forgave her. She apologized. But now I put away my recipe books whenever she comes over."

"If only things could be that easy with Eric."

"Of course I don't know all the details of your breakup, but I'm certain it was more serious than a pilfered pie recipe. But you've got a good head on your shoulders and I know you'll find a way to maneuver this little bump in the road. See you later, dear. I've got to go pick up a new tube of lipstick for Darci."

Sabrina shook her head. Strange as it seemed, Sunny actually liked running Darci's miscellaneous errands. She was a genuinely nice woman, and it was refreshing to have someone around who seemed to be unconcerned about office politics.

Sabrina decided to put off the call to Eric until after she got home. There was no way she wanted to risk an upsetting episode with him while there were other people around who might overhear.

"Hey, Sabrina."

She didn't have to turn around to know that Avery was standing in her cubicle.

"Hi, Avery."

"You busy?"

"Well, that's kind of what happens when I come to work. I have things to do, and that keeps me pretty occupied." Sabrina kept her back to him. If she couldn't see his face, she had a better chance of refusing to spend any more time with him.

"Then I'll be quick. I need to talk to you."

She had seen that one coming. "About?"

"Relax, Sabrina. I'm not trying to make you fall in love with me. It's about the show."

"Avery, I'm swamped. Can't you talk to Maris or Vincent or Darci?"

"No, I can't. And I don't want to talk about it right here or right now. How about tonight?"

She shook her head. "I'm going to a movie with a friend from church."

"It's important, Sabrina."

She spun around to face him. "I'm sorry, but I can't date you, talk to you, or spend time with you away from work. And I can't talk to you here because I have Darci breathing down my neck about whether or not you've ever kissed me. Please stop making my job more difficult and go away. You're the boss and I'm the employee. That's as far as things can go."

He tilted his head to the side. "So you're saying . . ."

"I'm saying a relationship between the two of us would never work."

He grinned. "I didn't come in here to ask you to be my girlfriend, but apparently, you've given the issue some thought."

Sabrina's face grew warm. She had blurted out way too much information.

"Relax, I'm not laughing at you. I've been thinking about it, too. And I disagree. I think it can work. If we both really wanted it to."

He put his hands up in defense. "Look, I really do want to talk to you about the show because I'm concerned about some things. But I also wanted to spend some time with you, and you've been making that difficult."

He sat in the spare chair. "Listen, no one's going to think any less of you if you go on a few dates. And, to tell you the truth, I doubt anyone will call you a failure if you somehow happened to fall in love this year. They might even be happy for you." Avery wiggled his eyebrows comically.

Sabrina giggled. "Okay, but I still have plans for tonight. Can we schedule this talk for tomorrow?"

"What time?"

"How about right after work? I've got an appointment with my trainer at eight and I can't be late."

"So we should meet somewhere?"

"Right. I won't be hungry, but we can talk over coffee. I know a great little shop that's nice and quiet."

He cocked an eyebrow. "I thought you were supposed to be giving up coffee."

"Wrong." Sabrina shook her head. "I'm *cutting down* on coffee, and I haven't had any for an entire week. But after what I've been through today, I think I deserve a latte."

"I'll bet you do. So, tomorrow after work I'll meet you at the shop. Where is it?"

"It's not too far." Sabrina got out a piece of paper. "I'll draw you a map."

Avery frowned. "I really dislike maps. They do nothing but confuse me. Why don't you just write out the directions and e-mail them to me?"

"Good idea."

He stood and backed out of the cubicle. "I'll get out of your hair now."

"Thank you."

Sabrina returned her focus to the work on her desk once again.

The phone rang.

"No big surprise there," she mumbled.

"Hello?"

"It's Maris. Can we meet for lunch?"

"Sure. My office or yours?"

"I was thinking more along the lines of out of the office."

"I was thinking along the lines that I have a million things to do. I can't leave this place today, especially since we're taping another resolutions spot."

"Really? Which one?"

"The one where I sit and nod my head while the financial expert tells me how to effectively save more money. I've been going to the classes once a week, but the film crew hasn't been able to tape any of it."

Maris sighed. "I was really looking forward to getting out of here, but I guess we can have sandwiches in your cube."

"Okay, let's play it by ear. I need to make about five million calls and get some things settled for next week's taping schedule. I definitely can't stop for lunch until I get that done."

"Sabrina, am I going to be hitting the vending machine every five minutes waiting for you to eat lunch?"

Sabrina laughed. "Come on, have some faith in me."

"You didn't answer my question. The last thing I need is one more bag of those mini chocolate-chip cookies."

"I'll do my best, and I'll give you a progress report at eleven thirty. If I'm still bogged down, I give you my blessing to have lunch without me."

"Well, I was really hoping we could talk about something."

"You, too? Everybody wants to talk to me today. I must be getting popular."

"Who's 'everybody'?" Maris asked, laughing.

"You, Darci—"

"That's a given," Maris interrupted.

"Eric—"

135

"Eric called?"

"Again."

"I hope you send him packing permanently this time. Didn't you already sell the ring?"

"And I sent his part of the proceeds last week. He'd better not be calling to say it got lost in the mail."

"I know that's right. So who else wants to talk to you?"

Sabrina opened her mouth to mention Avery, then thought better of it. Maris still made it clear that she thought even hanging out with Avery was a bad idea. She'd nearly had a fit the day Avery insisted on going hobby shopping with Sabrina.

"Sabrina? Are you still there? Who else is clamoring for your attention?"

"Um . . . Sunny."

"Sunny? What for?"

"I don't know, just giving me some advice about Eric, I guess. He called and she took a message."

"You didn't spill your guts to her, did you?" Maris's voice dropped to a dramatic whisper. "Certain people in this office think she's Darci's eyes and ears to find out what people are saying. Do you ever notice that she seems to always pop up out of nowhere? It's like she's hiding in the next cubicle, just lurking and listening."

Sabrina laughed out loud. "Lurking and listening? Maris, she wouldn't hurt a ladybug. Why is it that you and Avery are so convinced otherwise?"

Maris was quiet for several seconds. When she spoke again, her voice was even quieter. "Yeah. Well, you know what? She just passed by my doorway. Now she'll probably run to Darci and quote back everything I just said. If I lose my job today, you'll know why."

"Seriously, she just passed by?"

"Yep. And she had the nerve to turn and wave. I got up and closed my door."

"Hmm."

"'Hmm,' is right. And don't think I didn't notice that you just mentioned the big A."

Sabrina giggled at Maris's nickname for Avery. She sometimes resorted to code names for people when she thought someone might be listening, but Sabrina always laughed because she thought the code names were just as identifiable as the person's real name.

"You've been talking to him again, haven't you, Sabrina? Are you guys dating, or what?"

"How much did the queen pay you to ask me that?"

"What are you talking about? I'm not her spy. But we all know who is."

"No, seriously, Maris. She was in my office half an hour ago, demanding to know if I was dating him. What's the buzz?"

"If you must know, it looks ridiculous and everyone's talking about it."

"It?" Sabrina repeated. "There is no 'it.'"

"Looks like there is. There is obviously some kind of chemistry between you two. People can spot it a mile away. Even the guy who fixes the copy machines asked me if something was going on."

"Asked you? Why'd he ask you?"

"Everyone is asking me. I'm the best friend, so I should know this kind of thing."

"Maris, we're not dating. Trust me. I have very serious reasons for keeping my resolutions this year."

"Yeah, I'm still trying to crack the case and find out what in the world made you sign up for that."

"I'll never tell."

"So there is some big reason behind all of this? Is the queen blackmailing you?"

"No. But let's go back to the other thing. Define the sentence 'People can spot it a mile away.'"

"It means that this constant display of Avery stopping you in the hallways and you running the other direction is starting to look suspicious. Everyone—and I mean everyone—wants to figure out what you guys are trying to pull."

"What's suspicious about a man talking to a woman who is not returning his affections?"

"The thing is, Sabrina, you're not really turning him down. We've all seen women send major signals that they're not interested. But you're not doing that. You may be walking away from him with your feet, but your eyes give you away. I'll bet you can't deny that you feel something for him."

"I'm not in love with him."

"I didn't say you were. But do you like him? Have a little crush on him?"

"Does it matter?"

"Maybe not. Apparently Darci already knows, and she's the one you have to be concerned about. If you still have your job, I guess you're safe."

Sabrina scribbled on a piece of blank paper as she talked. "I just hate the idea that everyone is gossiping about me. Especially when essentially nothing is happening."

"And that's the reason I tried to talk you out of this crush ages ago. Anything that happens at the office is fair game for the rumor mill, and people can get vicious. Especially if they think they can exploit someone else to move up in rank."

"Okay, okay. I see your point."

"And I can tell by the tone of your voice that you're going to do what you want to do."

Sabrina didn't answer. Maris meant well, but she could handle this on her own.

"We've got a taping in twenty minutes, so I'm going to get off the phone now. And I have a feeling you're going to cancel on me for lunch," said Maris.

"Twenty minutes? Yeah, I think I'll be the one eating vending machine food today. Can we do lunch tomorrow?"

"You know, the more I think about it, I'd rather not discuss what I have to discuss here. Someone might—"

"Overhear," Sabrina interrupted, completing one of Maris's favorite phrases.

"Exactly. And it's really kind of personal, so maybe I'll just come over to your house."

"Okay. I'm seeing a movie tonight with Jasmine, but I should be home around nine."

"She's that woman you met at church, right?"

"Yes. And please don't start saying that I'm trying to replace you with her."

"Well, you never have time to go to a movie with me anymore. And how long has it been since we've gone shopping?"

"Maris, it's a little hard to shop when you don't have any money to spend. You and your husband both work, and I'm working with my own salary here."

"Okay, okay." Maris cut her off. "Have fun with your little holy friend; I'll be over around nine thirty."

"See you then."

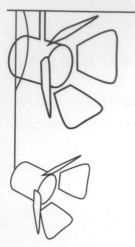

Chapter Thirteen

"He did *what*?" Maris sat at Sabrina's kitchen table and stirred another teaspoon of sugar into her coffee.

"Eric sold his story to some tabloid. When I called him back this afternoon, he said he wanted to give me a 'heads-up.'"

"That boy is sillier than I thought," Maris grumbled. "Did he say how all of this fell into his lap?"

"He claims they called him, but I don't know how they could have found him. I never mentioned him on *The Daily Dose,* and *Celebrity Journal* just said I had recently ended a relationship with my fiancé."

"So you think he saw *Celebrity Journal* and decided to go around fishing for somebody to buy what he had to say?"

Sabrina nodded, tears welling up in her eyes. "I promised myself I wouldn't cry over anything else Eric did, but—"

"And you won't." Maris handed her friend a tissue. "Wipe your eyes and stop crying. It's not worth it."

"But I have no idea what he said about me."

"So what? It's a tabloid, for goodness' sakes. Everybody takes those headlines with a grain of salt."

"What's Darci going to say when she finds out? And what about Avery?"

"They will react in the best interest of the show and put out a statement saying that they fully support you. You may have to give an interview to a more reputable magazine, though."

"Me? Give an interview? I'm not a celebrity, Maris. This is not what I set out to do with my life."

Maris shook her head. "Well, you pretty much signed up to be famous, at least for a little while, when you told Darci you'd do the show. If you hate it so much, then quit the resolutions program."

"I can't do that."

"Exactly. Everyone will think you're bowing out of the spotlight because Eric's telling the truth."

"So what do I do now?"

"We tell Avery, and we try to get an advance copy of Eric's interview. Then we look for the holes in it and find someone to listen to your story."

Sabrina pushed her cup of tea aside, and Maris's heart ached for her friend.

"Come on, don't look so worried. You're the new sweetheart of daytime television. America loves you, and the entire country isn't going to be easily swayed by the ramblings of a vengeful ex-boyfriend."

"It's not that I think Eric's going to say terrible things about me. I just know he's doing this to get some publicity about his book. He's just using me to get ahead, and that makes me angry."

"So write that down and put it in your interview. And in the morning I'll get you a meeting with Adrienne in PR so she can coach you."

"Great. Now I need a PR coach. If the press gets wind of that, they'll think I'm hiding something."

"Not necessarily. Everyone needs a little help in learning how to handle interviews and press conferences."

"Press conferences? Who said anything about a press conference?"

Maris shrugged. "You never know how much this could escalate, so we should get prepared."

Sabrina leaned forward and put her forehead on the table. "I can't do this. I'm not cut out to be in the spotlight. I haven't even lost my ten pounds yet. In fact, I gained two pounds last week."

Maris patted Sabrina on the shoulder and tried to sound positive. She tried to forget that she'd come over to get cheered up herself. But the last thing Sabrina needed to hear was Maris's problems.

"Listen, honey. Nobody's going to think any less of you. You look great. And a trip to the PR coach doesn't mean you're a phony. Although they have worked wonders on Darci. The public never really sees the real Ms. Oliver."

"Maris," Sabrina whined, "you're not making me feel better. I don't want to be compared to Darci right now."

"Okay, sorry. But don't let this Eric thing get you down. If anything, people will find him totally ridiculous and then they'll feel sorry for you."

Sabrina sat up and gave a wry grin. "Okay. But if he somehow finds a way to sell his book out of all this, I want a cut."

"That's the spirit." Maris picked up her mug and took a sip.

"So what's your big news that you wanted to talk about?" Sabrina asked.

Maris shook her head. "The timing's not that great, so we can talk about it later."

"What's bad about the timing? I'm here; you're here; we're not at work where someone might—"

"Overhear." Maris finished the sentence and chuckled. "I guess I'm a little paranoid about people eavesdropping on me, huh?"

"I'll say." Sabrina lifted the teabag from her mug and set it on a saucer. "So what's the news?"

"It's nothing major. But I'm not sure this is a good time, with all of the Eric stuff we just discussed."

Sabrina shrugged. "If I've learned one thing in the past six weeks since the year began, I've learned that nothing ever happens at a good time. But I'm learning to roll with the punches."

Maris blinked back her tears and reached for a tissue. Funny how the tables had turned. Five minutes ago, Sabrina had been the one crying.

"Maris, what's wrong?" Sabrina sounded alarmed. "Why are you crying?"

Maris shook her head. "I'm okay. I'm just . . ." She might as well get on with the truth. "I think my life is falling apart."

"What do you mean?"

"I mean everything. Sidney and I aren't getting along. He thinks I spend too much money." Indignation welled up inside Maris even as she spoke the words. "It's my money, Sabrina. I'm the one who puts up with Darci for hours on end to earn it. If I want to buy a dress or some shoes with the money, I think I should."

Sabrina didn't say anything but listened quietly.

Maris sighed. "You're being really quiet. What? Is there some Bible verse that says wives need to do everything the husband says?"

"I can't quote you chapter and verse, but there are several passages that talk about how husbands and wives should treat each other . . ."

Maris put up her hands in front of her face. "Don't tell me about it. I have a feeling the Bible would say I'm wrong."

"Why don't you tell me the reason behind this argument? Are you two still saving money so Sidney can start his bakery?"

"Yes. But now his brother is backing out of the deal. He was supposed to relocate to St. Louis, and they were going to start the business here."

"So he changed his mind."

"Yes and no. Now he thinks they should open a full-fledged restaurant, but he wants me and Sidney to move to Louisiana, where he lives."

"He wants to change the St. Louis bakery to a New Orleans restaurant?"

"A Cajun café." Maris shook her head. "I told Sidney there was no way we're moving there. And now he's mad because I haven't been putting any of my paycheck into the joint savings account."

"I see."

"But why should I? That's not the deal I agreed to. I may not have the best job in the world, but deep down, I enjoy it. Otherwise, I would quit."

"But weren't you going to take a sabbatical next year and help Sidney with the bakery?"

"Yeah. But 'was' is the key word. I was willing to take off eight months to a year to help him get off the ground, but I was supposed to be helping with the business side of the bakery. Now he and his brother want me to quit *The Daily Dose,* move to New Orleans, and be a waitress in their little café."

"Waitress?"

"Yeah, they think it'll be more profitable if Dexter's wife and

I are the waitresses. That way, we can take our tips and put it right back into paying off the mortgage on the place."

"Hmmm." Sabrina looked as though she didn't know what to say.

"Sabrina, stop trying to come up with a holy answer. This is ridiculous. Can you really see me as somebody's waitress?"

Sabrina smiled. "Not really . . ."

"Exactly. But try convincing Sidney. He's so bullheaded about the whole thing, and the more I complain about it, the more determined he gets."

"You said something about paying off the mortgage. Did they already buy a building?"

"They're pretty close. In fact, Sidney's down there right now. He left this afternoon, and we had such a big argument about it."

Maris grabbed another tissue and wiped at her eyes again. "Now, I don't like the idea of any of this, but I'm not sure it's worth giving up my marriage."

"Giving up your marriage? Are you guys splitting up?"

Maris shrugged. "I wish I knew. When I dropped him off at the airport, I asked him when his return flight was and he said he didn't know. He said he would be there indefinitely."

"Oh, Maris, I'm sorry."

"His whole family is there, and of course, they want him to move there. But my whole family is in Chicago. Do you see me trying to drag him there and start a flower shop with my sister?"

"No, I guess not."

"That's my point. I like living here. I was willing to sacrifice my job for a year to help him do this—but that was when he claimed he wanted to open a business here."

"Did you tell him that?"

"I tried, but he won't listen. He thinks I'm too scared to take a business risk. And he said I was too scared to step out of my comfort zone."

"And you disagree?"

"Of course." Maris blew her nose. "Maybe not. I mean, I don't want him wasting my money on something that won't work. What if he fails and we get stranded in Louisiana? You know how fickle Darci is. What if she won't give me my job back?"

Sabrina nodded silently.

Maris wiped away more tears. "And I think I made things worse. Last week I withdrew my half of the money from the account."

"Did you spend it?"

"A little. But I can take the stuff back and get a refund."

"Did you tell Sidney?"

"No. He found out when he went to get some money out for the down payment. At first he thought the bank had made an accounting mistake, so he got into an argument with the teller. The teller had to get the managers, and they told him that I was the one who made the withdrawal."

"So he was embarrassed because the bank knew and he didn't."

"Exactly. He came home and fussed about it and told me I had to put the money back. So I threatened to get a lawyer and sue if he tried to spend a cent of my money on some horrible little café. He got really mad and just wouldn't talk to me for the rest of the day."

"Do you really have a lawyer?"

"No, Sabrina. I was just talking. Still trying to talk him out of it. But maybe I went too far. I don't know."

"Does he know you were just talking?"

"I have no idea. I was just trying to hit a nerve, so he would cancel his trip. But he went anyway. Now he might not come back."

Maris put the tissue down and sobbed into her hands. "But if he doesn't come back, what will I do? I don't make enough money to make the house payment by myself. If we get divorced, his mother will say, 'I told you so.' She never liked me anyway."

"Maris, calm down, you're getting hysterical," Sabrina said.

"I think I have the right to be hysterical. My husband is spending an indefinite amount of time with his relatives, who don't really like me. They're trying to brainwash him."

Sabrina inhaled and exhaled. "Okay, Maris, tell me what you want me to do."

"I was going to ask you to pray for me, but what good would that do? If you have all of these problems and you can't make them go away, what good would it do for you to pray for me? I mean, I don't even go to church."

Sabrina patted Maris's hand. "No, no, that's not how it works, Maris. Of course I'll pray for you. I'll pray for myself, too. Saying a prayer doesn't always make problems instantaneously disappear, but it does get things moving."

"I don't know, Sabrina. You're the one always quoting the Bible. I laugh at you so much, I don't think God would be interested in trying to help me. For all I know, maybe He's punishing me for not agreeing with you."

Sabrina shook her head. "God will forgive you if you ask Him. He doesn't hold grudges."

Maris felt the hopelessness start to loosen its grip on her. "Does that mean you'll pray for me?"

"Of course I will. I'll pray for you and Sidney and both of your families."

Maris rolled her eyes. "Don't waste your prayers on his mother. She's impossible."

Sabrina pursed her lips.

Maris stood up and got her purse. Even Sabrina was turning on her. "I guess that means you *want* to pray for his mom." She put her hands on her hips. "What? Does it cancel out my prayer if I ask you not to pray for her?"

Sabrina stood, too. "Well, prayer has a lot to do with the attitude of your heart. It's our way to talk to God, and He wants to listen to us."

"So what's the holdup?"

"Well, God loves everybody. Even Sidney's mom. So it doesn't do much good for you to pray and ask for something good for yourself while you're wishing something bad for her."

Maris shook her head. "That's not fair, Sabrina. Not fair at all. Are you telling me that you can't ask God to make people stop picking on you?"

"No, not at all. In the Psalms, King David tells God all about the people who are plotting against him. But the thing is, you have to be willing to forgive these people."

"So, I have to forgive Sidney's mom, and then ask God to fix our marriage?"

"In a nutshell, yes."

"Well, that's unlikely to happen. I know she's the one who put him up to this. If she wants him to leave me, then I don't exactly want anything nice to happen to her."

"I know you feel that way, but really, Maris, do you want something *bad* to happen to her?"

Maris hated it when Sabrina had to take everybody else's side. "You know what? This is why I'm not a Christian. This whole turn-the-other-cheek thing."

"I never said turn the other cheek," Sabrina said.

"Well, you implied it."

"Maris, did you know that the Bible says I can tell a mountain to move? Think about it. A huge mountain, and all I have to do is have faith and say, 'move.' If it's God's will, the mountain will move."

That sounded pretty impressive to Maris, but she wasn't about to let Sabrina know it. "And what does this have to do with my mother-in-law?"

"The next verse says that when I pray, I need to forgive anyone that I haven't forgiven."

"And if you don't?"

"God won't forgive my sins."

"So the prayer is canceled out?"

"Well, sin hinders our communication with God, so my prayer won't be as effective as it could be."

Maris groaned. "Why is it so bad that I don't want you to pray for Sid's mom?" She sat down again, and Sabrina followed suit. "Doesn't the Bible also say do unto others as you want them to do to you?"

"Yes, but—"

"But nothing. Sid's mom picks on me, no matter how nice I am. For the past few months, I figured I might as well give her some of her own medicine."

Maris stopped and folded and unfolded her tissue. Sabrina was giving her a tolerant look, and Maris knew she was starting to sound like a spoiled, whiny brat. "Sabrina, you know I'm not a mean person. I hate conflict and I try to keep the peace. So I don't understand why this is happening to me."

"I know you're not a mean person, Maris, but being nice doesn't get anyone into heaven."

"Hold it. I didn't come here to talk about heaven. Why do you always have to turn everything into a salvation sermon?

Can't you just listen and be sympathetic for a few minutes without trying to evangelize somebody?"

Sabrina sighed and shook her head. "Okay, I'm sorry. You talk, and I'll sympathize."

Maris's temper flared. Sabrina was giving her a speech without saying anything. "You don't have to sound so facetious."

"I was *not* being facetious. But honestly, Maris, you need to calm down. I'm your friend, not your enemy, but it's really hard for me to comfort you while you keep accusing me of being against you."

Maris took a deep breath. Sabrina didn't look too happy. And she had good reason. She had her own problems to deal with, and now Maris had dumped her issues on top of the pile. "This isn't going as well as I had hoped," Maris said, feeling disappointed. "I think I should just go home."

"Maris, please don't leave and be mad at me. I'll pray for you no matter what. In fact, we can pray now."

Maris breathed a sigh of relief. "Thank you." Feeling self-conscious, she ran her hand through her hair. "So what do we do now?"

She hadn't prayed since she was a little girl, and that was only when she spent the night at her grandma's house. She wondered if she should kneel or clasp her hands together, but Sabrina didn't seem to be doing either one.

"Let's just sit here at the table," Sabrina suggested.

"The kitchen table? That's it?"

"Or we can go in the living room if you want," said Sabrina.

"Well, I just want to make sure it works."

Sabrina laughed. "You don't have to be in a special room to pray. I pray even when I'm sitting in the car, stuck in traffic. God is still listening."

Maris hoped Sabrina wasn't saying this because she was still upset about the mother-in-law thing.

They both sat at the table, and Maris waited expectantly. Sabrina closed her eyes, so Maris did the same.

"Lord, I thank you for my friend Maris, and I'm asking you to comfort her tonight . . ."

Sabrina's voice was strong and clear. She was speaking in plain English—no fancy words and phrases and no special tone of voice. It almost seemed as though she could be talking to someone sitting right across the table.

Maris opened her eyes for a couple of moments and looked around. There was no one in the room but her and Sabrina, and Maris was getting a little spooked out that Sabrina was talking to God as if He were sitting right next to Maris. But Sabrina didn't seem to be spooked at all.

". . . Please give her and Sid peace and understanding . . ."

Maris wondered if she should remind Sabrina to tell God that Sid was her husband. But Sabrina always said God knew everything, so she guessed there was no need to interrupt.

". . . and I ask You to open the lines of communication between them and heal their marriage. Help them to reach a decision they can both be happy about concerning their business . . ."

Maris liked the sound of that. Given the way things were now, nobody short of God Himself would be able to make her husband see the light.

If Sid kept going at his current rate, they would be bankrupt soon. And stranded in Louisiana. With Sid's mom. Ugh.

Oops, I didn't mean that, Maris thought. *All right, I did mean it. But only a little bit.*

She opened her eyes to see if Sabrina could tell she was thinking bad thoughts about Sid's mom. But Sabrina prayed on, seemingly unaware.

Way to cover, Maris thought, feeling relieved. She closed her eyes and listened again.

"... Show them the kind of business You want them to start ..."

What was Sabrina doing? Maris wanted to stop her before she went too far, but she didn't want to be rude. Plus, she didn't want to nullify the part about her and Sid getting along better. But really, did Sabrina have to go and ask God to pick a business for them?

Obviously, she and Sid couldn't agree at the moment, but surely they could come to a mutually agreeable conclusion soon. But if Sabrina kept this up, she and Sid would look up and find themselves running a Bible bookstore or something.

Is this what being a Christian is about? Asking God to tell you what to do all day, every day? Does Sabrina have to ask God if she can tie her shoes?

Maris felt frustrated. She liked the concept of being able to talk to God and ask Him to fix problems, but the price tag seemed a little steep. By nature, she was an independent person, and she didn't even like it when Sid got too bossy. The last thing she needed was a God who picked up where Sid left off.

Between God, Sidney, and Sidney's mother, her life would be ...

"Oh, great, I did it again," Maris mumbled. *There goes the prayer.*

Sabrina stopped praying and looked at Maris.

Maris wondered if they would have to start the prayer over again or if Sabrina would get fed up and call the whole thing off.

"What did you say?" Sabrina wanted to know.

Maris sighed. "I think I messed up the prayer. A couple of

times I couldn't help myself and I had some bad thoughts about Sidney's mom."

"Oh." The expression on Sabrina's face was difficult to read. Finally, she said, "Listen, Maris, do you want to stay bitter at her or do you want to have the upper hand?"

Upper hand. The phrase was music to Maris's ears. Had Sabrina lost her Goody Two-shoes somewhere?

"So there *is* some kind of power behind this whole God thing," Maris said. Perfect.

"Of course I want the upper hand. I want to march right into her living room and tell her—"

"Not that kind of upper hand," Sabrina said, interrupting. "I mean a spiritual upper hand."

"I guess," Maris said. Still not exactly what she'd expected, but a spiritual upper hand had to be better than none at all.

"Then you need to forgive her. Take your unforgiveness, hand it to God, and trust that He will make things right." Sabrina put up her hands, warning Maris to be quiet.

Maris took a deep breath and bit back her retort.

Sabrina continued. "Yes, it's difficult, and it doesn't feel very good at first. It makes you feel helpless and even angry. In fact, sometimes I even pick it back up again and hold on to it. Sometimes it seems like I can do a better job of fixing things than God can. But you know what?"

"What?" Maris braced herself for a holy answer.

"I always mess up. I usually go over the top and make myself look stupid and vengeful. Either that or I can never come up with a good enough plan. So I sit around stewing, trying to dream up a way to make somebody pay, and they keep running roughshod over me. I might get a few digs in here and there, but they always seem to win the big battles."

"So what happens when you let God handle it? I'm sorry, but

I'm having a hard time picturing God swooping down and giving Sid's mom what for."

"God's in charge of the universe. He usually doesn't do exactly what I *wish* He would do to someone, so He probably won't knock on your mother-in-law's front door and give her a lecture. And sometimes, even when I let Him have my problems and I don't keep taking them back, it seems to take a long time for anything to happen."

"So why give it to Him at all?"

"Because it's easier. It's less stressful. I don't feel guilty for trying to make something awful happen to someone. I don't worry about how God will work with that person, and that makes it easier for me to work on getting closer to God."

"So you're saying you let go of the problem, go on with your life, and God's got your back?"

Sabrina grinned. "Exactly."

Maris considered all this for several moments. Maybe she could try it for a little while. Just to see if Sabrina was telling the truth.

"Okay. I'll forgive her. Tell me what I need to do."

"Just tell God you forgive her. Tell Him that you trust Him to move in her life."

Maris closed her eyes and spoke. "Okay, God. I forgive Sid's mom. I don't really feel like it, but I will. I'm hoping that You will do something to show her that she doesn't need to treat me like I'm her enemy. And I'm hoping that You'll help work things out with me and Sid, too . . . Amen."

Maris opened her eyes and looked at Sabrina. "Did I do okay?"

"You did fine." Sabrina was grinning from ear to ear.

Maris checked her watch. "It's almost eleven. I guess I should get home and see if Sid might have called."

"All right, I'll see you in the morning."

Maris walked to the front door, and Sabrina followed. Maris stood in the doorway, not really wanting to leave. Despite her confusion and frustration at having to forgive Sid's mom, she honestly felt much better than she had when she'd arrived.

"Thanks, Sabrina. I know I can be difficult, but I really appreciate the time you spent with me."

"No problem, Maris, I was happy to help."

"Will you keep praying about it?"

"I will. And you should, too."

"Is there anything else I need to do?"

"Like what?"

"I don't know." Maris shifted from side to side for several moments. If she said what she was thinking, Sabrina would never let her forget it. Still, it might not be all that bad. Even Darci had braved it for the past few weeks. "Should I come to church?"

Sabrina didn't say anything at first, but a smile spread across her face. "If you want to," she said finally. "I'd love it if you did come. You can even bring Sid when he gets back."

"*If* he gets back," Maris said. The thought terrified her, and she blinked back tears again.

"Hang on." Sabrina ran back to the kitchen and brought more tissues. "Are you okay to drive? I don't want you getting so upset that you don't pay attention to where you're going."

"I'm fine." Maris grabbed the tissues and dabbed gently under her eyes. The skin was already raw from repeated rubbing. "But, yeah, I think I will come to church. Even if Sid doesn't want to." It was a given that Sid would refuse to come, even if he were home. He was more wary of religious people than Maris was.

"Well, you know where it is, and we start at ten."

Maris nodded. "Okay. Don't hold me to it, but I'm giving it some serious thought."

"I promise not to bug you about it," said Sabrina.

Maris said good-bye and got into her car. She felt empty inside, knowing that Sid wouldn't be there when she got home, but she could always call. He had his cell phone, so she wouldn't have to call his mom's house and deal with her first.

"God, please let this turn out okay. I don't want to lose my marriage," she said as she steered her car back out onto the main road.

Seconds later, she sat at a red light. The realization came to her in a stunning rush.

I just prayed. Without anybody else around. Without Sabrina showing me how to do it.

Was it really that simple? Had God heard?

The warmth that seemed to envelop her was unmistakable. She hadn't felt that on the way to Sabrina's house. In fact, she'd felt exactly the opposite.

Still, doubt wiggled its way into the edges of her thoughts. Had God really been listening?

According to Sabrina, He had. *I forgave Sid's mom, and I trust God to change things.*

And if there was more she needed to know or do, Maris was determined to learn it on Sunday.

"We'll see," said Maris. The light changed, and she drove forward. One thing was for sure. She hadn't felt this confident in ages.

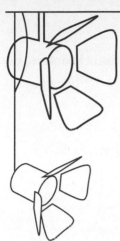

Chapter Fourteen

Sabrina stared up at the menu on the wall and changed her mind too many times to count. After almost a month of being coffee-free, she was about to have her first latte.

"You want to order first?" asked Avery.

Sabrina shook her head. "No, you go ahead. I'm still trying to make up my mind."

"Okay." Avery turned to the girl behind the counter and rattled off his order.

"Can I help you, ma'am?" the girl asked.

"Well, let's see . . ." Sabrina looked at the menu one more time.

The girl was staring at her curiously, and Sabrina knew she probably looked like one of those people ordering a specialty coffee drink for the first time.

Back in the days when she had two or three lattes a day, Sabrina hated getting stuck behind someone who was too overwhelmed by all the choices to make up their mind. Now, having been deprived of coffee for several weeks, she was reveling in the sounds and smells of the coffeehouse, and she didn't want to rush for anything.

She glanced up at the menu again. She wanted chocolate, no doubt about it. And maybe a little caramel. And definitely more than a single shot of espresso.

She looked at the girl. "I think I want to create my own latte, since I don't see exactly what I want on the board there."

"Sure, we can do that," said the girl.

"Okay. How about a medium mocha, triple shot of espresso? Throw in some amaretto, skip the foam, and top it with whipped cream instead. Then drizzle on some caramel."

The girl blinked. "Okay. Skim or two-percent?"

"How about whole? I'm feeling adventurous," she said to Avery, who stood nearby, waiting for his drink.

"I'll have to taste that one," he said.

The girl gave the order to the people making the drink, then turned back to face Sabrina. She was staring at her.

Sabrina felt a little uncomfortable underneath this teenager's scrutiny. She turned and glanced at the door, wishing some other customers would come in.

"Um, can I ask you something?"

Sabrina turned to face the girl again. "Me?"

"Yeah," she said, nodding.

With a shrug, Sabrina glanced at Avery, who was watching. "Go ahead."

"Aren't you that lady on *The Daily Dose?*"

Sabrina chuckled. Was the girl confusing her with Darci? She must not be a regular viewer.

"Oh, I work for the show, but I'm not the host," she explained.

"Oh, I know you're not the host. But you look like that woman, Sabrina, who's trying to keep the resolutions."

Another employee, the one who was supposed to be making

Sabrina's coffee, looked up. "Oh, the one who doesn't want to fall in love. Hey, you do look like her."

"Oh." Sabrina looked at Avery. "I am her. I mean, that's me." *Wow, my first fan sighting.*

The girl squealed. "It *is* you! I knew you looked familiar." She whipped out a napkin from behind the counter. "Can I have your autograph?"

"Me, too," said the other girl.

The customers already sitting down at their tables looked up to see what the commotion was about.

"So why don't you want to fall in love?" the first girl asked as Sabrina fumbled in her purse for a pen.

Sabrina didn't know what to say. She looked at Avery and sent him a silent plea for help.

Instead, he chuckled. "I've been wondering the same thing," he told the girl. "But she won't tell me. I'm guessing it's a big secret and she'll wait until later to reveal it on the show."

"Oh," the girl said. "Well, I'm usually at work when *The Daily Dose* is on, but I'll have my mom tape the next resolutions show for me. We made a joint resolution that she would brush up on her piano playing and I would keep up my voice lessons."

"I tape it, too," said the other girl. "I made a resolution to read a book every week, and so far, I've kept it. You know, that show is really inspiring me. I figure, if they can do it, I can, too."

Sabrina located a pen and began scribbling her name on the napkins.

"Well, that's good news," said Avery.

"Do you work for the show, too?" said the second girl. "Or are you just, like, her chauffeur or something?"

Sabrina laughed out loud. Avery, the chauffeur. She would tease him about that for a long time.

Now it was his turn to look flustered. "No, not exactly," he stammered. "I'm the executive producer of *The Daily Dose.* I created the show."

An older woman had gotten up from one of the tables and asked Sabrina to autograph her napkin as well. "And could you sign one for my sister, too? She's trying to lose fifty pounds this year, and the show really keeps her motivated."

Sabrina grabbed the napkins and kept writing.

"So, do you guys know Darci?" asked the older woman. "She's such a sweetheart, you know. I keep telling my son I'd love to have a daughter-in-law like her. She's just so sincere, and she really cares about people."

Sabrina smiled and nodded. She had to give it to the PR department. The public *loved* Darci.

"I'd love to meet her in person one day," said the first girl behind the counter. "I'm so jealous that you guys get to see her every day."

"If you go to our Web site, you can get tickets to come to a taping," Avery suggested. "Darci usually signs autographs after we finish an episode."

"Oh, that sounds lovely," the older woman said, clasping her hands together. "Maybe I can get my son to take the day off from work and come with me. He works for an advertising firm, but maybe . . ."

"Ooh, we should get an afternoon off and go on the same day," the girl behind the counter said to her fellow employee.

"Do you know if Darci has a . . ." The older woman blushed but kept going. "If she is seeing anyone? I'd love for her to meet my son."

Avery leaned his head to the side and spoke very kindly. "Oh, we're not at liberty to give out such personal details. Darci really values her privacy, of course."

"Oh, of course," the woman repeated. She put her hands over her mouth. "Forgive me for even asking."

"But I'm sure she'd love to meet you, so please feel free to come, and bring your son along. Darci loves talking to her fans," Avery said.

Sabrina was impressed with how smoothly he'd handled that situation. She doubted Darci would be interested in the woman's son, but she would certainly be gracious and sign a few autographs for them.

Darci was like a lightbulb. On the set and afterward when she met with fans, she glowed, full of warmth. But back in the production offices, away from the cameras, she shut down and grew cold. Sabrina didn't know how she could be so different from her on-air persona. But the important thing was, people liked the Darci they saw on TV.

And as long as people loved Darci, *The Daily Dose* stayed in business, and Sabrina continued to get a paycheck.

"Sabrina, here's your coffee." The girl behind the counter held it out, and Sabrina reached for it. It was a little odd to hear the girl use her first name, but she guessed that was one of the things that went along with being on the show.

Before she could grab the cup, the girl pulled it back. With a puzzled look on her face, she said, "But I thought you were giving up coffee."

The room went silent.

Avery cleared his throat, and Sabrina could tell by the look on his face that he was trying to hold back laughter.

All eyes were on Sabrina, waiting for an explanation.

"Well, not technically giving up coffee," Sabrina explained. "Just cutting back."

"Oh." The girl looked down at the cup.

Sabrina looked, too. It was piled wondrously high with

swirls of whipped cream, and rivulets of caramel beckoned tantalizingly. The scent of espresso was so heavy, she could almost taste it.

"I haven't actually had any coffee in almost a month," Sabrina said, feeling defensive.

"Oh," the girl said again.

"A triple shot," the other girl murmured.

"Darci says she drinks water when she has cravings," the older woman said. "My sister said it works for her," she added helpfully.

Avery started coughing and had to turn away.

Traitor. Sabrina wanted to glare at him but refrained.

Sabrina looked at the three women. How could she let them down? Far be it from her to dash their hopes.

Could she live with knowing that a high school girl decided it was impossible to read a book every week because she had to have a latte? What if the woman's sister gave up on her diet? And what about the mother-daughter musical duo?

"I thought I would make this a reward for staying away from caffeine for so long," she said, in a feeble attempt to redeem herself.

"Oh," the first girl said again.

Couldn't that girl say anything besides "oh"?

"You know . . ." the second girl began, "I could make you a decaf chai latte."

"A what?" Sabrina asked.

"It's a latte made with decaf tea instead of espresso. I can still put whipped cream and caramel on top. And you'll still be keeping your resolution."

Sabrina sighed. If she didn't take the chai latte, they would think she was a phony and a cheat. She was already feeling guilty enough to stay out of any coffee shop for the remainder of the year.

She pasted on a smile. "Okay, I'll try it."

The second girl didn't need any additional encouragement. She immediately went to work making the new drink.

The older woman clasped her hands together. "I'll have to tell my sister about it. She'll be so encouraged."

"I know," the first girl agreed. "I can't believe I was a part of this. How exciting. I'm going to tell my mom all about it when I get home."

Within minutes the drink was ready. Sabrina humbly and hurriedly paid her bill, then exited the shop. Avery followed.

"I take it you don't want to sit inside and talk."

"Not under that kind of scrutiny," she mumbled. "We can talk in my car." She unlocked the door and got inside.

As soon as the doors were closed, Sabrina couldn't contain herself. "When Darci has cravings, she drinks water," she said, mimicking the older woman.

"Ha! Maybe I should buy a huge tub of water and put it in her office so she can dunk herself in it whenever she has a craving to yell at somebody."

Avery didn't say anything.

"Is this how it's going to be? I can't even get a cup of coffee without somebody scrutinizing me?"

Finally, he said, "You know, this is what I wanted to talk to you about in the first place." His words were slow and deliberate. "It's kind of fitting that this happened, because I have a feeling you wouldn't have fully grasped the depth of my concern."

Sabrina took a sip of her drink. It was good—in a tea-and-milk kind of way—but it didn't really hit the spot the way the espresso would have.

Avery pointed to his own coffee. "You can have mine if you want. Or we can go to another coffee shop."

Sabrina shook her head. "That's okay. For one thing, I would feel like a criminal, sneaking around trying to find somebody who will sell me a real latte on the low. And with my luck, I'd probably run into somebody else who recognizes me from the show."

He snickered. "That was priceless. The look on your face when that girl wouldn't hand over the cup—I wish I'd had a camera." He put his cup on the dashboard and laughed heartily.

Sabrina found it only mildly amusing. Two months ago, she wouldn't have dreamed that putting her goals out for the world to see would prevent her from getting the kind of latte she wanted.

The whole celebrity life was overrated. Signing autographs was one thing, but having people dictate the choices she made for a simple hot drink was a direct hit on her personal freedom.

And there was nothing she could do about it, short of being totally rude. Of course, if she'd rolled her eyes and told them to shut up and leave her alone, they would no longer think she was such an inspiration.

But if the Sabrina on television was so perfect, that left no room for the real Sabrina. The Sabrina who craved coffee and sometimes ate too many cookies and still nibbled on her nails when she was really stressed. The Sabrina who hadn't picked up her knitting needles in four days and hadn't balanced her check-book in two weeks.

There was no way to be herself and please the public. To do so would almost be a deception. Otherwise, she would have to transform herself into someone she wasn't and stay that way, on and off camera.

Then it hit her.

"It just occurred to me how difficult things can get for Darci," she said.

For the first time in her years of working for *The Daily Dose,* Sabrina felt sympathy for her boss.

Avery nodded somberly. "You couldn't pay me enough money to take her job. Yes, she goes over the top in her private life. She abuses the fact that off the set she can be less than perfect, but consider what just went on in that coffee shop.

"You've only been on the show three times. Darci's been on every day for years. The minute she steps out of her house, people are watching everything she does."

Sabrina shook her head. "Poor Darci." She smiled sadly, considering the irony. Who would even have guessed she'd utter the words "poor" and "Darci" in the same sentence and actually mean it?

He continued. "I've been grocery shopping with Darci a few times. She hates it. People actually follow her up and down the aisles.

"You can hear them murmuring, 'What kind of laundry detergent does Darci Oliver use? What kind of deodorant does she buy? What kind of ice cream does she like? Does she even eat ice cream? Didn't she have a show last week about avoiding ice cream cravings? So why is she buying ice cream?'"

He sighed. "She likes to be around people. At least, she used to. But this really gets to her. Lately, she's been sending people out to do her errands for her. She says she's too busy and doesn't have time, but I think it's because she's tired of people watching her so much."

Sabrina tried to imagine going grocery shopping and having most of the people in the store scrutinize every item in her basket. Good grief.

"And that's what I've been wanting to talk to you about.

You've just experienced your first brush with a public who recognizes you. And, in a sense, that makes you vulnerable to them. How will you handle it if we have one resolutions show a week?"

Sabrina shrugged. "Darci's determined to do it, so that's what we'll end up doing. It's no big deal."

"Sabrina, I know you, and I know your workload. And with me cutting back on my time at the office, you and Maris have even more to do."

Sabrina held up a hand to stop him. "I appreciate your concern, but there are nine other people on the everyday-people panel. Shouldn't you be asking them how they feel, too?"

He grinned sheepishly. "I guess so. But you're prettier. It's a lot more fun talking to you."

Sabrina turned away and stared out the window. Was he flirting?

She turned and looked at him again. He winked.

Definitely flirting.

She willed herself not to get all googly-eyed just because he'd called her pretty. If he couldn't maintain a modicum of professional behavior, then she would.

She cleared her throat. "I appreciate your concern, but it might be better if you just e-mailed a survey to the rest of the people on the panel to see how they feel about extra shows. It would be an additional intrusion on all of our lives, but if it helps the show, I'm sure most of them will be willing to sacrifice that extra time."

Avery shook his head. "I give you one tiny compliment and you pull out the business-meeting voice. Come on, Sabrina, what are you afraid of? We were having a friendly conversation; then all of a sudden you start talking like you're trying to sell insurance or something."

"Well, think about how I felt," she countered. "We were having a good discussion and then, out of nowhere, you throw out a pickup line."

"That's not a pickup line," he protested.

"Oh, yeah? Sounds like it to me."

Avery shook his head. "No, that was a compliment. A pickup line would be something really ridiculous and unbelievable, like, 'Did it hurt when you fell from heaven?' or 'You must be tired because you've been running through my mind all day.'"

"Please tell me you have never actually used those."

"Not me. I know better," Avery said. "But I know some people who have. One brother back in college actually went up to a woman in church and said, 'Is it a sin that you stole my heart?'"

"No way." Sabrina tried to keep her jaw from hanging open.

"I kid you not. He also tried telling some girl, 'Excuse me, but I think one of your ribs belongs to me.'"

"This guy must be related to my ex-fiancé. The day I met him, he came up to me and said, 'Do you believe in love at first sight, or should I walk by again?'"

"And you fell for it?"

"Actually, I laughed at him, but I guess I thought he was kind of charming or something."

"Or something," Avery repeated.

"Exactly. I mean, he's not a bad guy or anything like that. He's just . . ."

"Silly enough to use a lame line to talk to a really beautiful woman," Avery supplied. "And if he called you right now and told you he'd made a mistake by letting you get away from him, what would you say?"

Sabrina deliberately didn't answer. Avery was always trying to work the topic of love and relationships into the conversation. She reached for her chai and took a long sip.

Avery nodded. "I see. You're ignoring my question."

"For now I am."

"Don't worry. I'll find a way to ask you again later."

"I don't doubt it. But maybe I'll be the one to ask you something really personal sometime."

"Why wait? Ask me now." Avery folded his arms and sat back, an expectant look on his face.

"Okay. Let me think about it." Sabrina racked her brain for something to say that wouldn't be too cheesy.

Silence hung heavily as several moments passed and Sabrina still had yet to come up with her question.

Avery hummed the tune to *Jeopardy!,* and from the look on his face, he was enjoying her discomfort far too much.

"You know what? I want a rain check," she said.

"For what?"

"The personal question. I'll think about it and then I'll spring it on you someday when you least expect it."

"Ooh, when I least expect it? Sounds pretty scary."

"Consider yourself warned," she said, laughing.

He drained the rest of the contents of his coffee cup, then looked straight at her. "So you couldn't come up with anything? Or you just didn't want to say what you were thinking? You didn't want me to think you were falling in love with me?"

Sabrina felt her face grow warm, and she knew he could tell she was blushing.

Avery reached over and patted her arm. "I'm sorry for embarrassing you. I'll shut up now."

"Thank you," she said, feeling genuinely relieved.

"Well, it looks like this conversation has come to a close."

"I agree."

"But getting back to my original subject," he said.

"Seriously, I'm fine with two more shows. If it's good for the show, then it's ultimately good for me."

"You're sure?"

"Yes. I'm actually a little frustrated that you keep asking. It's like you don't think I'll be able to keep up with things. It's almost kind of demeaning, if you think about it."

"That's not what I'm trying to say."

"Then what *are* you saying?"

"I'm saying that I'm concerned you might be taking this resolutions program too seriously. I know you're a perfectionist. How will you handle it if you keep biting your fingernails or don't succeed at your hobby?"

Sabrina looked out the window again. Things would be a lot easier if Avery knew the reason behind her involvement. She appreciated his concern, but she had gotten herself into this, and she could tough it out for the next ten and a half months.

But as things stood now, keeping the resolutions had become part of her job description, and she wouldn't flake out. No way would she give Darci the satisfaction of seeing her fail.

"Avery, I'm glad you care enough to be concerned, but I'm okay."

"And you still didn't really answer my question. How will you take it if you wake up one day and find you can't really do it all?"

"That won't happen. Believe me, I've got it under control."

"Sure about that?"

"Positive."

Sabrina checked her watch. "Well, it's almost six. I should get home and do a little knitting before I head to the gym."

"And I have paperwork back at the office. So I'll see you tomorrow."

"Yeah, we've got a seven a.m. taping, so I'll be there bright and early."

Avery got out, then poked his head back inside. "I forgot to ask you something."

"Oh? What?"

He seemed to hesitate for a bit, then finally spoke. "Well, you know, the Bible says, 'Give food to the hungry and drink to the thirsty.' Would you like to go to dinner sometime?"

Sabrina rolled her eyes and shook her head. "Nice try. That one's right on par with 'Nice Bible' and 'Do you want to come over and watch *The Ten Commandments* with me?'"

Avery laughed. "What would you say if I told you I didn't believe in angels until I met you?"

"I would tell you to go away."

"Can't blame me for trying," he said. "Valentine's Day is coming up in a few days, you know."

"I'll pray for you," she said, laughing.

Sabrina pulled out of the parking lot with a smile on her face. Leave it to Avery to turn a simple discussion into a comedy routine.

Handsome, successful, God-fearing, and funny. What a combination.

Valentine's Day morning, on her way out the door, Sabrina nearly bumped into a delivery man.

"Sabrina Bradley?" he asked, consulting his clipboard.

"That's me," she answered.

He held up a crystal vase packed with mixed flowers. "Then these are for you. Sign here, please."

Sabrina signed for the flowers, then took them inside. The vibrant colors were a welcome respite from the eight inches of snow on the ground outside.

She opened the card and had to smile when she saw Avery's familiar scrawl:

I knew you wouldn't go to dinner with me, but I was feeling chivalrous, so I sent you these. I was passing by the florist and this caught my eye. In fact, they reminded me of you—vibrant, dainty, feminine, and delicate (and, no, I'm not trying to be cheesy. I really meant that).

Please find it in your heart to accept them as a token of my friendship (NOT LOVE—therefore, I don't think that keeping them will be a violation of your resolution).

Happy Valentine's Day from your friend (not boyfriend!),

Avery

P.S. I'm really hoping you don't throw the vase back at the delivery guy, but just in case, I gave him an extra five dollars for dangerous work.

Laughing, Sabrina put the card down and stared at the flowers. The bouquet truly was gorgeous, and her stomach flip-flopped at the notion that Avery found her just as beautiful.

Despite her best efforts to ignore him, Avery was somehow getting pretty adept at picking the locks she kept on the door to her heart.

The flowers were nice, and Avery probably meant well, but she was going to find a way to discourage him from doing anything further.

He might be the closest thing to Prince Charming she'd ever met, but he wasn't worth losing a promotion over.

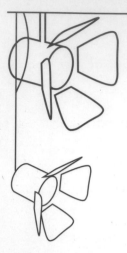

Chapter Fifteen

Well, you know they spend all of their free time together. At least that's what I heard."

"I saw them myself at the hobby store a few weeks ago."

"So are they dating?"

"They have to be. But does Darci know?"

"How could she not know?"

"You're right; she's smarter than that. And besides, Avery's her ex-boyfriend. She knows him well enough to see he's in love with someone else."

"But maybe she doesn't care. I heard *she* dumped *him,* so maybe she's thinking 'good riddance.'"

Darci stopped mid-step on her way to the ladies' room. She had a feeling she knew the identities of who the hushed voices on the other side of the cubicle walls were discussing.

She didn't bother to listen any longer. Office drivel had the tendency to be mostly fluff and little truth, and she rarely indulged in it. But this story didn't seem all that impossible to believe.

She turned on her heel and headed back to her own office. She needed time to sit and think.

Sabrina was ready to throw the knitting needles across the room. What in the world did "purl" mean?

She consulted the book again to see if the pictures would be more helpful than the dry paragraph of instruction. Two minutes later, she was ready to throw the book across the room. What a way to spend a Saturday morning.

The phone rang, and she rushed to it, relieved for a distraction.

"Hello?"

"Hey, it's me."

She knew the voice but decided to tease him a bit. "'Me' who?"

"Me, Avery. And I know you know it's me."

"What's up?"

"Nothing at the moment. What do you have going on?"

"Knitting. Or trying to. Remember that scarf I told you I wanted to make?"

"Yeah. How's it coming?"

"It's not. In fact, at this rate, it may be next summer before I get the first two inches done."

"Sounds like you picked the wrong hobby."

"Tell me about it."

"Well, how about we go find you something different?"

"I was thinking about that. But my resolution says I have to find a hobby and stick with it. So giving up knitting would be breaking it . . . I think."

"Or not. First off, it says 'find a hobby.' Then it says 'stick with it.' A hobby is generally something you like, so the way I see it, you haven't really found the hobby yet."

Sabrina liked his line of reasoning. "But do you think it's too late to change my mind?"

"Too late? It's mid-March. You have nine months until the end of the year. Of course it's early enough to change your mind."

"Maybe I could try quilting . . ." Sabrina mused.

Avery cleared his throat. Sabrina had a feeling he was holding back laughter. "Maybe you should try something that doesn't involve needles and thread this time."

"Is that an insult?" she playfully challenged.

"No. Just my opinion. Take it or leave it."

"I'll take it if you have a suggestion for a new hobby."

"I don't know. It's starting to get warm outside. Do you really want to sit inside crocheting all the time? Maybe you should pick something you can do outdoors."

Sabrina glanced out the window. It was starting to get warm, but the heat wave hadn't hit quite yet. The idea of spending a prolonged period of time outside didn't really appeal to her, but a glance at those knitting needles gave her pause.

"I'm not going to go hiking and I don't like tennis," she said.

"What about gardening?"

"Gardening. In the dirt. With bugs." It didn't sound all that fun.

"And fresh air and pretty flowers. And I'll help you get started."

Sabrina considered that for a moment. How bad could it be? In fact, it sounded fun . . . even a little romantic. Especially with Avery around.

She envisioned the barren flower beds in her front yard bursting with color. She could see herself in an oversized floppy hat and a lacy Victorian-style dress, clipping abundant rose blooms.

The summer sun was warm but not overly so, and a gentle breeze wafted through every few moments.

Avery hovered nearby with a frosty glass of lemonade to quench her thirst. When the basket of roses got too heavy to carry, he took over and held it, and all Sabrina had to do was cut them.

"Sabrina? Are you still there? If you hate the idea so much, just say so."

"No, no. I actually think it's a good idea," she told Avery. "And you'll help, right?"

"Of course. Now, put those needles up where you'll never find them again and I'll be over in an hour."

"Where are we going?"

"It's a surprise, but wear something comfortable that won't be ruined if it gets dirty. And wear shoes that don't hurt your feet."

"I'm getting the feeling we're going somewhere with lots of dirt and walking. I'm not sure I want to spend my Saturday like that."

"You are correct. Actually, we're going two places. The first place involves walking; the second place involves dirt."

"Avery, maybe I will stick with the knitting. I just need to find someone who can teach me to purl."

"Oh, come on. Admit that you hate it. My idea is better," he said. "And if you can stick it out through the dirt and walking, I'll take you to a movie tonight."

That didn't sound bad at all. Before she could answer, Avery added, "And it's not a date. You won't fall in love with me. In fact, I'm starting to wonder if you'll still even like me by the end of the day."

"That sounds pretty ominous."

"I'm hoping it won't go that badly."

"Me, too. Whatever it is. But I accept the movie invitation."

Sabrina gave him directions, and they ended the call. For the next hour, she rushed around the house, alternating between getting dressed and putting on makeup, and trying to make the house look presentable.

When Avery arrived, she stood waiting at the door, wearing jeans, a sweatshirt, and tennis shoes. She was relieved to see that he was dressed in similar fashion.

"You ready?" he asked. "Let's head out now."

"Can you tell me where we're headed?" Sabrina said as she seated herself in the passenger's seat of his car.

"Botanical gardens. And then the nursery. I figured the gardens can inspire us; then we can get the flowers and go home and dig."

She nodded. "Very well planned. I like that."

"Like or love?" he asked.

Sabrina gave him a sideways glance. He was forever teasing her about the love issue.

"Can we leave love out of the conversation for one day?"

"Maybe. If you tell me why you hate the idea of being in love."

"I don't hate it. It's just not for me right now."

"So you'd like to be in love someday."

"Of course. I've been in love before and it didn't work out, so I'm taking a break."

"A break from love." Avery repeated the words, sounding thoughtful. "I've heard people say that when you least expect it, love finds you."

"I've heard that, too, but I think it's pretty cliché."

"So tell me. If you were in the market for love, how would you describe your ideal mate?"

"Good try, but I'd never tell you."

"Why not?"

"Because in my experience, that's backfired on me. I told my ex-fiancé the type of man I'd want to marry and he somehow managed to transform himself into a pretty good imitation."

"But it wasn't the real him."

Sabrina shook her head. "No. The real Eric kept seeping out of the seams now and then, but I didn't pay attention. I just kept stuffing him back into the box I'd created for him, and he let me—for a while. Then he started complaining that my 'ideal' was stifling him and his creativity."

"So he turned into someone totally different?"

She shrugged. "I guess you could just say he was being the real Eric. But the real Eric was not compatible with the real Sabrina."

"You were being someone you weren't?"

"I think so. At first I told myself that I was just trying to learn about the things he liked, but pretty soon, he was dragging me to poetry readings and writing lectures and I realized I was bored out of my mind. When I started voicing my complaints, he accused me of being phony."

"I think I understand that. When you first meet someone, you want to learn all about them, so you get interested in what interests them."

"Because you want to make the relationship work, it's easy to just go along with it."

"While you're secretly hoping it's only a phase," Avery cut in.

"Exactly."

"I've seen a lot of couples look up several months later in the relationship and realize they don't have anything in common," he said. "But by then it's difficult to get out of it, because you've gotten so . . ." He stopped, apparently searching for the correct word.

"Attached?"

"Right."

"And you don't want to be alone anymore, so you wonder if you can make it work somehow."

Avery nodded. "It's happened to me before."

Sabrina wondered if he was referring to his relationship with Darci, but refrained from asking. "The bottom line is, you can only pretend to be another person for so long before your true self starts demanding to be set free again."

"Well said. I agree completely."

The conversation stilled for several moments, and they rode the next few miles without talking.

Avery finally broke the silence. "I'm a little concerned, though."

"About what?"

"Well, if you won't tell me what kind of guy you like, how will I find out?"

Sabrina laughed. This man never stopped trying. "You won't." She wiggled her eyebrows. "I keep my ideals to myself, and if somebody matches up, I'll know it's the real thing."

"Determined to make it hard on me?"

"Have you been in love before?" she asked, changing the subject.

"Trying to shift the attention away from you?" he asked.

"Not really. But you've been the one asking all of the questions. I feel like I'm at an interview when I spend time with you."

Avery was quiet for a long time, and Sabrina began to wonder if he was upset by her question. Either that, or he was deliberately ignoring it.

She watched him at work and paid attention to the way he interacted with Darci. Though he sometimes grew visibly frustrated when Darci acted like a child, he still treated her with a great degree of tenderness.

At first Sabrina convinced herself that it was just because he didn't want to lose Darci as an employee, but lately she wondered if he might still have feelings for her.

The thought was unsettling, because he seemed to work so hard at getting Sabrina to lower her defenses.

Was he only trying to make Darci jealous? Everyone pretty much assumed that she had been the one to end the relationship.

Sabrina's curiosity got the best of her, and before she realized it, the words were out of her mouth. "Did you break things off with Darci, or was it the other way around?"

He shot her a sideways glance. Had she overstepped her boundaries? After all, he was still her boss.

"Don't you want to give me a chance to answer the first question? Or did you forget you'd asked me if I'd even been in love?"

"I thought you were ignoring that question, so I thought I'd toss out another one."

"Another question, equally as difficult to answer."

"So are you going to sit here and analyze the difficulty of the questions, or will you actually answer them?" Sabrina was surprised at her own tenacity.

She didn't usually press people to answer questions if they started squirming, but she felt she deserved an honest reply from Avery. After all, *he* was the one who kept making comments about love.

"Why are you asking? Don't you believe the office grapevine?" The twinkle in his eye let her know he was still in a jovial mood.

"The office grapevine? Don't tell me you actually believe the stuff you hear," Sabrina said.

He looked sheepish. "I don't actually engage in gossip, but in this cutthroat day and age, it never hurts to keep an ear to the ground. I sometimes learn the most interesting things about myself."

"Like what?"

"For example, did you know that I cried in my office for a week after Darci dumped me? Supposedly, the janitor heard me sobbing away day after day. Of course, I had my office doors closed and no one could really see, but that's the story and they're sticking to it."

"I heard you ate nothing but ice cream because you were so depressed. And Darci went on a mega shopping spree because she was so happy to be rid of you," Sabrina added.

"I wouldn't doubt it. But don't worry about me. I'll be fine. In fact, I'm already doing better. Did you know that you and I are practically engaged?"

"I've heard." Sabrina rolled her eyes. "Or more accurately *over*heard." She'd been in the ladies' room and two women had walked in, chatting away. Sabrina had been so embarrassed that she couldn't bring herself to come out of the stall until after they left.

"The office grapevine is never more than fifty percent truth, but generally I've found it to be mostly fiction."

"I wish people wouldn't believe everything they hear. It's sad. Nobody has any respect for the truth because they spend so much time speculating. And I've noticed that people have never really come up to me and simply asked a question. If they would, I would tell them the truth and set the story straight."

"Oh, but it's so much more fun to be secretive about it."

"It's so much more ridiculous," Sabrina said.

"And"—Avery lifted his hand from the steering wheel—"it cuts down on productivity. As the boss, I can attest to it. People don't get nearly as much work done when they're busy playing detective with the details of their coworkers' lives. All of this gossip messes with my bottom line. That's what really makes me mad."

Sabrina cleared her throat. "Avery."

"Yes?"

"Since we're on the topic of honesty, and going directly to someone to ask a question, I'd like to point out that you never really answered my question about you and Darci. Or the question about you having been in love."

"Well, we sort of got off the subject," he said.

He was sidestepping the question, but why? Sabrina felt a surge of temper. Had he merely been toying with her emotions these past few months?

"Avery, if I'm crossing some line, just say so. Otherwise . . ." She grinned, hoping to keep the mood light. "You've left me no choice but to draw my conclusions from what I've heard at work."

He nodded. "You drive a hard bargain."

"Let's just say I'm smart enough to tell when I'm being taken for a ride."

"Ouch. That hurts."

"That's why I said it." She had been on the relationship merry-go-round long enough to tell when a man was being less than truthful. Right now Avery was exhibiting classic symptoms.

She decided to raise the stakes even higher. "And if you change the subject one more time, I'm not going to the movie tonight."

Avery sighed. "I know you think I'm holding something back, and I guess I am, in a way."

No big surprise there. Sabrina put on a tolerant look and tried to stay patient.

He continued, speaking slowly. "I'll admit that I don't really want to discuss my relationship with Darci, but I'll do my best to set the record straight. Without going into details, let's just say it was a mutual decision. We're just two different people. Thankfully, I realized that before I married her."

"You were planning to get married?"

"Eventually. Nothing was concrete, and Darci isn't ready to be a wife yet. It probably would have been three or four more years."

"Do you regret ending it?"

"A little. Sometimes I walk into the office and I see glimpses of what first attracted me to her. Those are the times when I wonder if I was too hasty. You know, maybe I should have been more patient, given her a second chance—things like that." He looked across at her. "I'm sure you've thought the same things about Eric."

"Do you think you'll ever fix things between the two of you?"

He was silent for a long time. Then he said, "I don't think so. Most of the time I'm happy to have gotten out when I did. We were terribly mismatched, and marriage would have been miserable for both of us."

"By mismatched you mean . . . ?"

"Most important, she doesn't share my faith. She used to act interested when I first met her, and I guess I always hoped she would wake up one day and just be ready to accept Jesus." He shook his head. "But she never did. And I finally woke up and realized that she probably wouldn't."

"But she seems to be considering it now," Sabrina probed

even further. She was interested in knowing what Avery thought of Darci's sudden interest in Christianity.

"Yeah, it's kind of ironic, isn't it? After I back off and stop begging her to follow Jesus, she wants to go to church. Lately, she's even been asking me to take her to New Believers' class."

"That's great." Sabrina forced herself to sound cheerful, but inside, she felt anything but happy. And to top it off, she felt guilty.

In all honesty, what she really wanted was for Darci to stay the same and still refuse to go to church. As long as that was the case, Avery would still consider a relationship with Darci out of the question.

As things stood now, no matter how much Avery denied it, Darci still had him hooked. Three months ago, Avery's true feelings about Darci wouldn't have mattered to Sabrina. But now she was remembering how it had felt to see Eric with Sharon.

Avery's voice broke into her thoughts. "It's a good thing, if she really means it. But the faith difference isn't the only reason I can't see myself marrying her. She's got a lot of maturing to do, and I'm still not certain this sudden desire for all things religious isn't part of some larger scheme."

Sabrina nodded. Maybe Avery wasn't as clueless as she thought. Or maybe Darci was making a sincere change and would surprise them both.

"Then you still consider her to be your friend?" she asked, hoping to shift the conversation away from love.

"Are you still friends with Eric?"

Sabrina laughed. "We said we would be friends, but I'll know for sure once this interview of his hits the newsstands."

"Then you could say the same about me and Darci. We're nice to each other, but I'm always wondering if she's going to do something when I'm not looking."

"You seem to get along okay at work."

"We do. But we almost have to. But my situation with Darci is a lot like a couple who breaks up after they have a child. You and Eric could just break up and go your separate ways. You can be friends with him if you want to, but you don't necessarily have to. But Darci and I created this business together, and even though our relationship is over, the show still exists.

"We might not feel like getting along, but we have to be civil to each other for the sake of the show. If we have a difference of opinion, we try to resolve it away from the office. We don't always succeed, but that's our goal. We're both smart enough to realize that our livelihood is dependent on how we conduct ourselves at work."

They had reached the parking lot of the gardens, so Avery found a space, and they spent the next few minutes paying their admission and getting a map of the grounds.

Sabrina thought the conversation about Darci had been put to rest, but Avery surprised her by bringing it up again.

"I still respect her professionally. She's incredibly talented, and I admire the Darci she used to be before all the pressures of the show started to change her."

"What was she like?" Sabrina found the notion of the pre-celebrity Darci intriguing.

"I don't know . . . vivacious, charming, adventurous. She cared about other people back then. She was kind of timid about some things. Over time, she's gotten a lot more confident—maybe too much so."

He glanced at her. "I know you won't believe this, but in some ways, she was a lot like you."

Sabrina stopped walking and just looked at him. "Please tell me you're kidding."

Avery had an amused look on his face. "It's not an insult,

Sabrina. Don't be offended. If you had met Darci back when she was a freshman in college, you would have really liked her."

Sabrina pointed her finger at him. "You're walking a fine line, buddy. Keep it up and you'll be going to that movie by yourself tonight."

Avery made a big display of opening the map. "Okay. Change of subject. Which gardens do we want to see first?"

"Does it matter?" Sabrina wasn't ready to let go of her irritation just yet. The nerve of him, comparing her to Darci.

"As a matter of fact, it does. And I'm sorry." He reached out and wrapped her in a gentle hug.

Just as suddenly as he began the embrace, Avery ended it, dropping his arms to his side. "We're here to soak up inspiration for your garden, and instead we've gotten on edge talking about Darci and Eric."

He held out his hand. "Let's make a deal. No more talking about old relationships today."

Sabrina reached for his hand, and they shook. "Deal." Although she was disappointed that he had never admitted whether he had been in love with Darci, she was relieved to see the subject come to a close.

She didn't know if her nerves could take another comparison to Darci.

She smiled and suggested they tour the international gardens first. Determined to enjoy her day, she made a conscious effort to relax and have fun spending time with Avery.

After walking so long that they both complained of aching feet, Avery declared it was time to leave and head to the nursery.

There they spent nearly an hour picking out various seedlings that could be planted when the weather got a bit warmer.

"If I can't put these in the ground now, what will I do with them? Shouldn't I wait until the end of the month to buy all this stuff?" Sabrina suggested.

"Maybe you're right," Avery admitted. "But we should get you some gardening tools. I checked out your flower beds this morning, and they are in dire need of some rake-and-fertilizer action. When was the last time you planted anything in there, anyway?"

Sabrina pretended to be deep in thought. "Oh, let's see . . . I think it was around the fifteenth of . . . *never.*" She laughed. "This may be a bad idea. I don't think I have a green thumb."

"But I do. So you can learn from me."

"If you say so."

After Sabrina paid for her purchases, Avery insisted on actually going back to her house and doing some preliminary work on the beds.

He made a preliminary inspection of the largest section and decided that Sabrina should rake the leaves and brush; then he would follow with the shovel and try to soften the ground.

Sabrina looked at him incredulously. What he was suggesting could take hours.

"When you called this morning, you neglected to mention that I would have to participate in hard labor," Sabrina teased him. "I thought today would be a leisurely Saturday, but no. First you dragged me around miles and miles of gardens, then we went to a store and looked at every rake and shovel ever invented, and now you're actually making me dig in the dirt."

"I wasn't exactly forthcoming with the information, was I?" he said.

"Nope."

"I'll compromise with you. We work on this for an hour; then we take a break. I'll go home and come back, and we'll go to dinner and a movie. Monday after work, I'll come over and we can finish the rest."

"Dinner and a movie? That sounds a lot like a date."

Avery plunged the shovel down into the dirt so that it stood upright on its own. "You know what? It is. Our first date." He didn't say anything but remained quiet, apparently waiting for her reaction.

Sabrina wondered what she should say. He had already pointed out that her resolution didn't say she wouldn't go on a date, so technically, she wouldn't be breaking it.

But could she go on a date with him without falling in love? The answer was yes.

She didn't need to go on a date with him to fall in love.

What should she do? Her heart was already opening up to the man who now stood in her flower beds making plans for her future garden. The man who had already volunteered to come over and help her finish raking on Monday. The man who was once in love with the very woman who had made it impossible for Sabrina to fall in love for an entire year.

Darci.

Sabrina thought of her deal with Darci. The pending promotion, the ten-grand bonus—her big chance to make it to the top.

She glanced at Avery and felt her stomach do cartwheels when he smiled at her.

In that moment, Sabrina finally admitted to herself what she'd spent the past month trying to ignore. Her resolutions were all attainable. All except one.

She'd have to deal with that later.

"Our first date," she repeated. "I'll go," she told Avery, not quite believing she had actually said yes.

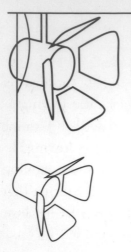

Chapter Sixteen

Maris arrived at church before Sabrina did. She sat down in a seat in the same area where she and Sabrina had sat the previous week.

Feeling awkward, she checked her watch and hoped Sabrina would come soon. This was only her second Sunday at church, and part of her wanted to get up and go home.

While Maris sat debating whether to go or stay, Avery passed by, Darci at his heels.

Avery stopped to say hello, while Darci smiled tolerantly.

As they walked away, Maris shook her head. She had never imagined she'd see the day when she *and* Darci were in church at the same time.

Church was due to start in less than five minutes. Maris gave Sabrina two minutes to arrive or else she would leave. Two minutes came and went, and still no sign of Sabrina.

Maris put on her coat and was exiting the row when Sabrina's friend Jasmine came bustling toward her.

"It's Maris, isn't it? Do you remember me? We met last week."

"I remember you," Maris said.

"Do you have an extra seat?" Jasmine asked.

Maris shrugged. "I guess so." There were probably at least six or seven empty seats in the row, and besides, she was leaving.

"My goodness, it's raining cats and dogs out—" Jasmine stopped mid-sentence and stared at Maris. "Are you leaving?"

Maris froze. How could she get out of here without looking like a total heathen? Jasmine would no doubt tell Sabrina that Maris had come and gone, and Sabrina would never let her hear the end of it. There was no way out.

Sighing heavily, she removed her coat for the second time and sat back down. "No, I'm here to stay."

Jasmine sat next to her, and just as Maris was getting comfortable again, the lady leading the songs told everybody to stand up and sing.

Maris did her best to follow the words on the projection screen, but she didn't sing much louder than a whisper. She had never had delusions of being a professional singer, and Sid always joked that she was tone-deaf. No sense in scaring the living daylights out of the people around her with her attempts at carrying a tune.

Personally, she didn't understand the need for the singing part of the service, but most of the people around seemed to be really getting into it. They had their eyes closed and their hands up in the air. Some people swayed back and forth, and others actually jumped up and down occasionally. Maris hoped she never felt the urge to do so.

Sabrina had said the people were doing that because they felt the presence of the Lord—whatever that meant. Maris didn't want to sound stupid, so she didn't ask for any further explanation, but now she really wished she had.

Ten minutes after the songs began, Sabrina slipped into the seat next to her.

"I'm so glad you came," Maris whispered. "I almost left twice."

"I'm glad you stayed."

"What took you so long?"

Sabrina shrugged. "I had trouble deciding what to wear." Without stopping to remove her coat, Sabrina closed her eyes and joined right in with the other singers.

During the rest of "worship service," as they called it, Maris kept sneaking glances in Sabrina's direction. Something was different about her friend.

Her eyes sparkled more than usual, and her cheeks were positively rosy. If she didn't know any better, she'd tease Sabrina that she looked as if she was in love.

But with whom? Surely Eric hadn't sweet-talked his way back into her life. Sabrina was too smart to fall for that.

And Maris had already warned her to stay away from Avery, so surely he wasn't the reason. Or was he?

Maris had done plenty of warning, but Sabrina had never seemed particularly willing to listen.

I'll have to look into this later, she decided. Maybe she could talk Sabrina into going to lunch after church.

As soon as the service ended, Maris asked Sabrina if she had plans for lunch. Sabrina didn't, and they decided they would go to a nearby Mexican restaurant.

Unfortunately, Jasmine invited herself to come along. Maris's irritation level went up a notch. Maris tried to send silent signals to Sabrina that she didn't want company. But apparently, Sabrina didn't notice.

Wonderful. There was no way she could discuss anything of substance with Jasmine listening in.

Out of the corner of her eye, she noticed Avery and Darci in the near vicinity. The last thing she needed was to have a run-in with Her Highness.

As she turned, she saw a flash of salt-and-pepper hair styled in a familiar looking pageboy. Maris could only see the person's back, but she knew without a shadow of doubt whose hair that was.

Sunny.

But why was she *here?*

"I'm ready to go," Maris announced.

Sabrina and Jasmine didn't seem to hear. Instead, they stood around chatting with other people. Did they think they were on the hospitality committee or something?

Moments later, Avery made his way over, Darci close behind.

"Hi, Sabrina, Maris," he said.

"Oh, Avery. Hi."

Maris's intuition kicked in. There was something a little unusual about the small talk between Avery and Sabrina this morning.

Sabrina laughed a bit more than she normally did, and Avery seemed more attentive than usual toward her.

Maris wasn't the only one who noticed. Avery and Sabrina carried on a rather lengthy conversation about gardening while Maris, Jasmine, and Darci stood listening.

From what Maris could gather, the two of them had been planting something in Sabrina's flower beds the day before. Apparently, Sabrina had ditched the knitting project for something totally new.

Darci didn't seem at all happy to hear this bit of information. She stepped closer to Avery and looped her arm through his.

"What's this about?" she said, interrupting the conversation. "Did you give up on one of your resolutions, Sabrina?"

"I haven't given up. I just decided that knitting wasn't really for me. I'm going to try gardening."

"Oh." Darci blinked. "I kind of figured you wouldn't be able to keep them all." Her voice was laced with a twinge of superiority.

"Technically, she's not giving up," Avery said. "As far as I know, there's no rule against finding a hobby that she actually likes."

"Well, no. I guess not," Darci said almost grudgingly.

"Who cares?" said Maris. This whole encounter was growing more tiresome by the moment. "It's just a list of resolutions. You all are going over the rules and minute details as if Sabrina gets some kind of prize if she keeps them all."

"Now, that's a good idea," Darci said. "I wonder if it's too late to add some kind of incentive to the show."

"Incentive?" asked Avery. "Like what?"

"Oh, I don't know . . ." Darci put a finger to her chin and stared off in the distance.

Something was up. Maris instantly recognized Darci's pretending-to-think-about-something tone of voice and facial expression.

"How about . . . ten thousand dollars?"

"Wow," said Jasmine, her eyes wide. "For keeping New Year's resolutions? Tell me where I can sign up."

Maris had almost forgotten Jasmine was standing there, she'd been so quiet.

Avery shook his head. "That may be overdoing it, Darce. Ten grand is a lot of money. How about something a little less . . . extravagant?"

"Being able to keep all of your resolutions is no small feat," Darci persisted. "I think the person who can really stay focused and meet their goals should be able to win something of value. I vote for the money."

Avery chuckled. "I can tell already that you won't be easily talked out of this. But let's discuss it tomorrow in the production meeting."

"Thank goodness," said Maris. "I don't understand how you people can talk work every day of the week. Doesn't the Bible say you're supposed to rest on Sundays?"

"It does," Avery admitted. "And I'll be the first to admit that I need to leave my work at the office."

"I used to be a workaholic, but the stress was too much to handle. I've had to force myself to only get wrapped up in work during working hours," Maris said.

Avery was a good guy, but she had noticed that the stress of operating the company was beginning to wear on him in recent months.

Darci gave Maris a condescending look. "That's the difference between an employee and the person who actually runs a company. We can't afford to just skip off and forget about things at the office." Looking up at Avery, she said, "Can we, sweetie?"

Avery didn't answer. Instead, he stepped away from the circle. "I guess I need to get you home," he told Darci.

Nodding toward Sabrina, he said, "See you at the office."

"Okay." Sabrina still had that dreamy look in her eyes.

He waved at Maris. "Later, Maris."

As they walked away, Jasmine watched. "Your bosses make such a cute couple, Sabrina. How long have they been dating?"

"Oh, they're not dating," Sabrina said.

Jasmine looked puzzled. "They're not? Well, you can certainly tell they like each other. I bet it'll only be a matter of time before they realize it."

Sabrina didn't say anything but turned around to get her

coat. When she turned back to face them, she didn't look pleased.

"You know, I really don't feel that hungry," she said. "I think I'm just going to go home and try to get some rest before work tomorrow."

Jasmine looked concerned. "Are you coming down with something?"

"I don't think so. Just sore from being out in the garden. My arms need more muscle tone, I guess."

"Looks like we're canceling lunch, then," said Jasmine. She looked at Maris. "Unless you still want to go."

Maris shook her head. If Sabrina was going home, she couldn't envision herself spending any more time with Jasmine. Besides, Sid was supposed to get home later today, and she wanted to fix him a nice dinner.

"I'll call you later this afternoon," Maris said.

They definitely had things to discuss. Avery was a great guy, but he didn't seem in any hurry to be fully rid of Darci. If he didn't make up his mind soon, her pal Sabrina was on a course to getting her feelings hurt if she didn't watch out.

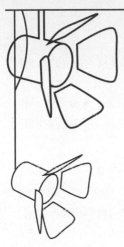

Chapter Seventeen

Sabrina lay on her sofa with a heating pad on her back. All that raking had taken quite a toll on her. The television was tuned to an old movie channel, but she couldn't concentrate on the plot.

Her emotions were vying for attention. One minute she was happy, remembering her date with Avery the night before; and the next, she was feeling jealous of the way he always treated Darci so kindly.

"Am I that delusional for thinking he likes me?" she wondered aloud.

She stared at the phone, wishing Maris would call. It was three thirty, and Sid was supposed to get in some time today, so maybe Maris and Sid were busy talking and she wouldn't have time to talk to Sabrina.

Still, Sabrina wished she had someone to talk to. Jasmine was nice, but she was a new friend, and Sabrina didn't know her well enough to share her feelings for Avery with her.

Besides, Jasmine had rankled her nerves this morning with her comment about Avery and Darci making a "cute couple."

Whatever. It's so obvious that he doesn't love her. He sees Darci as a friend and business partner.

Or did he? Was she missing something that everyone else could see? From the look on Maris's face, Sabrina could tell that her friend had reservations as well.

And she hadn't missed Darci's subtle reference to the ten-thousand-dollar bonus. If Darci even suspected that Sabrina had feelings for Avery, she was sure to cancel the agreement.

But then again, who could prove that she loved him? And the resolution didn't say anything about *liking* anyone. Right now she just liked Avery. All she had to do was make sure her feelings for him didn't progress beyond the liking stage.

But she had a feeling Darci wouldn't stand for it.

Sabrina was beginning to wish she had gotten her deal with Darci in writing. But then it wouldn't be a secret, would it?

Sabrina glared at the phone. "Maris, call me," she said.

As if on cue, the phone rang. Sabrina grabbed it.

"It's about time," she said.

Silence greeted her from the other end.

"Hello? Hello?"

"Sabrina? It's Eric. I take it you've been waiting for me to call?"

Her heart sank. Not today. "I have nothing to say to you. Not after you shamelessly went running to the tabloids to spread gossip about me."

"I didn't spread gossip, Sabrina."

"Eric, listen to yourself. You went to a tabloid. Of course it's gossip. Are you that delusional?"

"You know I wouldn't do that. In fact, I only told them how great a person you are. They tried to get me to say bad things about you, but I didn't."

She sighed loudly. Hopefully, he would realize she didn't feel like talking to him. "I sent you the money from when I sold the ring. Did you get it?"

"I did, and thanks."

"And you're still strapped for cash, I take it?"

"Well, yeah. How did you know?"

"Oh, I'm just guessing. I hope the tabloid paid you well because I want a percentage."

Eric was quiet for a long time. Sabrina smiled indulgently. He was one of those people you could yell at until you were blue in the face, and it wouldn't faze him in the least. But threaten his wallet, and he snapped to attention.

"You're not serious, are you?" He actually sounded worried.

"So they did pay you." Sabrina tossed the heating pad aside and sat up. "Yes, I am serious."

"I'm sorry, but I already spent it. I had bills to pay . . ."

Sabrina didn't bother to listen as he listed the assorted reasons he couldn't afford to give her a penny of the money.

When he finally stopped talking, her patience had worn thin. "Can I ask you a question?"

"Sure. Anything."

Ding-ding-ding!!! Warning bells went off in her head. The words "sure" and "anything" were not a part of Eric's regular vocabulary. He wanted something.

Sabrina tried to sound as no-nonsense as possible. "Why did you call me?"

"Why did I call you?"

Yep, he was definitely up to something. Now he was repeating sentences, a clear sign that he needed to stall for time.

"Yes, why did you call me?"

"I want to see you."

Sabrina laughed. That statement didn't even deserve an answer.

"I'm serious. I miss you." He was quiet for a few seconds, then added, "I saw you on *The Daily Dose.* I even taped the shows you were on. You looked beautiful."

Whatever. He was really pouring it on thick.

"Sorry, Eric, but I don't think I miss you."

"Please. We can meet for coffee and talk. No strings attached."

"No."

"I broke up with Sharon."

That got her attention. She waited for him to say more. Not that she wasn't surprised, but this seemed pretty sudden. Could he really truly be missing her?

"Let's just get together and talk," he pleaded.

"That could be arranged. But I'm pretty busy lately. My workload has picked up."

"I'm flexible. You pick a time and I'll be there."

"Let me think about it and call you back." She'd probably go, but it wouldn't hurt to let him stew over it for a while.

"When will you call?"

"I don't know. Maybe tomorrow. Or Tuesday." If anything bothered Eric more than the threat of someone being after his money, it was not being able to schedule every detail of his entire life.

He sighed, apparently resigned to the fact that Sabrina wouldn't give him a clear answer. "I'll be waiting."

The call-waiting beep sounded, and Sabrina was happy for an excuse to get Eric off the phone.

"Someone's calling in on the other line."

"Oh." He was quiet. Surely he did not think they had anything more to discuss.

"So, I'll let you go so I can get that call," Sabrina said.

"Oh, okay."

"Bye." She clicked over without giving him a chance to say anything else.

"Hello?"

"Hi, it's me."

"Maris! I was wondering if you would ever call."

"Well, I was kind of busy after I got home from church. I had to clean the house, cook dinner, then pick up Sid from the airport."

"How's it going?"

Sabrina could sense Maris's hesitation, even on the phone. "At the moment, it's going rather quietly."

Whatever that meant, it didn't sound good. "I'm sorry, Maris. I'll keep praying for you guys."

"Thanks. The dinner was a bust. I cooked his favorite meal and he picked at it. It seems that when he got to New Orleans without my half of the money, his brother got cold feet. While Sid tried to convince him that I would come to my senses and eventually agree with them, someone else outbid them on the building."

"They didn't get the café?"

"No, and he spent the last week and a half looking for an alternate location, but without any success."

"That's what you wanted, isn't it?"

"Yes. But I didn't ask for a pouting husband."

"He's still upset with you, then."

" 'Upset' is an understatement. I tried to bring up the possibility of opening the restaurant here in St. Louis, but he's not interested. At the moment, he is in the study, sulking."

"Maris, I'm sorry," Sabrina said again. She knew she was repeating herself, but she didn't know what else to say.

Maris sighed into the phone. "Sidney wants to move to New

199

Orleans, Sabrina. Whether or not we open the business. I told him I won't go."

"And?"

"He's threatening to go without me. He wants to be there by Christmas."

Sabrina was stunned. It felt as though someone had knocked the wind out of her. Her best friend might be gone by Christmas. "Wow," she said quietly.

"No kidding. And, honestly, I don't want to talk about this anymore. Let's talk about you."

"Me?" Sabrina had been hoping to discuss the situation between herself and Avery all day, but Maris's news had taken the joy out of it.

"What's going on with you and Avery? I know I've asked you this question before and you always deny, but today there was definitely something going on. There was chemistry between the two of you."

Sabrina got right to the point. "We went on a date last night. A real date."

"You're kidding me. Please tell me you're kidding."

"Dinner and a movie."

"You're not kidding."

"No. I had a great time, actually."

"I could see that. Did he kiss you?"

"Now you sound like Darci," Sabrina joked. "But, for the record, no, he did not kiss me."

"I bet you would have let him."

"I plead the Fifth on that one."

Maris's voice became serious. "Sabrina, I can tell you're happy and all that, but you have to end this now. Darci's already starting to get overly perturbed. If she finds out—and you know she will—"

"Wait a second," Sabrina interrupted Maris, feeling irked. "Why do you always have to assume that Darci knows, or will eventually know everything? She's not God, you know."

"You got that right. But she's got eyes and ears in the right places. Oh!" Maris exclaimed. "For example, guess who was at church this morning?"

Sabrina didn't feel like playing guessing games. "Okay, who was at church?"

"Sunny."

"Really? How do you know?"

"I saw her. Well, I saw her back. She left as soon as church was over. You were too busy batting your eyelashes at Avery to notice."

"I was not batting my eyelashes."

"Flirting, simpering, whatever you want to call it," Maris said.

Sabrina felt her face get warm. "Was it really that noticeable?"

"Yep."

"Darci is going to make my life miserable," Sabrina said, thinking aloud.

"You just realized that? Why do you think I've been telling you to stay away from him?"

"Do you think he still likes her?" Sabrina ventured.

"What did he tell you?"

"That he respects her professionally, and he has to get along with her for the sake of the company. But he said he couldn't marry her."

"Unless she starts agreeing with him about the Bible," Maris finished.

"Well, yes. And no. But he's not sure about her motives for being at church."

"My best guess would be that her motive for coming to church is to keep an eye on you and Avery. At least right now. And I bet you a million dollars that Avery knows this, too, but he's secretly hoping that some religion will sink in. That way, he can go ahead and marry her."

"You think so?" Sabrina felt helpless. If Avery cared about Darci so much, why was he sending signals to Sabrina?

Sabrina didn't know what else to say. She couldn't reveal the details of her deal with Darci to Maris. Maris would probably slip and tell someone, and if word got out, Darci would cancel the deal and deny she'd ever made it.

"I may be a little biased right now, Sabrina, but he's a man. He'll wiggle and squirm and keep from telling you the whole truth for as long as he can. Look at Sid. When we got married, he told me that he had no intentions of ever going back down south to live. Now look at him. He's practically packing his bags as we speak.

"Avery may be a Christian, Sabrina, but you tell me all the time that Christians aren't perfect. I wouldn't believe everything he says."

Sabrina took the advice with a grain of salt. Maris was right—she couldn't be unbiased about Avery, because she was upset with Sidney right now.

Sabrina heard Sidney's voice in the background. "Is he calling you?" she asked.

"Apparently. Listen, I have to go, but please hear me out on this. You're a good worker, Sabrina. You're valuable to the company, and I think Avery would do his best to keep you there no matter what. But if you deliberately prance around in front of Darci, parading the fact that you've got a crush on Avery, you'll wish you hadn't."

"I'm not prancing around in front of—"

"Semantics. Whatever," said Maris. "If I still end up taking my sabbatical, or if we actually end up moving, you are next in line to get my job. And that's what you're wanting, right? A promotion?"

"Yes."

"My point is, either keep it on the low—which would be almost impossible—or end it altogether. I prefer the latter. I just don't think that a brief romance with Avery is worth you possibly losing your job."

Sabrina remained silent. Her best friend had almost no sympathy for her.

"Hey, Sid just called me again. I'll talk to you tomorrow," Maris said.

Sabrina hung up the phone and repositioned the heating pad on her back.

She felt alone. No one knew what was *really* going on in her life—the secret agreement, the constant threats from Darci, her new feelings for Avery, and her worries that he still loved Darci.

Who could she talk to?

Sabrina closed her eyes and tried to fall asleep, but she was too worked up to relax.

She picked up the remote and channel-surfed.

Shampoo commercial.

Kids' movie.

Home-decorating show.

Car commercial.

Cooking show.

Cartoon.

A church service.

Sabrina paused.

The preacher's voice resonated through the speakers: ". . . You think no one listens, no one cares, nobody knows what's really going on." He paused, then continued in a sing-song voice, "Nobody knows the trouble you see." He grinned, and the congregation tittered.

"Well, God knows. He's ready to listen. And you know what else? He can give you more help than anybody else."

Sabrina was instantly encouraged. He was right.

She clicked off the television and poured out her heart to the One who would listen to all her problems.

The One who already knew what she couldn't tell anyone else.

The One who could provide the resolution to her problems.

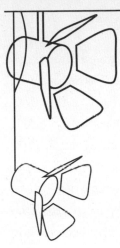

Chapter Eighteen

Darci tapped her fingernails on the edge of the desk. She pressed the intercom button to speak to Sunny. "Is she here yet?"

"Not yet. But I'm on the lookout. I told the guard at the front desk to buzz me when she comes in. As soon as she gets off the elevator, I'll be standing there waiting for her."

Darci leaned back in her chair, relaxed for the moment. Sunny certainly had things under control.

Not ten seconds had passed when Sunny poked her head in the door. "She's on her way up."

Darci stood up. "I'll get Sabrina. Can you go ahead and send for Annette?"

"Will do." Sunny was gone as quickly as she had come.

Darci straightened her suit and headed down the corridor to the elevator.

Perfect timing. The doors opened as soon as Darci reached the landing.

Sabrina's eyes widened at the sight of her.

Darci took that as a good sign. At least the girl still realized that Darci ran the show around here.

"Sabrina, I'd like to speak with you for a moment."

Sabrina adjusted the strap of that gigantic purse she lugged everywhere. "Okay." She glanced around. "Right now?"

"In my office." Darci turned and started walking back toward her office and motioned for Sabrina to follow her.

Sunny and Annette had just reached the doorway when Darci and Sabrina got there.

"Sabrina, Annette, please come inside and have a seat."

Darci sat in her chair and placed her hands on the desktop. Both Sabrina and Annette wore scared-rabbit expressions. Darci wondered how they had made it this far in their careers.

As far as she was concerned, they had yet to master the first rule of being successful in the business world: Everyone needs a game face.

"Ladies, we tape in an hour, so I'll be quick. Sabrina Bradley, meet Annette Walters. Annette, meet Sabrina."

The two women gave each other tentative smiles.

"Annette has been with us for four months as an intern. I've been kept apprised of her progress, and I'm pleased to announce that she will be getting a promotion, so to speak."

Annette smiled, relief written all over her face.

Sabrina still looked tense. Darci decided to leave her in suspense for a bit longer.

"With Avery cutting back on his workload, it's fallen to Maris and Sabrina to take up the slack. Avery and I have decided that Annette will become Sabrina's assistant."

Darci made eye contact with Sabrina. "She will work directly with you, and my desire is that you teach her all aspects of your job. That way, in the event you can't come to work or need to take vacation time, we won't be dead in the water without you."

Darci hoped Sabrina understood the full impact of her words.

She addressed both women now. "Given the nature of this work, it's imperative that you two share a workspace. I've cleared out the small meeting room across the hall from my own office and made it into a joint workspace for the two of you.

"You two have the rest of the day to move your belongings from your old space into this new one."

Neither Sabrina nor Annette said anything. Both seemed to be in shock, but Darci was satisfied to note that Annette's shock was a happy shock, while Sabrina seemed less than pleased.

"Any questions?"

None. Good.

"Annette, you are free to leave. Sunny will give you a key to the office on your way out. Sabrina, I'd like a few more minutes of your time, if you don't mind."

Annette jumped up and hurriedly made her exit.

"Close the door behind you," Darci called out.

As soon as the door was closed, she got right down to business.

"I take it you understand the impact of this new arrangement."

"I think I do," said Sabrina.

"I don't know what you're trying to pull with Avery, but you're not going to get away with it. Don't delude yourself; he's not interested in you."

Sabrina visibly bristled. "Then why are you going to so much trouble to keep me away from him?"

Darci grinned. So there was some backbone underneath that church-girl exterior.

Finally, a worthy opponent. A fight wasn't really fun if the opposition rolled over and played dead—and that's what usually happened around here.

Darci surmised that Sabrina had decided that Avery was worth fighting for.

Too bad she would lose.

For the moment, Darci ignored Sabrina's question. "Perhaps you can clear up some confusion on my part. Do we or do we not still have a deal?"

"Why don't you tell me?" Sabrina countered.

Darci was briefly taken aback. Who was this woman, and what had she done with Sabrina? Keeping her composure, she smiled. "You remember the rules. Keep the resolutions; make me look good. But it looks like you're developing some feelings for Avery. That's a violation of one of your resolutions."

"But you have no way of knowing whether or not I love Avery—or any other man, for that matter. So how do we decide if I keep that resolution?"

"I guess that's up to my discretion. If I think you failed, then you don't get the money."

"I see. A little arbitrary, don't you think?"

Darci shrugged. "I invented the game, so I guess I make the rules." She leaned forward and tried to soften her approach.

"Sabrina, if you're confused about Avery, you can talk to me. I know him well, probably better than anyone else in this office."

Sabrina's face betrayed her. The mention of Avery had definitely piqued her interest.

Darci continued. "When I ended our relationship, I was deeply hurt. I really loved him. But he led me on."

Sabrina's eyes widened. Darci kept going.

"He talked about marriage all the time, and he led me to believe that someday he would set a date, but all he ever did was talk."

Darci saw tears welling up in Sabrina's eyes and struggled not to allow any expression of triumph to put this little charade in jeopardy. Thankfully, Sabrina was actually taking all of this in.

I knew the girl was gullible, but not this gullible. But at least it's working in my favor today.

"Between the two of us, I think he's afraid of commitment," Darci whispered.

Sabrina suddenly sat up straight in her chair. "I don't think this deal is really about me making you look good," she said.

"Oh? Then what is it about?"

"I think it's about you losing Avery and then deciding that you want him back. But he doesn't agree. I think you invented this deal to keep me away from him." Sabrina paused, then added, "Since you couldn't keep *him* away from *me*."

Darci's chest tightened with anger. Sabrina was smarter than she looked. Her theory hit where it hurt.

Darci swallowed the hurt and probed for a chink in Sabrina's armor. "I can assure you, dear, that if I really wanted Avery back, he would come running. He's always hinting, hoping, hanging around to see if I would take him back."

She shrugged. "And maybe one day I will. But he has a lot of growing up to do before I'll even consider it."

"So why should it matter to you if he likes someone else?"

Darci slapped her palm against the desktop. "Get out of here. How dare you come into my office and mock me!"

Sabrina stood slowly. "Do I still have a job here?"

Darci wanted nothing more than to escort Sabrina to the front door herself. She would take great pleasure in telling her that she was no longer a part of this company. Unfortunately, Avery would have a conniption if she actually fired Sabrina, and would fall all over himself trying to get her back on staff.

He was falling hard for this girl, and so far, Darci hadn't been able to stop him.

Darci refrained from lashing out any further. To do so now would reduce her advantage. Better to make Sabrina's time at work absolutely miserable than to actually fire her. Maybe she could make it so difficult that Sabrina would willingly resign.

"Consider yourself on probation, Ms. Bradley. Watch your step, because I guarantee that I will be watching."

Sabrina gave a terse nod and asked if she could be excused.

"Of course," Darci said, regaining her cordial tone. "Sunny will get you a key to your new office, and if you need anything, feel free to pop over and ask." Darci gestured toward her windows. "Since I can see your office from here, it'll be that much easier for us to keep the lines of communication open."

Just as Sabrina reached the door, Darci called her name. Sabrina turned around. "As far as I'm concerned, our agreement still stands. I'm still committed to holding up my end of the bargain."

Sabrina left without saying another word. Darci closed her blinds, then sank back into her chair. She was so upset, she was actually trembling.

The resolutions deal had gone horribly awry, thanks in part to Avery's relentless pursuit of Sabrina. But Darci could and would find a way to make it work. Hopefully, Sabrina wasn't so fed up that she had lost interest in trying to keep her resolutions.

Despite her stoic front, Sabrina obviously harbored some doubts about Avery. A comment here, a suggestion there, and before either of them realized it, Sabrina and Avery would be at odds with each other.

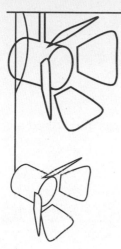

Chapter Nineteen

Just one more rep," Nadia suggested.

Sabrina groaned and shook her head. Her shoulders felt as if they were about to fall off.

"Come on, you can do it."

Sabrina eked out one last repetition. Her triceps screamed in agony. Nadia's cheery encouragement was beginning to get to her.

On one hand, she appreciated having a personal trainer who pushed her to achieve all she could, but on the other hand, sometimes Sabrina wanted to sit cross-legged in the middle of the gym and refuse to do "just one more" of anything.

"Now we need to work your abs."

"Please, no crunches," Sabrina said. She knew it sounded like begging, but she didn't care.

Nadia smiled cheerily. "You may not like doing crunches, but you'll like the results. What's the current tally anyway? Seven pounds lost since we started?"

If Nadia spoke a little louder, people in China would know how much Sabrina weighed. Enough was enough.

Sabrina shook her head. "No crunches, no leg lifts, no aerobics." She gave Nadia her best apologetic look. "I'm sorry, but I need to cut this session short."

"Bad day at the office?" Nadia ventured.

"An understatement." Sabrina grabbed a towel and wiped her neck.

"Well, you know your body's limits better than I do. If we need to stop early today, it's your call."

Nadia was always rambling on and on about the "body's limits." Sabrina secretly wondered if she was some kind of robot endowed with superpowers.

Her body apparently knew no limits. Sabrina had never seen a woman with triceps so firm. And Nadia's thighs probably thought "saddlebag" was a word in a foreign language.

Sabrina let out a resigned sigh. "I think my body needs to call it quits."

Nadia nodded sympathetically. "Don't beat yourself up about it. We all fall off the wagon sometimes. But don't worry—we'll get back on track the next time you come in."

Sabrina willed herself not to read too much into that statement. Nadia meant well, but sometimes she failed in the tact department.

Sabrina forced a smile. "I'll be in Thursday for my one-hour session."

"Perfect." Nadia paused, then said, "Hey, I read that article about you and your ex-fiancé."

Sabrina stopped in her tracks. The article was finally out.

"I didn't actually read it," Nadia qualified. "I mean, I don't *buy* those kinds of magazines. Most of the stuff is too sensational to be true, but I saw your face on the cover, so I picked it up and kind of skimmed through it."

My face is on the cover? I hope it's a good shot. "So what did you think?" Sabrina tried to sound casual. She had already decided to take a detour to the grocery store on her way home. This she had to see for herself.

"He seems nice enough." Nadia grinned. "And he's pretty good-looking. I'm guessing he's the reason behind the no-love resolution?"

"You could say that," Sabrina mumbled.

"There were some really cute pictures of you two," she said.

Pictures? Eric had sold personal pictures of her? He was going to get a piece of her mind when she saw him tomorrow.

"He seems really nice," Nadia said for the second time.

Why in the world did Nadia suddenly have a million questions and comments about Sabrina's personal life? Sabrina liked their relationship much better when all their discussions were about lunges and treadmills.

"Are you guys still friends?"

Sabrina considered the question, trying to answer truthfully. "I'm not sure. I'll know after I read this article."

"Do you know if he's seeing anyone?" Nadia pressed.

Sabrina wanted to laugh. Eric must have really painted a saintly portrait of himself. Women who were total strangers now wanted his phone number.

Weird.

"I'll see you later, Nadia." Sabrina left Nadia standing by the recumbent bikes and headed for the locker room.

She felt bad about dodging the question about Eric, but she couldn't see Eric making a love connection with Nadia. For one thing, he hated going to the gym. He couldn't stand to be around people he thought were fitness fanatics. Nadia, on the other hand, spent all her free time doing push-ups and crunches.

After a quick shower, Sabrina got in her car and headed to the nearest grocery store.

During the ride, she ate two meal replacement bars and wished she'd had one candy bar instead.

Just as she pulled into the parking lot, her cell phone rang.

It was Maris.

"Hello?"

"I'm at home now, so we can talk. What in the world is going on?"

Sabrina chose her words carefully. She had to tell the story without including details of the resolutions deal.

"I got an assistant. Her name's Annette. She's a new intern and I'm supposed to teach her everything about my job."

"She's going to fire you." Maris's voice was matter-of-fact.

"No way. You think so?" Sabrina didn't bother to hold back her sarcasm.

"I've seen her do this before. She's just making you agonize over it while she waits for the perfect time."

Sabrina shook her head. "She hasn't shown me the door just yet."

"I told you to stay away from Avery. Now look at this mess."

Sabrina cleared her throat. She knew she should feel worried beyond belief, but for some reason, she had felt as though she were in a cocoon all day. Apparently, she was well on her way to getting a pink slip.

Somehow, it didn't feel real. Either that, or she truly wasn't afraid of Darci anymore.

Maybe I'm in shock.

"Maris, do you know the symptoms of shock?"

"What?"

"The actual physical symptoms of shock. Real shock. Not shock as in 'I'm so shocked that that store doesn't have that dress in my size,' but shocked as in 'My body has physically gone into shock.'"

Maris giggled. "Did you know that when you say 'shock' over and over again, it sounds funny?"

"Thanks for the help, Maris."

"Sabrina, are you okay?"

"I hope so. I should be a nervous wreck, but it hasn't really hit me yet. I'm a little worn out from a long day, and adjusting to having to share an office with a college student whose boyfriend calls her cell phone every hour on the hour, but other than that, I'm good."

"What are you going to do?"

"About what?"

"About Darci? She's obviously threatening you, and everyone knows it. But everyone also knows that you haven't done anything wrong."

"'That's good to hear. But it's never stopped her from firing people before." Sabrina laughed.

"Sabrina, are you listening to yourself? The thing you most feared has happened and you're acting like it's a big joke."

Sabrina shook her head. "Believe me, Maris, I really don't think it's funny. But in a way, I'm actually relieved it's finally come down to this."

"What are you talking about?"

"I'm saying her bark is worse than her bite—at least so far."

"Please elaborate. I don't fully understand."

"I don't, either. All I know is that yesterday I prayed for almost three hours about everything that was bothering me. I handed it all to the Lord, and went to bed. In the middle of the night, I woke up and this Bible verse kept coming to mind."

"Which verse?"

"'God hasn't given me a spirit of fear, but power, love, and a sound mind.'"

"That's nice, but is there a verse anywhere that says, 'God

will not let Darci fire Sabrina'? Come on, we all think you should fight."

"We who?"

"We as in everybody in the office. We're behind you one hundred percent. And we think you should go to Avery. In fact, we're all willing to sign a petition to let him know that we think you're doing a great job."

Sabrina considered this information. The news was encouraging, but she wondered if taking immediate action would be wise. "I don't think I should actually do anything until she officially tries to fire me. As it stands now, I'm just in limbo. Kind of like a warning."

"Sabrina, swallow your pride. Everyone knows you're in big trouble."

"You know how she lies. If I go to Avery saying that Darci hinted she wanted to get rid of me, she'll deny it and find a really clever way to set me up later."

"Maybe you're right about that. So what is the plan?"

"The plan is not to be afraid of her. To do my work. To keep my resolutions. To have fun for a change. To come home from work and enjoy life instead of worrying about what Darci will do next."

"I'm impressed with the way you've decided to handle this," Maris admitted.

"I am, too. I've imagined what I would do if this ever happened, and I was never this calm."

"Do you really think it's because you prayed?"

Sabrina thought for a while. "Yeah, I do. Otherwise, I'd be running around like a chicken with my head cut off."

"I know I would."

"Listen, I've got to run in the store for something, so I'll let you go."

"I'll call you in the morning before I leave for the office," Maris said. "And from now on, we don't discuss anything but work while we're there. Especially in your new office. I bet she has the place bugged."

Sabrina nodded, even though Maris couldn't see her. "Probably. But then again, she can see my office from her office. Why would she need to bug it? She's practically within earshot."

"Amen to that. Hey, Sabrina, one more thing." Maris's voice turned somber. "Promise me you'll be careful around Avery. I know you like him and everything, and in my heart I want you to find the man of your dreams and be happy forever."

"I hear a 'but' coming," Sabrina broke in.

"*But,*" Maris emphasized the word, "consider this. I'm sure Avery's heard what's going on by now. If he's half the man you think he is and he really does care about you, he'll do everything in his power to save your job."

Sabrina had been thinking along the same lines, but she didn't admit that to Maris.

Her relationship with Avery—if it could even be called a relationship—was just beginning. The last thing she wanted to do was dive in too fast and make him feel overly pressured.

"I know, Maris. I will be even more careful than I usually am."

"Good for you. Later."

"Bye."

Sabrina put her phone in her purse and got out of the car. She was halfway to the door before she wondered if anyone would recognize her. Nadia had mentioned that her picture was on the magazine cover.

I wish I had a hat and some sunglasses.

Sabrina pictured herself ducking into the store wearing a trench coat and dark shades. The mental image made her laugh out loud.

A disguise like that worked in movies, but in St. Louis, Missouri, she would stick out like a sore thumb wearing that getup in the supermarket.

Sabrina went straight to the checkout stand and scanned the tabloids. She finally found the one with Eric's story.

Nadia had said Sabrina's picture was on the front, and it was. But it was only a tiny photo in the bottom corner. The caption was tempting enough, though:

SABRINA'S FIANCÉ TELLS ALL. WHY SHE'S AFRAID OF LOVE!

How utterly ridiculous. Sabrina wondered who in the world sat around making up these headlines. Nevertheless, she picked it up and flipped through the pages to get to Eric's piece.

As she searched, a few passersby gave her looks that could probably be translated to mean, "You actually read those things?" Sabrina didn't care.

If her picture on the cover was unexpectedly small, the article was equally minute. It consisted of no more than three or four hundred words.

The headline screamed: SABRINA'S EX SPEAKS! WHAT AMERICA'S FAVORITE RESOLUTIONER IS LIKE AT HOME.

Sabrina skimmed it and found nothing incredibly damaging or even embarrassing. Eric had actually been telling the truth when he claimed that he hadn't told any lies. The headline was the juiciest thing about the story.

Sabrina glanced at the cover. If people actually paid $4.99 to find out that she liked to bake cookies and watch old movies in her spare time, that was their right. But she wouldn't waste her money on this—not even to put in her scrapbook.

On her way out of the store, she nearly ran into a customer headed inside.

"Oh, sorry! Excuse me," Sabrina said.

The woman's eyes widened with recognition.

Sabrina said a silent prayer, thanking God that she hadn't been caught red-handed with a giant latte. The fact that she wasn't wearing any makeup didn't bother her so much.

"Are you Sabrina?" the lady exclaimed.

"Yes, I am," Sabrina said. This time she wasn't flustered at being recognized. Funny how quickly she was learning the ropes of the celebrity life.

"You know, I used to bite my fingernails all the time, and I'll tell you how I finally stopped."

Sabrina leaned closer and tried to look attentive. The nail biting had been a real struggle for the past few weeks. She hoped the lady didn't tell her to try deep breathing, as Darci's expert had suggested.

Sabrina wondered if the viewers of *The Daily Dose* noticed how many things could be remedied simply by mastering the art of deep breathing. Apparently, it was the newest cure-all.

"Get a manicure and have them paint your nails in a color you like. You'll like the way they look, and you won't want to mess them up. That'll cure the urge to nibble on 'em."

Sabrina nodded appreciatively. Now, *that* was sound advice. "Thank you. I'll try that."

"God bless you, dear. I'm praying for you and I wish you all the best in keeping those resolutions."

"Thank you." Sabrina knew she was repeating herself, but she didn't know what else to say. She hoped the tone of her voice conveyed how thankful she truly felt.

The woman blushed. "Oh, I don't mind. But don't be too hard on yourself if you can't keep 'em all. Especially the last one. Everybody wants to fall in love, and you don't want to run in the opposite direction if God sends Mr. Right your way this year."

Now Sabrina was beginning to feel flustered. It wasn't every day that she discussed her boyfriends, or the lack thereof, with a complete stranger in the entrance to the grocery store.

"I'll . . . well . . . thanks. I'll remember that," she finally managed to say.

The woman nodded. "Don't forget. If true love comes your way, you just forget you ever had that resolution. I know you were probably hurt when you wrote it, but you get over the hurt." The woman patted her on the arm and continued on her way.

Sabrina stood in the same place for a few moments, letting the woman's words sink in.

Eric had hurt her deeply, but sure enough, the bad feelings were beginning to fade. In fact, she was actually looking forward to seeing him tomorrow.

But at the moment, she was looking forward to going home and finding some liniment for her aching muscles.

Chapter Twenty

When Sabrina pulled up to her house, Avery was in the front yard, raking her flower beds.

She slapped her hand to her forehead. She'd totally forgotten about his promise to finish the garden work.

She parked her car and walked over to join him.

"Do you think this is a good idea?" she asked.

He shrugged. "I said I would come back and do the rest today."

Sabrina couldn't believe he was being glib at a time like this. She wouldn't believe for one minute that he hadn't heard about what had happened at work.

She lowered her voice a notch, hoping to better convey the fact that she meant business. "Avery, I know you must have heard what Darci did today."

"Yeah. The assistant. Do you like her?"

Sabrina blinked. His expression indicated that he thought it was a good thing. "I'm getting the feeling you think that's a good idea."

"Of course." He gave her an incredulous look. "I'm getting the feeling you think it's a terrible idea."

"Well, yes. I do."

Avery didn't say anything but put his shovel aside. Then he dusted his hands off on his pants and put the back of his palm against her forehead.

Sabrina brushed his hand away. "What are you doing?"

"I'm checking to see if you're delirious. You must be if you're upset because I insisted that you have some help."

"What are you talking about?" Sabrina's thoughts swirled in a million directions at once. Annette had been Avery's idea? Was this good or bad? Were Avery and Darci jointly plotting to get rid of her?

She thought back to her meeting with Darci and vaguely remembered Darci mentioning Avery when she explained that Annette would be helping Sabrina.

"Come here." Avery grabbed Sabrina's hand and led her to the porch steps. He sat down and patted the space next to him.

Sabrina sat.

"Now, look at me," he said. "Tell me what's bothering you."

"I just thought . . . well, everyone's been saying . . ." She didn't finish.

There was nothing she could say that would help her prove her point. Avery wouldn't take her seriously if she started recounting hearsay, and she couldn't tell him about the agreement with Darci.

"Now, I'm aware of a general buzz going around the office today that Darci promoted Annette to show you that she can replace you any time she gets ready." He grinned. "But I seem to recall us having had a conversation about how ridiculous it is to actually believe everything you overhear at work."

Sabrina nodded, feeling slightly better.

"Back when Darci first wanted to add two more shows every month, I told her I wouldn't let her do it unless she either reduced your workload or found you an assistant. In the end, I decided it would be unfair to Maris to give her more work, so we agreed on Annette."

"So you played a part in this?"

"Yes. But why does 'this' sound like you don't like it? I thought you'd be happy. You can have more free time."

Sabrina finally worked up enough nerve to ask a more difficult question. "You don't think Darci is trying to get rid of me?"

"I don't know. I hear a lot of stories and I don't know what to think. I know Darci's changed a lot over the years, but I guess I'm not willing to believe that she's gone so far as to fire people arbitrarily.

"Is she trying to get rid of you? I don't think so. I do think she's a little jealous because you and I spend time together."

"But you don't think she's jealous enough to get rid of me?"

He took both her hands and clasped them in his own. "Even if she is, I won't let her do it. I have the last say, so I would have to be the one to decide to let you go." He leaned closer and kissed her cheek. "And that won't happen, because I don't want you to go anywhere."

He didn't move away immediately. Sabrina smelled the woodsy scent of his cologne and felt the stubbly roughness of his cheek. Two inches closer and it would have been a real kiss.

Right on the front porch. Sabrina felt like a high school kid holding hands with her first crush.

Funny how the initial awkwardness of falling in love never seemed to change.

Love.

She was falling in love with Avery.

Sabrina jerked away so quickly that she lost her balance and fell backward off the steps.

Avery grabbed her arms and pulled her up just before she hit the ground.

Sabrina stood up and tried to compose herself. That first crush feeling still hadn't subsided. Avery stood right in front of her.

"Are you okay?"

She could only nod yes.

"It's been a while, so I'll admit I'm out of practice, but was the kiss that bad?"

Sabrina looked up into his dark brown eyes, and her knees went wobbly. He leaned over her, eyes full of concern, and the look on his face suggested he might kiss her again at any moment.

She had to get away. Fast.

"I need to go inside," she said, stepping away.

He sighed. "Please don't tell me this is about the resolution."

She looked at the ground. The resolution was just the tip of the iceberg.

"I think it might be a good idea for you to go home now," she told him.

"Why?" He took a step closer. "Sabrina, are you embarrassed to be seen with me?"

Embarrassed, no. Scared, yes.

Sabrina's heart ached as she realized she couldn't tell him how she really felt.

"No, I'm not embarrassed," she managed to say.

"But you're not happy."

"I . . . I'm not unhappy."

"Then why do I get the feeling you only want to talk to me when no one else is around? You dodge me at work, and you get upset because I kissed you on the *cheek* in your front yard?"

He put his hands up in surrender and stepped back. "You're

hiding behind this silly resolution, and I'm beginning to feel I'm not really wanted here."

"Avery, please, that's not what this is about."

"Then what is it about?"

When she didn't answer right away, he kept talking. "I feel like I'm walking on eggshells around you. One minute you're smiling; then the next, you're frowning and imagining reasons why we shouldn't be a couple."

Sabrina felt her eyes burning, but she blinked back the tears. She wouldn't let him see her cry. "I have my reasons, Avery. I wouldn't lie to you about this."

"You wouldn't lie to me?"

She shook her head. At this moment she was willing to tell him the truth about Darci if she had to.

"Then please tell me what's going on," he pleaded. He held up a hand and shook his head. "And please don't try to blame it on Darci. I know you don't like her, but have you realized that you and Maris are always trying to convince me that she's up to some unknown evil?"

"That's not true," Sabrina shot back, feeling indignant.

He crossed his arms in front of his chest. "Then give me a real reason why we can't be together—a reason that doesn't involve Darci."

Sabrina tried to find something, anything honest she could say that would satisfy his need for a reason. "It would be too awkward if everyone at work knew we were dating. Eventually, someone would accuse you of favoritism. Or they would say I was dating the boss to get ahead at work."

"I don't buy that. I dated Darci for years and our relationship was never an issue at work."

Only because everyone was too scared of her to say anything, Sabrina silently shot back.

"But we can compromise," he suggested. "If keeping our relationship separate from the office is really important to you, then we don't have to advertise that we're a couple. What we do away from the office is nobody's business."

She shook her head. "That won't work for me. I don't like the idea of sneaking around."

"I think you just like seeing Darci as a big villain."

Sabrina gasped. How in the world did he come up with such unbelievable drivel?

He nodded and kept right on going. "It's easier to blame your problems on her rather than actually solve them," he challenged. "And I think you have trouble believing that I really like you. Instead of just listening to what I say, you keep fishing for compliments by bringing up Darci over and over again." He sighed. "I can only tell you so many times that I like you."

Sabrina felt her temper surge, and she didn't bother to suppress it. He had no right to accuse her of slandering Darci. Anything she had ever said to him about that woman had been true. "You know what I think? I think you're blinded by her and you regret that you broke up. You're trying to find a replacement for her because she won't take you back."

He laughed. "*She* won't take *me* back? Where in the world did you hear that line?"

Sabrina narrowly refrained from telling him that Darci had told her. If he wanted to believe the woman was a saint, then let him. Obviously, his loyalties were to Her Highness. Sabrina wouldn't be the one to burst his bubble.

Sabrina walked to her front door and opened it. This argument was over.

"Sabrina? Is that it? Are you just going to walk away?"

She didn't even turn around. "Go home, Avery."

She stepped inside, closed the door, and watched out the peephole as he strode to his car and drove away.

So much for falling in love. Her heart had deceived her.

But on the positive side, he had just made it that much easier for Sabrina to earn her ten grand.

Keeping her resolution would be a lot easier as long as Avery was being so childish. Who wanted to love a man like that?

Darci couldn't believe her luck.

It was Friday, four days after her Monday morning meeting with Sabrina, and she couldn't remember the last time she'd had such a stress-free week.

From the looks of things, Sabrina and Avery had not spoken to each other since Annette arrived on the scene.

At least, Avery hadn't been in Sabrina's new office all week. This much she knew just from sitting and watching, and from Sunny's updates when she hadn't been around to see.

A week earlier, she would have surmised that they were putting on an elaborate act for the eyes in the office. For the past few weeks, their previous tactic had been to keep away from each other while at work, but in their free time, they were all lovey-dovey.

Not this week.

Something about the look in their eyes when they did encounter each other in the halls or in production meetings suggested this was the real deal. There was genuine animosity between them, and the air no longer sparked with chemistry when they were together.

Too bad. Darci put her hands over her mouth to keep from giggling. *Too bad for Sabrina.*

Darci knew for a fact that Sabrina and Avery had gone on a date last Saturday night.

But she also knew with great certainty that as of Monday night, the happy couple was no more.

She didn't know the exact details of what had happened, but apparently Sabrina had taken Darci's warning to heart and decided that winning the bonus was more important than winning Avery.

Good girl.

After only four days, Darci could see the positive effects of Avery and Sabrina's spat. Avery was being much nicer to Darci than he had in weeks. They had gone to lunch together twice, and Avery hadn't said Sabrina's name once.

Music to my ears, Darci mused.

A glance at her watch revealed it was almost noon. Her goal for the day was to get Avery to ask her on a date tonight, but she hadn't seen him all morning.

It was time to go on the hunt.

The husband hunt.

If she expected to get Avery and keep him for any extended period of time, Darci knew she would have to prove she was ready for a serious commitment. She'd already been faithfully serving her time at church. Now it was time to get him thinking about marriage again. Marriage to her.

She stepped out of her office, and Sunny called her name.

"Ms. Oliver?"

Darci inhaled and fought to keep her irritation in check. This better be serious. She wanted to find Avery before he went to lunch.

"What is it, Sunny?"

"We just got a phone call from the people at the *Morning Coffee* show."

Now Sunny had her full attention. *Morning Coffee* was the top-ranked early morning show. It featured three hosts: two women and one man. Working as a team, they reported a smidgen of news and generally did little else but chat about everything under the sun, interview celebrities, and provide up-to-the-minute fashion and entertainment news for three hours every morning.

Darci really wanted to be on the show but had yet to be invited.

"They said they want an interview."

"Really? That's wonderful." Darci didn't try to hold back her elation. She almost wanted to hug Sunny. At this moment, she could probably even hug Sabrina.

"When?" Her mind kicked into overdrive with details. She needed a new suit, new shoes, maybe a manicure and a hair trim. She might have to rearrange her taping schedule in order to fly to New York for the interview.

Or maybe they would do a satellite interview, with Darci in her own studio.

That would be easier, but she really wanted the experience of sitting around the coffee table with Daphne, Gordon, and Renee.

"Ms. Oliver? Do you want to tell Sabrina, or should I let Mr. Benjamin break the news?" Sunny interrupted her train of thought.

Darci frowned. What in the world did Sabrina have to do with any of this?

"What?"

"I said, do you want to tell Sabrina or should—"

Darci cut Sunny off mid-sentence. "Tell Sabrina what?"

"About the *Morning Coffee* interview," Sunny said.

"The *Morning Coffee* interview," Darci repeated.

Sunny gave her a quizzical look. Darci rolled her eyes. Sometimes the woman was the perfect employee, and other times she was absolutely clueless.

"They want to interview Sabrina."

What? Why did she have to share her shining moment with Sabrina? Of all the people . . . Darci took back her earlier sentiments. She didn't want to hug Sabrina; she wanted to strangle her.

She sighed loudly. "Okay, Sunny, run this by me again. I wasn't listening."

Sunny recounted the story at a snail's pace.

Darci zoned out until Sunny got to the part she wanted to hear.

". . . people have been calling in and asking for them to feature Sabrina on the show. They want to do a ten-minute live interview with her in twelve days. They're booked solid until then; otherwise they'd have her on sooner."

"Hold on. They just want to interview Sabrina?"

"Well, let me see . . ." Sunny consulted her notes for an agonizing twenty seconds. She looked up, glasses perched on the bridge of her nose, looking more bug-eyed than usual. "As far as I can tell, yes. Just Sabrina."

Darci now understood the meaning of the phrase "blood began to boil."

Had all her hard work been for nothing? Had she sweated and toiled eighty-hour weeks in the early days just so people like Sabrina could get famous and go on *Morning Coffee?*

I will not cry. I will not cry. I will not cry. Darci silently repeated the words over and over in an attempt to keep her composure.

Sunny didn't seem to notice that she was on the verge of tears. "Or do you want me to tell her?" Sunny was still wrapped up in the details of breaking the news to Sabrina.

Darci stalked toward the ladies' room. "Let Avery tell her," she called out over her shoulder.

Once she reached her destination, she made sure no one else was inside, then locked the main door. If anyone needed to use the facilities right now, they were out of luck. Besides, there was another lavatory on the floor below.

She stared at her reflection in the mirror. Wasn't she good enough?

Until last fall, Darci had never even entertained such thoughts.

She had always considered herself prettier, smarter, more ambitious.

She had the good job, the nice house, the perfect boyfriend. Then it started to unravel.

First she pushed the boyfriend away. Then he noticed Sabrina. It was all downhill from there.

Darci sank down to the floor, emotionally exhausted. She didn't care if her suit got smudged or her shoes got scuffed. It didn't seem important right now.

How embarrassing. Sabrina gets invited to Morning Coffee, *but not me.*

She buried her face in her hands and sobbed.

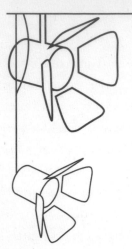

Chapter Twenty-One

Avery sat at his desk, wishing he could go home. He wanted nothing more than to escape the two women plaguing him at work.

One plagued him openly, purposefully. Darci repeatedly came to his office whining, sometimes even crying, begging for comfort and mumbling about retribution.

The other plagued him silently, unknowingly. Sabrina was a nervous wreck. Everyone could see it. She buried herself in her office and spent her free time being prepped for the interview by the people in the PR department.

He wished she would let him comfort her. But she wouldn't even let him talk to her.

It had only been three days since the *Morning Coffee Live* call. Avery closed his blinds and locked the door. That should keep Darci away for a while.

He wadded up sheets of paper and practiced his three-pointer with the wastebasket in the corner.

He chewed pencils while pretending to review the budget.

He told the secretary to hold his phone calls and refuse all visitors—even Darci.

He turned on the television in his office and watched *Sports Center*—something he never did during regular office hours. When *Sports Center* went off, he channel-surfed.

Three hours and three soap opera episodes later, Avery wished he had a time machine. He could think of ten ways he could benefit from it, right off the bat. For one thing, he would zoom forward and get this interview over and done with.

But first he would go back and try to fix the argument with Sabrina. He would take back all the things he'd said about Darci. He had known it would infuriate her, but he'd been too frustrated to care.

Then maybe he could go back and somehow convince the *Morning Coffee* people to interview both Sabrina and Darci.

Darci wouldn't be thrilled with that arrangement, but it would be loads better than the current situation.

Sabrina would still be nervous, but she deserved the publicity far more than Darci. She was the kind of celebrity Americans loved to love pretty, nice, wholesome. Even her ex-boyfriend couldn't find anything bad to say about her.

Avery considered the novelty of a time machine once again. Finally, he would travel back three hours and reclaim the time he'd wasted watching the soaps.

His own life teetered dangerously close to the same level of drama. Who needed to watch a television show about it when all he had to do was get up and go to work?

Sabrina lay on her couch, worn out. After leaving work, she'd spent the rest of the evening at the mall with Maris and Jasmine, shopping for the perfect ensemble to wear on *Morning Coffee Live*.

She had finally located a suitable outfit but had walked away much wiser. The trip would have been much easier had she gone on her own.

Sabrina couldn't envision herself going shopping again with both Maris and Jasmine any time soon. They agreed on nothing and argued about everything.

She could have gone shopping without either of them and fared just as well. They hadn't been much help anyway.

She had located the chic black pantsuit while Maris and Jasmine argued about whether she should wear her hair up or down.

She had found the perfect shoes while the two of them debated whether she would wear gold or silver jewelry.

The scent of chocolate-chip cookies wafted from the kitchen. Sabrina heard the sound of the oven door being opened.

"They're done," Jasmine announced.

"No, they're too soft," said Maris. "Five or six more minutes."

"The bottoms will be black if they stay in much longer," Jasmine countered.

"We'll get salmonella if we eat them now. They're nothing but warm dough. They need to brown," Maris argued.

"Nobody wants a cookie that has the texture of a rock."

"And nobody wants to eat gooey flour and eggs. It's gross."

Sabrina could picture Maris with her hands on her hips and Jasmine with a perturbed look on her face.

If I tell them I have a headache, will they go home now? she wondered. She grabbed a pillow and put it over her face in hopes of drowning out the sound.

Moments later, they entered the room. Jasmine carried glasses of milk on a tray. "Look what we brought for you," she said.

"We'll have cookies in a few minutes," Maris added. From

the look on her face, it was apparent that she had won the cookie argument.

Sabrina sat up and tried to look pleased.

"How do you feel?" Maris asked.

"Okay, I guess. If I don't think about it too much, I don't feel so nervous."

"Do you know what you're going to say?" Jasmine wanted to know.

Sabrina took a sip of her milk. "Not exactly, but the PR people at work have been running me through all kinds of scenarios."

"This is so exciting," said Jasmine. "I can't believe that somebody I know is actually going to be on *Morning Coffee Live.*" She curled up into one corner of the sofa and hugged a pillow in front of her. "I think you should definitely say something about Jesus. Think how awesome that would be."

Maris frowned. "Please tell me you are not going to get on national television and start preaching a sermon. Sabrina, you'll look ridiculous."

"But how will anyone know she's a Christian if she doesn't say something?"

Sabrina closed her eyes and listened while Jasmine and Maris went back and forth. She really was starting to get a headache.

". . . that won't be a very good witness." Jasmine's voice sounded a little uneven.

"Witness?" Maris's tone was heavily laced with sarcasm. "What are you talking about? Sabrina's the nicest person I've ever met. Why would she want to ruin a perfectly good interview by sounding like some kind of religious freak?"

"Ruin? Freak?" Jasmine had definitely reached her limit. Her voice was high and shrill.

"That's why I don't like religious people." Apparently, Maris had reached her limit, as well.

"What do you mean, religious? You're religious, too."

"No, I'm not." Maris was indignant. "You couldn't pay me to be like you."

Sabrina opened her eyes and watched the sparks fly, amused.

"What do you mean, you're not religious? You're a Christian, aren't you?"

"Technically, I guess not. I haven't prayed that prayer, if that's what you mean."

Jasmine gasped, taken aback. She gave Sabrina an incredulous look. "She's not a Christian?"

Sabrina felt weak under the scrutiny of their stares. Both women wanted her to take their side.

She shook her head. "Well, no. Not yet."

Jasmine's eyes grew wide. "Why haven't you led her to the Lord yet? Don't you feel convicted by the Spirit?"

"Led me to the Lord? Convicted by the Spirit?" said Maris. "Why is it that Christians have to speak in a totally different language? Sabrina, if you use these kinds of phrases on television, people will get freaked out."

Then she turned her attention to Jasmine. "Have you even considered that the reason you're not winning enough souls—whatever that means—is because nobody understands what you're talking about?"

Jasmine huffed.

"I like the Bible, I like church, and I even like *some* of the Christians I've met there," said Maris. "But I don't feel ready to sign my life away just yet."

Jasmine ignored Maris and turned her attention to Sabrina. "Haven't you told her that her soul is in danger? Don't you want her to spend eternity in heaven with us?"

"I do, Jasmine. Believe me, I've preached at Maris since the day I met her. But that approach wasn't working."

Jasmine looked as though she didn't quite believe Sabrina.

"She's telling you the truth," Maris said. "A few months back I told her to stop it because I didn't want to hear it anymore."

"Then what are you doing at our church?" Jasmine challenged.

Maris inhaled sharply. "So now I have to have some kind of Christian membership card to get in?" She shook her head. "Don't worry, I won't be back." She crossed her arms and looked away.

Sabrina decided to intervene. They were acting like spoiled little kids.

"Look, you guys. Can we settle down and try not to get so riled up? I'm getting a headache."

Maris arched an eyebrow at Jasmine. "We were supposed to be cheering her up, and look who had to ruin everything."

"It's just as much your fault as it is mine," she shot back.

"Please!"

Jasmine and Maris stopped talking and looked at Sabrina as if she'd grown two heads.

Even Sabrina was surprised at the vehemence in her tone.

"Guys, this was supposed to be fun, but I'm just getting stressed . . ." She stopped and sniffed the air. An acrid scent drifted from the direction of the kitchen.

"The cookies!" Jasmine and Maris screamed in unison. They ran to the kitchen, and Sabrina followed.

Maris yanked open the oven door, and thick puffs of smoke poured out. The cookies were burned far beyond the crisp stage.

"I predicted this would happen." Jasmine wore a defiant expression.

Maris placed her hands on her hips. She spoke quietly, slowly.

"This wouldn't have happened if you hadn't distracted me with that argument about being religious."

"I didn't *start* that argument."

"Oh, yes, you did. In fact, you started it and *then* you fanned the flames . . ."

Sabrina quietly backed out of the kitchen. They wouldn't even notice she was gone. Maybe they would both get so angry, they would give up and leave. She went to her room and curled up on her bed.

Now the headache had ballooned into a full-fledged pounding nightmare. She got up, found a bottle of ibuprofen, and swallowed two capsules along with a glass of water.

I could go for a latte right now. A real latte.

She fluffed her pillow and lay down again. An overwhelming sense of loneliness enveloped her.

Lord, I could really use someone to talk to. The two people who came over to cheer me up are having a knock-down, drag-out fight in my kitchen over cookies and church.

My head hurts, and I have to go on national television in nine days. My palms are already sweaty, and my stomach is party central for a truckload of butterflies. Please help me get through this without looking absolutely silly in front of the entire nation.

The phone rang, and Sabrina checked the caller ID.

Avery.

He had called at least once a day since their argument, but Sabrina wouldn't answer.

She held the cordless extension in her hands and listened to it ring.

Judging by the rise in volume coming from the kitchen, Maris and Jasmine were having a full-fledged argument and hadn't even heard the telephone.

Should she talk to him? Although she had taken great pains to ignore him, he had seemed apologetic all week.

Before she could change her mind, Sabrina clicked the phone on and answered. Talking to Avery was bound to be more pleasant than listening to Jasmine and Maris fussing.

"I'm surprised you answered," he said.

"I am, too. But there are extenuating circumstances on my end."

"Such as?"

Sabrina stopped talking and held the phone in the general direction of the kitchen. "Hear that?"

"Yeah, what is it? Alley cats?"

"Maris and Jasmine having an argument about burned cookies."

"Seriously? Maris doesn't seem like the type to lose her cool over something so . . . trivial."

"Actually, it started when we were discussing the *Morning Coffee* interview. Jasmine thinks I should work the plan of salvation into my answers, and Maris says I'll look completely stupid if I start spouting Christianese."

"What do you think?" he asked.

"Me? I don't know. I hadn't thought that far in advance, so they've just given me one more thing to stress about."

He laughed.

"What do you think?" she asked. "What would you do if you were in my shoes?"

"Hmm. Tough call." She could picture him shrugging.

"I mean, I'm not trying to hide the fact that I'm a Christian—although I may be hard-pressed to convince Jasmine otherwise. And even though Maris would be mortified, I'd love to be able to talk about Jesus somehow, but I don't want it to sound forced or contrived."

"I understand exactly how you feel," said Avery.

"Might you have some advice to accompany your empathy?"

"I just remembered something one of my professors in college told me once."

"Really? What?"

"Let me give you a little background first. At the time, I was really on fire for the Lord. I was running around campus preaching to anyone who would listen.

"One day, I visited this church and found out my humanities professor attended there. I was pretty surprised because he never said he was a Christian in class. I always thought he was nice—just your basic, all-around good guy.

"A few weeks later, I was still really bothered by the fact that he wasn't openly proselytizing, so I confronted him after class."

Sabrina chuckled. "That was pretty bold of you."

"It was close to the end of the semester and I pretty much knew I was going to get a B-minus, so I figured I didn't have much to lose.

"Anyway, I told him as respectfully as I could that I thought he was hiding his light under a bushel. I was shaking like a leaf on a tree, since he was old enough to be my grandpa."

"What'd he say?"

"He thanked me for expressing my concern and he told me that he really admired my zealousness. As it turned out, he'd been watching me all semester."

"So what's the moral of the story?"

"He said that he probably could step things up as far as witnessing to other people. But he also said that he had grown to understand that many people respond pretty negatively to an outright salvation message."

"Like Maris," Sabrina said.

"Exactly. Maris watches to see how people act, how they react in certain situations. I see her scrutinizing everything you and I do at work and in church. She's the analytical type, and she'll go home and cross-reference the things she sees us do to what she already knows about the Bible."

"And sometimes she'll come back and ask me questions."

"Right. But there are a lot of people like Maris out there who just watch without even asking questions. They form their impressions of Christians by seeing how the people who claim to be followers of Jesus live their lives."

"That's pretty humbling," Sabrina said.

"Yeah. It keeps me on my toes, especially when I'm at some fast-food place and the kid behind the counter puts mustard on my burger when I specifically asked for no mustard."

"Or when the lady at the coffee shop decides I should have tea instead of my espresso," Sabrina said.

"Right. Like my teacher told me, sometimes we plant seeds by speaking the gospel directly to someone, and sometimes we plant seeds with our actions. Either way, the seed is planted, and hopefully, it will come to fruition."

"I like that," Sabrina said.

He went on. "In the words of Saint Francis of Assisi, by way of my humanities professor: 'Preach the gospel at all times, and when necessary, use words.'"

Sabrina didn't say anything but sat quietly, soaking in the depth of his words.

"You still there?"

"I'm here. Just thinking."

"About what?"

"Everything."

Avery cleared his throat. "Everything, huh?"

"Yeah."

"Can I change the subject for a bit?" he asked.

"I think I know where you're heading."

"Well, it's been four days, and I was beginning to think that you were never going to speak to me again."

Sabrina sighed. More conflict. Just what she needed before the big interview.

"Avery, I forgive you for what happened the other day, but I can't go into this right now. I need to focus on getting ready for this interview."

"And after the interview? Do you think we might be able to pick up where we left off?"

She pursed her lips. How could he ask her this after their discussion about people watching their actions?

The whole country knew she was trying not to fall in love, and she had already made the deal with Darci.

If Sabrina lied to Darci and all the viewers by sneaking around with Avery, her actions would undermine her witnessing. She couldn't do that.

"Avery, I can't. You know I can't."

"Sabrina, just say you have a boyfriend. Say you don't want to keep that resolution anymore. Nobody's going to be mad at you."

Darci would be.

"No, I want to keep it." And she did. Mostly for the money and the promotion, but a part of her wanted to prove she could do what so many people thought would be impossible.

"Sabrina, please."

"No. I won't break it. We have to be friends or nothing else. No flirting, no kissing, no dates.

"My heart already proved I'm not ready for another relationship right now. You saw how upset I was on Monday. Everyone's right. I'm too hurt and too scared to fall in love right now. Let me have some time to heal."

He didn't answer.

"Avery?"

"Yes."

"Do you understand?"

"I hear you, but I can't say that I understand you. I think you have other reasons for saying no."

"And if I did, I'd still want you to respect my choice. If you can't even do that, I guess you're not someone I'd want to date anyway."

He sighed. "All right, I give up. You win."

"Let's not declare a winner or a loser," she suggested. "It's not a contest, you know."

He laughed. "Sabrina, you have a really interesting way of looking at things."

"Sabrina? Where are you?" Maris's voice carried through the house.

"They're looking for me. I'd better get off the phone."

"I'll see you at work?"

"Yes, I'll see you at work. But that's it."

"I got it. Just friends. I don't like it, but I don't think you're giving me a choice," he said. "And relax about the interview. If the right opportunity comes for you to say something, you'll know it. And if not—"

"Preach without using words," Sabrina finished the sentence for him.

"See, I don't even have to tell you. You already know."

"Sabrina?!" This time Jasmine called.

"Gotta go."

Sabrina hung up the phone and hurried to the kitchen. If Maris and Jasmine couldn't resolve their differences in the next ten minutes, she would send them both home.

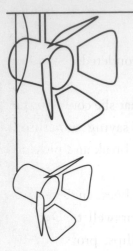

Chapter Twenty-Two

The next two days passed almost uneventfully. Maris and Jasmine were still not the best of friends, but at least they weren't upset with Sabrina.

Sabrina kept her interactions with Avery short and businesslike and shifted all her available energy to getting ready for *Morning Coffee*.

She taped the show every morning and watched it when she got home from work.

She sat in a chair in front of her bathroom mirror and talked to her reflection, pretending she was in front of the *Morning Coffee Live* studio audience.

She rearranged her living room to look like the *Morning Coffee* set—complete with the round table she dragged in from her kitchen. She put giant pillows in the seats where the hosts sat, then taped paper-plate faces onto the pillows.

Sabrina put on her new high heels and practiced entering the room and saying hello to hosts Daphne, Gordon, and Renee, and pantomimed shaking hands with them.

Sabrina was grateful for the invention of curtains, because if anyone had seen her walking in and out of her living room and shaking hands with air, they would have wondered about her sanity.

Just when Sabrina was feeling confident that she could do the interview without tripping or sweating or saying something that didn't make sense, she decided to take a break and pick up some essentials at the grocery store.

She took off the heels, put on her tennis shoes, and grabbed her purse. As she left the house, she bade farewell to Daphne McGuire, Gordon Mitchell, and Renee Phillips, promising to return within the hour.

She was standing in line at the grocer's, her arms full of high-fiber cereal and ready-to-eat salad, when she caught her first glimpse of the headlines: SABRINA'S SCINTILLATING SECRET!

Another beckoned with the words: RESOLUTIONER FAILS AT LOVE AGAIN.

A third tabloid read: SABRINA DISCREETLY DATING "DAILY DOSE" PRODUCER.

Yet another proclaimed: THE REAL SABRINA. HEARTBREAKER OR OWNER OF A BROKEN HEART—AGAIN?

This time, her story was juicy enough to fill the covers of all three magazines. And now there were pictures. Lots of them. But how? And when?

In shock, Sabrina stared at the collage of photos splashed across the covers. Some had been taken the night she and Avery had gone to dinner and the movie. There were photos of them at the botanical gardens and at the nursery. And finally, photos of them arguing in her front yard.

Someone's been trailing me, she realized.

The man behind Sabrina in the line cleared his throat. She pulled her attention away from the magazines long enough to realize that she was holding up the line.

They were all staring at her—the clerk, the bag boy, the other people in line.

She thought she saw the glint of recognition in some of their gazes.

Could someone please pass me the mortification pills?

Now everyone knew. And it wasn't even 100 percent true—at least not anymore.

Mumbling an excuse about having forgotten something, Sabrina exited the line and ran for cover in the relative anonymity of the aisles. There, no one would be able to match her face to the front of a cereal box or a jar of applesauce.

How did movie stars go grocery shopping? Even if they consciously refused to look at those headlines, the people behind them might not hold similar convictions. How could they stand there, right next to those outrageous headlines, while the people around them devoured every word as the gospel truth?

Sabrina was torn between putting a grocery sack over her head and slinking home, and going back to the front of the store to prove her innocence.

She wanted to pick up those awful pages, hold them over her head, and yell, "It's not true! It's not always the way it looks!"

Maris would never let her hear the end of it if she did.

Forget Maris—she herself would be embarrassed for life.

Presumably, someone would end up calling a news crew, and then her outburst would be preserved on film for all posterity to view.

Sabrina pretended to be engrossed in comparing the prices of three brands of canned tuna while she planned her escape.

Somehow, she had the presence of mind to return her items back to their proper places in the store before she bolted for her car.

As she drove to her house, she dialed Maris on her cell phone.

From the sound of her voice, Maris already knew. "Sabrina? Where are you?"

"I'm in the car, driving home from the grocery store. Can you come over? Or maybe we can meet somewhere."

"Uh, no. I don't think we want to meet anywhere. Have you seen the news today?"

Sabrina's heart sank. "The news?"

"Yeah. You're . . . kind of a big story."

"No, I've been too busy pretending to talk to Daphne, Gordon, and Renee to actually watch TV. But I'm guessing the news is telling the same story as the tabloids."

"Then you already know."

"Basically. I saw headlines that made me blush. And they only contain a grain of truth," she protested.

"Sabrina, you're preaching to the choir."

"Can you come over?" Sabrina knew she sounded pitiful, but she didn't care.

"I can't right now. Sid just got home from work, so I need to get his dinner. Why don't you come over here? You can have dinner with us."

Sabrina almost said no. Sidney hadn't been in the best of moods since his failure to buy the New Orleans building.

But dinner with Sid sounded much more exciting than a night sitting at a table and talking to pillows with faces.

"I'll be there in fifteen minutes," she said.

❦

"Obviously, somebody staked out your house," Sid said. "Maris, pass me the mashed potatoes."

Maris passed the potatoes.

Sabrina considered the stakeout idea. "But who? And how? I don't remember seeing anything out of the ordinary that day."

Sid shrugged. "Cameras are pretty high-tech these days. They could have been a couple of blocks away on the upstairs floor of some house."

"They did seem to be kind of fuzzy, so I doubt that whoever took them was sitting right in front of your house," Maris added.

"More roast beef?" Sid asked.

Sabrina buried her face in her hands. "You guys don't understand how embarrassing this is. A first kiss is a private thing. But now everybody's seen it."

"Technically, it wasn't really a kiss. It was on the cheek," said Sid.

Sabrina realized he was trying to be helpful, so she refrained from rolling her eyes.

She turned pleading eyes to Maris. "How am I going to face everyone at the office tomorrow?"

"Better yet," Sid broke in, "how are you going to handle the *Morning Coffee* interview? You know they're going to be asking questions."

"I'll just have to cancel the interview. I'll say I'm sick."

Maris shook her head. "They'll know you're bluffing and assume the tabloids are telling the truth. You have to do the interview."

Sabrina shook her head. "I can't do it. I need to go away, disappear, take an extended vacation. I need to fall off the face of the earth without anyone noticing."

"I have an idea," Sid jumped in. "Why don't you move down to New Orleans and come be a waitress in our restaurant?"

"Sid . . ." Maris shot her husband a warning look.

Sid took a bite of his roast beef and put his hands up in defense. "Hey, it was just an idea. She said she wanted to get far away, and you somehow have the idea that New Orleans is one of the four corners of the universe . . . I figured that if she came, you could both be miserable together."

Maris stood and started clearing dishes from the table. "I have peach cobbler if anyone wants dessert."

Sid pushed away from the table. "I'll get some later." He put his arms around Maris's waist and kissed her. "Great dinner, sweetheart."

"Thank you," Maris said.

Sabrina felt a pang of envy. She wanted a husband who would kiss her and tell her she was a great cook.

After Sid left for the family room, Maris gave Sabrina an apologetic look. "I'm sorry Sid made fun of you. He just gets in those moods sometimes and thinks everything he says is funny . . ."

"It was kind of funny," Sabrina admitted.

Maris chuckled. "Your little friend Jasmine would probably have a conniption if she ever met him. Five minutes into their first conversation, she'd probably tell him how he needed to get his soul saved."

Sabrina tried to picture such a conversation. Sid was generally easygoing, but she had a feeling Jasmine probably *would* rub him the wrong way.

Maris ran her hand through her hair. "Although, if I could get him to go to church, maybe he would get some religion and drop this silly New Orleans café idea."

Church.

"Oh, no!" Sabrina put her fork down.

"What is it?" Maris leaned over, looking concerned.

"Church. The people at church are going to see those tabloids."

Maris arched an eyebrow. "I thought holy people aren't supposed to be reading that trash. If anybody says anything to you about it, you can tell them they should have been reading the Bible instead."

Sabrina didn't have the energy to counter Maris's barb. "They're going to think I'm a complete floozy."

Maris doubled over in laughter.

Sabrina felt a surge of irritation. Maris was supposed to be commiserating with her, not laughing. "I'm in pain here. What's so funny about my being the laughingstock of church?"

Maris straightened and opened her mouth, but no words came out. Instead, she was overtaken with another fit of giggles.

Sabrina watched, feeling annoyed.

Maris gasped for breath and finally uttered, "Floozy!" before dissolving into another laughing fit.

"What in the world?" Sid came running in from the family room.

Sabrina shrugged. "I have no idea. I was telling Maris that I worried about going to church, and she's been laughing ever since."

Maris gasped loudly and finally stopped laughing.

Sabrina and Sid looked to her for an explanation.

"Sabrina just said the word 'floozy.'" She shook her head. "I haven't heard that word in years, not since I was a kid."

Sid chuckled. "That is an old-time word. I used to hear my grandmother sitting around talking to her friends and they would say things like 'That floozy had the nerve to walk in here and—'"

Maris burst out laughing again. "My grandmothers used to do the same thing. And I didn't know what a floozy was, but I was too scared to ask anybody, because it sounded like such a horrible word."

Sabrina nodded, having experienced similar scenarios in her own childhood.

"All I knew was that I never wanted to be one," said Maris.

"I guess I'll go back to the family room," said Sid. "The conversation here has definitely segued into girl talk."

"I don't care about the pictures, Sabrina. You're too good for them to get any real dirt on you. For goodness' sakes, you actually used the word 'floozy.' I mean, that word is so . . . so *Gone With the Wind.*"

Sabrina leaned her head to the side. "I'm trying to decide if that's a compliment or a put-down."

"It's a compliment, believe me. The worst word you can come up with is 'floozy'? You're such a Goody Two-shoes." Maris continued clearing the table. "And don't worry; I mean that in an endearing way."

"Thanks, I think," said Sabrina.

"Hey, hurry up! Come in here!" Sid yelled from the family room.

Maris and Sabrina hurried to see what the commotion was about.

"*Inside Entertainment* is getting ready to show a story about Sabrina," he explained. "After the commercial."

Sabrina sat and waited for the show to come back on. When the commercial break ended, Maris turned up the volume.

"Shh," said Sid.

As if any of them were planning on talking during the segment.

"Welcome back to *Inside Entertainment.* I'm Lilia Jacobs, and we have a new development in the Sabrina Bradley story for you tonight."

The screen filled with clips of Sabrina taken from *The Daily Dose* shows, while Lilia continued speaking.

"Most of you are already familiar with Sabrina, the woman who has resolved not to fall in love for an entire year. She's one of the panel of people *The Daily Dose* talk show is helping to keep their New Year's resolutions.

"But recent revelations have shown that Sabrina may be finding this resolution too much to handle."

Lilia's image returned to the screen. "For more information, let's go to Stephan Frazier, live in St. Louis."

An image of a man standing outside a dark building popped on the screen. It took a moment for Sabrina to register exactly where he was.

"Hey, he's standing in front of my condo!"

"No way," said Maris. "I can't believe they'd actually stoop that low."

"Shh, be quiet," said Sid.

"Stephan, what do you have for us?" asked Lilia.

"Well, Lilia, not much at the moment." He gestured to the building behind him. "I'm standing in front of the condominium that Sabrina Bradley calls home, but unfortunately, not much seems to be going on. It appears that she isn't here at the moment."

"I see," said Lilia. "Well, can you tell us any more about those pictures that surfaced this morning?"

Stephan nodded. "Several papers ran a number of photos picturing Sabrina and a man. In some of the shots they were talking amiably, one showed the two kissing, and others showed them involved in an argument of some kind."

"Any definite word on the identity of that man?" Lilia asked. "There was a rumor going around earlier that the man was someone involved in the production of *The Daily Dose.*"

Stephan nodded emphatically. "Yes, and in fact, one paper went ahead and ran a story based on that rumor. As for us here at *Inside Entertainment,* our sources have now confirmed that the man pictured *is* Avery Benjamin, the executive producer and creator of *The Daily Dose.*"

"That would mean he's Sabrina's boss," said Lilia.

"Yes, apparently so."

"Can you tell us how long they've been involved, Stephan? Was the relationship in place before she began the resolutions program?"

Stephan gave an apologetic look. "That much we haven't been able to confirm yet. We *do* know from an earlier story that as of last August, Ms. Bradley had just ended the relationship with her fiancé, Eric Stover."

"This is certainly shaping up to be an interesting story," Lilia mused. "Some people are starting to say that the resolutions program is nothing more than a sham, complete with paid actors and phony goals. If Sabrina and this Mr. Benjamin are indeed a couple, then it would seem that she's either already given up on her resolution or she never meant to keep it in the first place."

"Yes, I agree," said Stephan. "It is certainly a possibility that the resolutions program just might be a highly scripted play.

"We've also heard that the staff at *The Daily Dose may* have instituted the resolutions program in order to prove to the critics that Darci Oliver, the show's host, is making a positive impact on viewers' lives."

Lilia pursed her lips and shook her head, a solemn expression on her face. "And Ms. Bradley is an integral part of that production staff, am I correct?"

"Yes. She has said in her segments on *The Daily Dose* that she is an assistant to the assistant producer."

"Do we know this producer's name?"

Stephan consulted an index card. "Yes, we do . . . The assistant producer's name is Maris Russell. Unfortunately, we have not yet been able to locate Ms. Russell in order to speak with her."

Lilia's face flitted on the screen for a brief moment. "I guess we'll all know soon enough what the true story is behind all of this. Do we have a statement from Sabrina?"

"No, we don't. The *Daily Dose* offices are closed, and

Ms. Bradley isn't answering her home telephone. We *have* learned that she is scheduled to be a guest on *Morning Coffee Live* next Wednesday."

"I see," said Lilia. "Perhaps she'll take that opportunity to tell her side of the story and set things straight if need be."

"Most likely," Stephan agreed. "And we, the investigative team for *Inside Entertainment,* will continue to uncover the truth as this unusual story progresses."

"Thank you, Stephan. I certainly hope that by this time tomorrow, the details of what exactly is happening in those photos will be clear. Now, let's preview movies opening this weekend . . ."

Maris turned down the volume and looked at Sabrina. "Of all of the inane things to report. No offense to you, but is it really that important that they need to set up camp at your front door?"

"I can't believe the serious look on that guy's face," said Sid. "You'd have thought he was breaking the Watergate story."

"I can't go back there," Sabrina murmured. "Not now. I can't face them like this. I'm not even wearing any makeup."

Maris went maternal. "Of course you don't have to go back there tonight. You'll stay here in the guest room. And tomorrow morning we'll call the police and see what can be done to get those people off your property."

Sabrina tossed and turned for a long time in Maris and Sid's guest bedroom. She was grateful for their hospitality but missed the comfort of her own bed.

Within a matter of hours, Sabrina's life had gone topsy-turvy. She wondered if it would ever return to normal.

Her stomach twisted with worry.

A familiar Psalm came to mind.

When I am afraid, I will trust in You.

Sabrina wished she had a Bible, so she could look up the rest of it.

She sat up, clicked on the lamp, and scanned the bookshelves in the bedroom. It was unlikely that Maris and Sid, of all people, would have a Bible lying around, but then again, you never knew. It never hurt to check.

Sure enough, tucked between the complete works of Shakespeare and an anthology of Jane Austen novels, Sabrina located a Bible.

Apparently, Maris and Sid held the book in high respect, though they didn't necessarily feel the same toward all Christians.

Sabrina carried the Bible back to bed with her and got comfortable. She flipped through the Psalms and found several verses that applied to her situation, including the verse she'd remembered from the fifty-sixth chapter.

She sat back and prayed the words of the Psalm over her own life:

Be merciful to me, O God, for men hotly pursue me; all day long they press their attack. My slanderers pursue me all day long; many are attacking me in their pride. When I am afraid, I will trust in You. In God, whose word I praise, in God I trust; I will not be afraid. What can mortal man do to me? All day long they twist my words . . . they conspire, they lurk . . .

It was an uncanny reminder of how unsettled her life had become. It almost felt as though it had been written to encourage her right at this exact moment.

What a comfort to know that God had control of every situation—even days like today that seemed to be completely out of her own control.

Sabrina finished praying the chapter, her confidence bolstered with each passing sentence.

. . . Record my lament; list my tears on Your scroll . . . then my enemies will turn back when I call for help. By this I will know that God is for me. In God whose word I praise, in the Lord, whose word I praise—in God I trust; I will not be afraid. What can man do to me?

Thank you, Lord, Sabrina prayed. *I'm sorry for ever doubting that you would take care of me.*

Sabrina lay down again. She needed rest before she had to face the office in the morning.

This time, peace came and sleep followed.

Chapter Twenty-Three

Darci made a trip to the store on her way to work, to see the news for herself.

At six thirty in the morning, the store was relatively empty, so the risk of being bothered by fans would be low.

Under the ruse of getting a bottle of nail polish, Darci had the satisfaction of seeing Sabrina's name splashed across the cover of every tabloid on the market. What a scandal.

Unfortunately, Avery's name was mixed up in the mess, but that wouldn't be a major issue. He'd be forgiven and forgotten soon enough. Men tended to walk away from these things a lot easier than women.

Darci made her way back to her car, feeling happier than she had in weeks. Yes, there was the little issue of Sabrina and Avery keeping their relationship a secret from her, but now it was out in the open.

Darci had heard many celebrities complain about the questionable tactics of some reporters, and in the past she had agreed with them.

But in a situation like this, questionable reporting tactics weren't so bad.

Although Darci had been curious about what was going on behind her back with Avery and Sabrina, she hadn't been able to uncover the truth without looking conspicuous.

She didn't try to conceal the grin that formed at the corner of her mouth.

It was certainly amazing what a well-timed anonymous tip to the media could do. Freedom of the press was a beautiful thing.

Avery was running late. He'd gone home exhausted the night before. Too exhausted even to watch sports scores on television. Besides, his three-hour soap opera stint had been enough to make him swear off all television for a while.

He rushed around getting ready and nearly forgot his brief-case in the process.

Ten minutes before he reached the office, his stomach began protesting the fact that he'd skipped breakfast in his haste.

Avery pulled into the parking lot of the nearest grocery store. He'd run in, get a doughnut and orange juice, and still make it to work in time.

He strode to the bakery, grabbed a couple of glazed, then headed to the coolers in the front to get a small bottle of orange juice.

While he bent over to select his drink, a little old lady with a million groceries in her cart pushed past him in line.

Avery sighed. Sometimes the most unlikely people could be so rude.

He looked around to weigh his options. There was only one other checkout lane open, and the lady in that line had twice the amount in her cart than the lady in front of him had.

There was nothing he could do but wait.

Avery couldn't stand grocery shopping, especially when there was a long line. What was he supposed to do while he waited?

Women could gaze at the fashion magazines and learn how to make their boyfriends love them more or steal some celebrity's latest hairstyle.

A man would look ridiculous if he looked through one of those books. Avery made a mental note to write a letter to the grocery store manager and suggest that the local newspaper be placed in the same place as the fashion magazines.

Avery liked the idea of being able to read the *Post-Dispatch* headlines while he waited. It would be nice to catch up on what was happening, since he'd been too rushed to turn on the local newscast.

Avery shifted his weight from side to side a few times and perused the vast assortment of candy bars.

". . . Now, I have a few coupons," he heard the lady say.

Avery stifled a groan and checked to see how things were progressing.

In his peripheral vision, he saw some celebrity posed in a bikini. It was barely April, for crying out loud. Couldn't they hold the swimwear until June?

Avery was about to turn away when a familiar name caught his eye.

Sabrina.

Sabrina?

Her name was on the cover of at least half a dozen tabloids, along with pictures of the two of them together.

Avery knew his jaw was hanging open, but he couldn't quite bring himself to close his mouth.

He saw his name on one of the covers and blinked: MEET AVERY, SABRINA'S SECRET BOYFRIEND!

Avery snatched the magazine out of the rack. What in the world?

The pictures were the real thing. They were a little fuzzy, but he couldn't deny that he and Sabrina were in those photos.

Somehow, he had always assumed that all the pictures in this type of paper were doctored or contrived, but these weren't.

Someone had obviously been following them last Saturday and had gotten a load of pictures. There were also photos of their argument on Monday in Sabrina's front yard.

Avery lost his appetite. He wondered if anyone in the store had recognized him as the secret boyfriend of Sabrina.

We aren't even dating, he protested silently.

How long had this news been out? He wondered if Sabrina knew.

Or Darci.

Or the people in the office.

Was he the last to know?

Had people been talking about this behind his back?

Avery felt sick. Would it be obvious if he called in sick and skipped work today?

"Sir? Are you ready to check out?"

The clerk was looking at him. The lady who had been in front of Avery was gone.

Avery stepped forward, then realized that he still held the tabloid in his hands. He felt as guilty as a kid caught sneaking cookies out of the jar at Grandma's house.

He was too embarrassed to keep it and even more embarrassed to put it back.

After a moment of hesitation, he placed it facedown on the conveyor belt. Maybe the clerk wouldn't actually look at the cover.

He handed over his doughuts and juice and tried his best to look casual.

The clerk looked at the cover anyway to locate the price.

He shifted his gaze to Avery, then back to the paper, then back to Avery again.

From the look on the guy's face, he had just put two and two together.

The clerk gave him a wry grin and slid the paper into the sack with the other items.

Avery wished he had superpowers so he could make himself invisible.

A throng of photographers stood on the periphery of the *Daily Dose* parking lot.

"Maybe you should duck, or put papers in front of your face," Maris suggested to Sabrina.

They'd decided to ride together in Sabrina's car in order to prevent the press from learning too much about Maris right away.

Sabrina frowned. "If I do that, I'll look guilty."

"Good point." Maris kept her head held high as she drove past the photographers. They pressed in toward the car, and flashes of light erupted as they vied for the best photo.

"Ready?" Maris said before they exited the car.

"I think so," said Sabrina.

"Okay, here's the deal," Maris said, opening the door. The shouts of the press could be heard. "We walk fast but we don't run. These are new shoes, and I don't want to scuff them."

Sabrina laughed. "Maris, you are a real treasure. It's nice to know you value your new shoes above my privacy."

Maris was glad Sabrina was able to keep the mood light. "If we run, they'll think we're hiding something," she said, only half joking.

"Let's go," said Sabrina, climbing out of the car.

Inside, the security guard at the desk gave them a sympathetic look. "I told 'em they couldn't come past the entrance of the parking lot," he said.

"And we are grateful for that," Maris said.

He shook his head. "But that doesn't stop 'em from inching closer and closer. They did the same thing when Ms. Oliver and Mr. Benjamin got here."

Maris chuckled. "It's kind of funny that they feel the need to get so close. I bet that they can get a pretty decent picture of us standing here talking to you, even from three hundred feet away."

Sabrina nodded. "No kidding, thanks to the huge wall of glass."

Maris walked over to the elevator well and pushed the Up button. The door opened immediately. "Our ride is here," she told Sabrina.

On the way up, neither of them talked. The reality of having to face everyone was starting to set in.

Sabrina would be the one who had to deal with most of the fuss, but everyone would expect Maris, as her friend, to be privy to inside information.

She sighed, just imagining how many people would probably find their way into her office "just to chat."

They stepped off the elevator and onto the landing of their floor.

At first no one even noticed that they had arrived. The entire floor seemed to be in a general state of frenzy.

It sounded as if every phone on the floor was ringing nonstop, and no one appeared to be actually working. Instead, they stood around in clusters, talking and gesturing with their hands.

People from the PR department whizzed back and forth, talking on cell phones, presumably carrying out their PR duties.

Sunny came into view just then. "Oh, there you are," she said to Sabrina. "Ms. Oliver and Mr. Benjamin would like to speak with you in his office."

"I'll be there momentarily," Sabrina told Sunny.

Sunny hurried off in the direction of Avery's office.

Maris patted Sabrina on the back. Sabrina lifted her eyebrows and said, "Here goes."

"I'll pray for you," Maris said. She was trying to be helpful, but as soon as the words came out of her mouth, she regretted them.

Sabrina looked surprised.

Not as surprised as I feel, Maris thought dryly. What was she thinking, telling Sabrina that she would pray? What would she pray? And for how long? The entire meeting?

She wished she had kept her mouth shut.

A hush fell over the office as people began to realize that Sabrina had arrived. The clusters grew silent, and other people silently peered over the tops of their cubicle walls.

Maris wished she could say something encouraging before Sabrina left, but in this atmosphere you could hear a pin drop.

Sabrina didn't seem too rattled. She marched off to Avery's office, leaving Maris alone and in open view of everyone else.

Maris ignored their curious looks and went right to her office. She locked the door, not caring if it made her look guilty.

Taking a seat at her desk, she closed her eyes and started to pray. She didn't know what she would say, but there was no way she would let Sabrina down at this stage of the game.

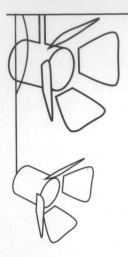

Chapter Twenty-Four

Darci finally felt in control of things again.

She sat in one of the empty chairs in Avery's office while they waited for Sabrina.

In all her years of knowing Avery, Darci had never seen him so unsettled.

When she came into his office ten minutes earlier, he'd been clutching one of the papers that featured the incriminating photos.

"Have you heard about this?" he asked, sounding tense.

Darci knew she had to spin things just so. "I did hear some things here and there," she said slowly. "But I assumed it was just worthless tabloid drivel."

She reached for the pages and tried to look concerned. "Oh, my," she said in her best surprised voice. "They really doctored these photos to look like you and Sabrina." She shook her head and handed the paper back to him. "It's a shame what people will do to make money."

Avery groaned. "Sit down," he said.

Darci sat and watched him squirm. Sooner or later, he would

have to break down and tell the truth. Avery was far too churchified to do anything else.

And if by chance he didn't admit it right away, Sabrina would break down and tell the truth.

The two of them were so painfully honest that they would never have what it took to truly get ahead in the business world.

Darci didn't consider herself to be an advocate of blatant dishonesty, and she would never tolerate such from one of her employees. However, in this competitive marketplace, a strategic little white lie every now and then could actually help a person get ahead of the pack.

Avery stared out the window. "These pictures are real, Darci."

She gasped quietly and opened her eyes wider. "What?"

He looked at her this time. "They didn't fake these. It happened last week."

"Oh." She sat back in her chair. "So . . . all of the talk . . . the things people have been saying about you and Sabrina . . . it's true?"

"Yes," he admitted, sighing. Suddenly, he sat up straighter. "No."

Darci arched her eyebrows. Was he really trying to take it all back this late in the game?

"I mean, I'm not sure. It depends on what people have been saying."

"I'm not sure I understand you." Time to make him sweat it out a little.

"We spent time together, yes. But we only went on one real date. It was all completely innocent, of course." He stumbled over his words but kept going. "I mean, you know me, Darci, and you know I wouldn't . . . we—Sabrina and I wouldn't . . ."

He trailed off. From the look in his eyes, Darci could tell he was hoping she would understand.

Oh, I know you, all right, she thought.

He was nothing less than a gentleman. Had he even kissed Sabrina on the lips yet?

She pasted on a concerned expression. "Oh, Avery, of course I never meant to imply anything . . . untoward."

He sank back in his chair, looking relieved.

Sabrina entered just then.

Darci had to hand it to the girl. She didn't seem nearly as flustered as Avery.

But then again, why wouldn't she be gloating? She stole my boyfriend.

"Good morning, Sabrina," she said cheerily. Her voice was light-years away from how she really felt about Sabrina.

"Good morning, Darci."

"Why don't you sit down?" Avery said, gesturing toward the other empty chair.

Sabrina sat, and for several moments no one said anything.

Darci cleared her throat. As interesting as this little meeting was shaping up to be, she did have work to do today.

"I assume we've all seen the pictures?" Avery said. "The head of PR has informed me that several television shows aired segments about them as well."

Sabrina nodded knowingly.

Amazing that little Miss Prim and Proper isn't at home, crying her eyes out, Darci mused.

"We've gotten numerous calls for interviews and statements this morning, so we need to decide what plan of action we will take."

No one said anything.

Darci cleared her throat. "Can I say something?"

"Go ahead," said Avery.

"This is deeply disturbing to me, as far as the show is concerned. It almost puts us back at square one. If I can't help my own employee keep her resolutions, then who will believe that I can help anyone do anything worthwhile?"

Avery frowned. "Darci, I understand your concern for the show, but I was thinking more along the lines of keeping Sabrina's and my reputations intact." With a wave of his hand, he dismissed her concerns. "I seriously doubt that finding out Sabrina went on a date will convince anyone that you're not . . . 'helpful,' as you put it."

Darci felt heat wash over her face. He was belittling her right in front of Sabrina. Of all the nerve.

Now she was no longer amused. She wouldn't let him get off the hook so easily. Or Sabrina.

Besides, that creepy Stephan Frazier from *Inside Entertainment* had already blabbed that he thought the resolutions program was a big joke.

She wouldn't let Avery drag her and the show down because he was too enamored of Sabrina to realize that *The Daily Dose* was in danger.

"I'm sorry, Avery, but I have to disagree. Perhaps your recent extracurricular activities have caused you to lose touch with what is happening with the show." She stopped and let the meaning of the words sink in.

It sank in, all right, and he didn't like it.

"Darci, I told you nothing happened," he shot back. "And I don't appreciate you implying that I don't care about the show. I created it, remember?"

"Then what are we going to do?" she shot back.

"I'm not sure." He looked off into the distance. "Maybe

Sabrina and I can get out there and do some interviews, answer some questions—put the truth out and let America decide."

Sabrina cleared her throat. "I'm not so sure I'd be willing to do a lot of press. I'd rather just release a statement."

Darci rolled her eyes. Sabrina and Avery doing interviews? Clearly, she was the only one of the three of them who was really prepared to deal with television crews.

"I completely agree with Sabrina," Darci said.

Avery looked surprised.

Now that she had his attention, she continued. "Let's be serious, Avery. You and Sabrina are not that . . . media-savvy. I, on the other hand, spend my time at work in front of a television camera. I think I should go out and handle the press for this. You and Sabrina can put out as many statements as you like, but when it comes to giving interviews, let me do the talking. In fact, maybe we should pull Sabrina from the *Morning Coffee* interview and let me do it instead."

Even as she spoke, Darci knew it was a long shot, but it didn't hurt to try.

Avery shook his head. "No, Sabrina's definitely still doing *Morning Coffee*. It'd look really odd if you went."

Darci shrugged. She hadn't really thought he'd go for it. "Well, what about all the other people who want to talk to us? I can handle those questions."

Avery didn't appear to be fully convinced. "In theory, that sounds okay, but I'm concerned what it will look like if we send you out to tell our story." He looked at Sabrina. "What do you think?"

Good grief. Does he always have to ask Sabrina what she thinks?

"I'm not necessarily happy with the idea of doing interviews to explain what happened. I'd rather release an honest statement and get on with my life.

"But if you still want me to do *Morning Coffee,* I will. But as far as Darci answering the press's questions, I'd say it's a bad idea."

Darci wanted to put a piece of duct tape over Sabrina's mouth. What in the world was she talking about?

"Would you be kind enough to tell us why you think it's a bad idea?" Darci said, trying her best to sound civil.

Sabrina looked at her evenly and said, "I was thinking about the things you said—how you were concerned about the show and people seeing you as a good host. I think that you should stay as far removed from this issue as possible. Let Avery and me take the heat, which frees you up to keep the show going without getting tossed into the fray."

"But I'm the host," Darci said.

"I like your reasoning, Sabrina," said Avery. "You're right. We should compartmentalize this as best we can. Darci is the host and she shouldn't have to answer for her coworkers."

He consulted his daily planner. "Let's see . . . today is Friday. We'll release brief statements today, say the relationship has already ended, and by Wednesday, when you go on *Morning Coffee,* a lot of the commotion will have probably blown over."

"As for you," he said, looking at Darci, "just stay focused on the show. If anyone asks you anything, tell them that your job is to host *The Daily Dose,* not to report gossip."

Avery crossed his arms and leaned back in the chair. "I guess that's it for now."

Darci was stunned. Sabrina had somehow brainwashed Avery into agreeing with everything she said.

But how?

Darci had a feeling that little Miss Sunday School wasn't as holy as she would like everyone to think. There was no way someone who was supposed to be turning the other cheek should come out on top. Consistently.

Sabrina stood, presumably to leave. Darci crossed her legs and gave Sabrina a tolerant smile. As soon as that girl left, she had something to discuss with Avery.

"Sabrina, don't go yet," he said. "I'd like to talk to you about something."

Darci lifted an eyebrow. "Do you think that's wise, given everything that's happened?"

Avery didn't look worried. "So we'll leave the door open. And, if it makes you feel any better, you can have Sunny sit right outside the door and eavesdrop. Don't think I haven't noticed that her 'errands' for you seem to coincide with other people's private conversations."

Darci inhaled sharply. "How dare you imply that I . . . I—"

"That you have spies in the office? I've known about it for ages but never said anything to you about it."

Darci bristled. Of *course* she had office spies—what smart employer didn't? But why did Avery have to throw it in her face in front of Sabrina?

That girl was working her last nerve.

"I need to talk to you, too, Avery," she said, not bothering to mask her irritation.

Avery's secretary poked her head in the door. "I'm sorry to bother you, but you told me to tell you if any more stories came on television. You might want to turn on Channel Seven."

Avery clicked on the television set.

Stephan Frazier from *Inside Entertainment* was standing in a coffee shop. Darci had been there two or three times and realized it was only five minutes away.

"I'm Stephan Frazier with a special report for *Inside Enter-*

tainment. I'm inside a coffee shop known to St. Louis locals as The Bean.

"We're only a few minutes away from *The Daily Dose* production studios, and I've learned some information from two employees about the secret relationship of Sabrina Bradley and Avery Benjamin."

Avery groaned.

Sabrina sank back down in the chair.

Darci braced herself for whatever was coming next.

The camera pulled back to reveal two girls standing next to Stephan.

"I have with me Nikki and Dana, two young ladies who work here at The Bean. They tell me that a few weeks ago, Sabrina and Avery came in together to get coffee." He held the microphone in front of one of the girls.

"Nikki, could you tell our viewers what happened that day?"

The girl nodded. "They both walked in and ordered coffee. I thought she looked familiar, but I didn't know who he was. When I realized that she was Sabrina from *The Daily Dose*, I asked for her autograph."

Stephan nodded. "And how did you find out that the man with her was Avery Benjamin?"

"We asked if he was her chauffeur, and he said that he was the guy who created *The Daily Dose.*"

"I see. Now, what happened next?"

Dana spoke up then. "Well, Sabrina was signing the autographs when I remembered that one of her resolutions was to not drink coffee, but she had just ordered a latte with a triple shot of espresso."

"Triple shot?" Stephan repeated.

"Yes, sir," said Nikki. "We offered to make her a chai latte instead, and at first it seemed like she didn't want it, but finally she said she would take it."

"So you were under the impression that she really wanted that espresso but decided against it because you confronted her about her resolution?" prodded Stephan.

Dana shook her head. "We didn't exactly confront her; we just asked her if she was sure she wanted the coffee."

"And then what happened?"

"We gave her the chai and they both left," said Nikki.

"Together?"

"I guess so."

The camera zoomed in so that only Stephan was visible. "So there you have it. Not only did Sabrina break her resolution not to fall in love, but it seems that when no one was looking, she broke various other resolutions as well. Back to you, Lilia."

Avery turned off the television. "She said she was *cutting back* on coffee, not giving it up completely," he mumbled.

Avery was right, but Darci didn't admit it aloud. In fact, she was starting to feel a tiny bit sorry for Sabrina.

That Stephan Frazier had a reputation for making mountains of molehills. A lot of people in the business laughed at him behind his back, but the viewing public lapped up his ridiculous special reports and investigative scoops, so he wasn't likely to go away soon.

Darci stood and walked to the doorway. She looked at Sabrina and decided to get in one last dig. "It looks as though you never took *any* of the resolutions seriously." Avery shot her a sharp look, but Darci didn't really care at the moment.

"I'll be in my office if anyone needs me."

Neither Avery nor Sabrina acknowledged that they heard her.

Fine, ignore me all you want, she thought. By the time the press finished running with this story, Avery would willingly come back to her. He was not a man who craved publicity, and she could tell he was quite perturbed about the whole situation.

What better way to disassociate yourself from Sabrina than by getting back together with your ex-girlfriend? she mused.

Let him talk to Sabrina all he wanted for now. In the end, Darci would be the one with the job *and* the man.

Sabrina would have neither.

Sabrina breathed a sigh of relief after Darci left the room. Her Highness had been in rare form this morning. She turned to Avery, who slouched in his chair, one hand to his forehead.

Sabrina wished she could do something to help him.

"Resolutions," he grumbled. "It sounded like such a good idea in the beginning."

"Do you want me to quit the resolutions program?"

He looked up. "What? You? Quit? I wouldn't ask you to quit. You love the torture of keeping them."

Sabrina hoped he was being sarcastic. She continued, trying to be helpful: "If people really think I was sneaking around drinking coffee whenever no one was looking, they're never going to believe that you and I only went on one date."

"I know."

"So what do we do?"

Tell the truth. "Someone somewhere is exaggerating things, and the longer we wait to say our piece, the more believable they look."

Sabrina had her doubts. She knew the way the media machine worked. "Do you really believe that?"

"I have to. The Bible says so," he said.

"Then, 'You will know the truth, and the truth will make you free,'" she said, quoting the verse he'd referred to.

"Precisely." He reached for the phone on his desk. Picking it up, he asked his secretary to bring him a bottle of aspirin.

"Now," he said, sitting up straight, "what does this mean for us? Are you still upset with me?"

Sabrina shook her head. "I'm not angry. But I'm still not ready to date you. Especially if we have to sneak around to do so. If you want me to stay in the resolutions program, I will, but there's no way I would consider dating you until it's over."

"Or you could just simply get rid of that resolution. I've told you all along that it would probably be impossible to keep, and I think the public agrees." He threw his hands in the air. "Otherwise, why would they be so eager to prove that you have a boyfriend?"

Sabrina wished she could. But there was no telling what Darci would do if she tried to get out of the deal this late in the game.

"I can't."

Avery huffed in frustration. "Sabrina, why are you so intent on keeping this resolution?" He put up a hand before she could say anything. "And don't tell me it's because you don't want to fall in love."

Sabrina looked away from him. Why did he have to keep prying into her reasons for making and keeping the resolution?

"Sabrina, look at me."

She looked.

"You can break this resolution. Go on *Morning Coffee* and say you made a mistake. Tell them you changed your mind. No one will call you a failure. They'll probably call you a hero."

Sabrina wanted nothing more than to tell him about Darci and the ten thousand dollars and the promotion.

But he'd already claimed that she accused Darci of more than the woman actually did. He wouldn't understand.

He shook his head. "You would think someone is paying you not to fall in love."

He was so close to the truth that Sabrina had to bite her lip to keep from telling him.

"Won't you admit that you like me—even a little?"

"I do." She was on the verge of telling him the whole story when his secretary came with the aspirin. Sabrina took the interruption as an excuse to escape.

"I've got work to do, so I need to go. Besides, Darci's right. The longer I stay in here, the more we'll feed the rumors. Since we're truly nothing but friends, we musn't do anything to raise people's suspicions."

Avery nodded, but he didn't look happy. "Fine. If that's what you want, I won't argue."

Sabrina left his office, her heart heavy.

She trusted the Lord to work everything out, but at the moment she had a hard time believing it.

After work, Sabrina and Maris drove by Sabrina's house to see if the coast was clear.

It wasn't.

Stephan Frazier and his team, along with several other reporters, were still camped out in front of Sabrina's house. And legally, there was nothing to be done about it.

They weren't technically on her property, but lined the streets and sidewalks.

"I'm not letting you stay here," Maris said, peering out the windows.

Sabrina shook her head. "I can't infringe on your and Sid's hospitality any longer. Besides, I need to get my own clothes and things."

Sabrina felt like a nomad, with no place to sit down and rest or even think clearly. How long would it be before she could go to her house without people sitting in front, watching her every move?

Maris continued driving and pulled to a stop on a street a few blocks over. "I have an idea," she said.

"I'm all ears."

"Do you have your house key?"

"Yeah."

"Call your friend Jasmine and ask her if she'll go in, get what you need, and meet us somewhere."

The idea actually sounded good.

"But I hate the idea of dragging someone else into this. They'll follow her and ask her a million questions, and I don't think she could take it."

Another, more sobering thought occurred to Sabrina. "Besides, I have no idea if she would believe me or the tabloids. She may not want to be associated with me."

"We could ask Eric to get what you need," Maris suggested.

Sabrina found that idea laughable. "There is no way I'm going to let Eric into my house unattended and ask him to go through my stuff. For all I know, he was the one who put the reporters on my trail in the first place."

"Yeah, you're right."

Sabrina weighed her options for a few moments. "Listen, we've got my car. Why don't we just go back to my house, pull into the garage, get what we need, and leave again?"

"And how do we keep them from following us back to my house?"

"Take detours? Go out of our way and hope they get lost? Drive fast?"

Maris's eyes lit up. "I like the 'driving fast' part. As someone who has more than a few speeding tickets, I think I can handle this task with a certain amount of ease." She wiggled her eyebrows. "Are you ready?"

"I'm ready."

"Then here we go."

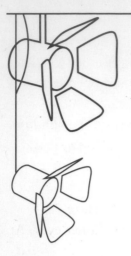

Chapter Twenty-Five

Maris couldn't remember the last time she'd watched television for longer than an hour at a time. Regardless, she didn't think she'd ever stared at the tube for seven hours straight.

Until today.

"I feel like a hermit," Sabrina said from her spot on the other sofa.

"Me, too," said Maris. It was late Saturday afternoon, and they were camped out in Maris's living room, eating ice cream and watching old movies. "I feel like a chubby hermit who's had way too much ice cream," Maris added.

"Me, too. I need to go to the gym."

"Why don't you call Nadia and see if she'll make a house call?" Maris suggested.

"Why don't I just throw the press a giant bone? Who knows what kind of spin they would put on that?" She spooned another scoop of ice cream out of the container. "Let's channel-surf."

Maris picked up the remote and clicked through channel after channel. "You know, we're almost out of ice cream. Maybe I should send Sid to get more."

"Maybe you should go," said Sabrina. She giggled, then said, "You speedster, you."

Maris threw a pillow at her. "Oh, shut up."

Sid walked into the room. "Maybe we should open the windows. The whole house feels like a dungeon."

Maris arched an eyebrow at Sid. "I *ought* to open the windows just so they can get a picture of you in that ugly sweatsuit. I thought I threw that out months ago."

"You did, and I rescued it."

"Oh, look," said Maris. "Stephan Frazier is getting ready to give another special report. Oh, goody." She rolled her eyes. At this very moment, Stephan Frazier was one of her least favorite people in the entire world.

Thanks to him, she was missing out on a major shoe sale at her favorite boutique.

Sid paced to the front door and peered through the peephole. "I feel like going out there myself and giving that Stephan Frazier a little special report of my own."

"Sid," she said in a warning tone. "Don't make things worse than they already are."

Inside Entertainment's special-report music boomed through the television speakers.

"I'm Stephan Frazier, live in St. Louis, reporting on the Sabrina Bradley story."

Maris made room for Sid on the couch and turned up the volume.

"Behind me is the home of Maris Russell, associate producer of *The Daily Dose*."

Sid huffed. "What about me? He didn't say anything about Sid Russell." Sid looked at the television set. "I live here, too, you know. Investigate that!"

Maris nudged him. "Be quiet, honey. I'm trying to hear this."

". . . Through a string of unusual incidents, I and my investigative team have learned that this is where Sabrina is staying, at least for the time being."

"Ho, ho," said Sid. "Did you hear that? A string of unusual incidents." He shook his head. "This guy is a real piece of work. He probably thinks he could work for the CIA or something."

"Can you tell us exactly what happened?" Lilia's voice came through loud and clear.

"Actually, I can show you what happened," said Stephan. "Let's roll that footage . . . As you can see here, late yesterday evening, Sabrina returned to her home with her friend Maris Russell. They pulled into the garage, and we weren't sure for a time if they were planning to stay or leave."

"Stay or leave," said Sid. "Wow. All of two choices. Time to start an investigation."

". . . As you can see, we soon realized they had apparently come to get some things from the house. Now, watch carefully and you'll see them leaving the house."

"Watch carefully, boys and girls," Sid mimicked. "Because it's so difficult to see an *entire* garage door move."

Maris half wanted Sid to shut up and be quiet, but the other half of her was happy for his unique brand of humor. It helped to make the situation more bearable. Besides, when he got going like this, no one could tell him to be quiet—not even his mother.

". . . We, of course, took one of our vehicles, along with a cameraman to follow them. At first, we had difficulty keeping up with them, as Ms. Russell seemed to be driving quite fast. But watch . . . About six minutes into the pursuit, a police officer pulled Ms. Russell over for speeding."

"That's *Mrs.* Russell to you, buddy," Sid interjected. "Because she's married. To Sid—the other person who lives in this house you're standing in front of."

". . . We waited patiently while the officer issued the ticket, and then resumed following them. A few minutes later, Ms.

Russell decided that she would attempt to lose us once again, so she picked up her pace.

". . . Watch the tape and you'll see that she was pulled over a second time."

"I can't believe they actually filmed me getting a ticket," Maris said. "And look at the close-up. You can practically see the blackheads on my nose."

Sabrina shook her head. "They made us look like criminals. The film quality is horrible—like a home video. It looks like it could be one of those car chase TV specials."

"And they don't even know I exist," Sid added. "Since this is live, I'm thinking I should open the front door and tell him that Sid Russell lives here, too."

Stephan's face filled the screen once more. "After the second citation, Ms. Russell decided to abide by the law and drove the speed limit. She and Ms. Bradley stopped at several places, probably hoping that we would lose interest, but we kept right on, determined to bring you this story."

"Wow," said Lilia. "That's some dramatic footage you've captured. Exactly how long did it take before you finally reached Ms. Russell's home?"

"Around four and a half hours," said Stephan. "They were determined, but so were we."

Maris wanted to open a window and throw the remote at Stephan. "Sid, would you go out there and punch that man?"

Sid put an arm around her. "Honey, calm down. It's okay. He'll go away eventually."

Maris couldn't hold back the tears any longer. She buried her face in Sid's chest. "Does that mean you won't do anything to him? I can't stand him anymore!"

Sid was quiet for several moments. Then he said, "If we move to New Orleans tomorrow, he might not be able to find us."

Maris sat up and stared at her husband. Sid was incorrigible. Since he and his brother hadn't been able to locate a building in New Orleans that had the square footage and the price tag they were looking for, they had now started searching St. Louis real estate for a property that could work.

In all likelihood, they probably wouldn't be moving to New Orleans—much to the chagrin of Sid's mother. But he still liked to tease Maris about it now and then.

"You okay?" Sid asked.

Maris nodded, wiping away her tears. She felt embarrassed now. She didn't usually break down so easily—it must have been the stress of the past two days catching up with her.

"This is all my fault," said Sabrina. "I'm sorry. I really didn't want to drag anyone else into this."

Sid dismissed her concerns with a wave of his hand. "Don't worry about it. This will blow over soon enough. It'll be so quiet around here that you two will get bored. I'll have to send old Stephan a bogus tip to get him over here again."

Maris and Sabrina laughed.

Maris hugged Sid, thankful he was here for support.

Sabrina's prayers for their marriage must really be working. Things weren't perfect, but at least he wasn't still determined to move to Louisiana, with or without her.

As for Sid's mom, well, that was another story. She'd called several times since Sid had returned, and the brief conversations she and Maris had were anything but pleasant.

Just thinking about some of the cutting remarks that woman made was enough to upset Maris.

But even in the midst of all this turmoil, Sabrina kept insisting that Maris not hold a grudge against her.

It was difficult, and sometimes Maris had to bite her lip to keep from saying something bad about Dolores, but she was determined to stay the course and keep praying until something good happened.

"Did you hear that?" Sid asked, pulling Maris from her thoughts.

"It sounds like a phone."

Sabrina sat still and listened. "I think that's my cell phone ringing." She jumped up and headed toward the guest room.

Just then Maris's home phone rang.

"Do you suppose Mr. Stephan has located our home number?" she asked.

"It was only a matter of time," said Sid. "Do you want me to answer it?"

"No, I'll get it. I've been wanting to talk to him anyway."

"Maris," Sid warned.

"I'll be nice," she promised.

She picked up the cordless extension. "Russell residence."

"Maris? I just saw the front of your house on national television. What in the world have you gotten yourself into? I warned you about gallivanting around with all those TV people."

It was Dolores. Maris sighed quietly and somehow refrained from rolling her eyes.

"It's your mother," she mouthed to Sidney, who was giving her a questioning look. He nodded knowingly and reached for the phone.

Maris shook her head, indicating that she would give it to him as soon as Dolores gave her a chance to say good-bye. If she just handed over the phone to him now, Dolores would complain that Maris had been rude and uncaring.

She did, however hold the phone away from her ear so Sidney could hear what she was saying.

". . . you need to put that floozy out of your house before she soils my Sidney's reputation . . ."

Maris put a hand over her mouth to keep from laughing aloud, remembering her conversation with Sabrina when the story first broke.

She was grateful that Sabrina wasn't in the room. Her worst fears had come to fruition. Someone had called her a floozy.

As soon as Dolores paused to take a breath, Maris spoke up. "Here, let me get Sidney for you."

"No, I don't want to talk to Sidney. I called to speak to you."

Maris's stomach went jittery. First Stephan and now Dolores. What next?

"Oh, you want to talk to me?" she repeated so Sid would know what was going on.

"Yes. Is there something the matter with that?"

"No, no. Not at all."

Sid patted her knee.

Maris lifted her eyebrows and shrugged.

Sid got up and left the room.

Maris got comfy on the couch. Dolores was probably in one of her lecturing moods, so this could take a while.

"Thanks for calling, Jasmine," Sabrina said. "Maris and I have been in the house all day, so it's good to hear from the outside world."

"I just wanted you to know that I hadn't deserted you because of all the negative press."

"Thanks, I really appreciate that. I wish I could tell you exactly what's going on, but I'd prefer to wait and tell everyone at once when I go on *Morning Coffee.*"

"Oh, I understand," Jasmine said. "I still can't wait to see the interview."

Sabrina wasn't excited at all about the interview, but she

didn't want to put a damper on Jasmine's enthusiasm, so she said nothing.

"Is there anything I can do for you?" Jasmine wanted to know. "Run errands or bring something to you at Maris's?"

"Oh, no, we're fine, but thanks for asking. Besides, if you came here, you'd just get thronged by reporters." Sabrina smiled at the thought of Jasmine being chased up and down Maris's driveway by Stephan Frazier and his team.

"Oh, I guess you're right about that," said Jasmine. "Will you be at church tomorrow?"

"I'm not sure. I suppose the media could hope to follow me to worse places than church, but I'm not sure they'd have the decency to not come in and disturb the congregation."

"Oh, that's sad," said Jasmine. "To think that those pesky people are keeping you from going to church. I'll pray about it."

"Thanks. That would be great," Sabrina said.

"Well, I didn't want to take up too much of your time. I know you're busy preparing for the interview, so I'll let you go. Hopefully, I'll see you at church in the morning."

"Hopefully. Bye," Sabrina said, then ended the call.

She had just put the phone back in her purse when it rang again. This time the caller ID indicated that Eric was trying to reach her.

Since they'd met to talk a few weeks ago, Eric had started calling Sabrina once or twice a week just to say hi. At first she'd been wary, but eventually she decided that he meant no harm. He was still the same old Eric: fun-loving, creative, and more than a little immature. If he ever grew up, he'd make some woman a good husband eventually.

For now he made subtle attempts at trying to rekindle a romance with Sabrina, but she'd made it clear that she was not interested.

The funny thing was, seven months ago, before the fateful day when she wrote the resolutions, she would have jumped at the chance to get back together with him.

Now it seemed that her resolution not to fall in love had wiped away any remaining feeling she had for Eric. Of course, her feelings for Avery had multiplied, but she tried not to think about it.

"Eric, what's up?" she said.

"I'm calling to see how you're holding up. I just saw on *Inside Entertainment* that you're holed up at Maris's house. You guys need anything?"

"We're fine, but thanks for asking."

"I could come over and keep you company," he suggested.

Sabrina laughed. "I think you just want to come over to get on TV. I wouldn't put it past you to show your book to Stephan Frazier, hoping he can help boost you to the big time. In fact, I'm not entirely sure you didn't start this mess. You and your tabloid interview."

"No, Sabrina, I wouldn't do that." His tone was far more serious than usual. "And I'm really sorry about selling that first story to the tabloids. I promise I didn't say anything to anyone about Avery—I mean, I didn't even know you were dating him."

Sabrina wondered where he was going with this.

"But that's beside the point," he said. "I only realized how special you were after we broke up."

"What's your point, Eric?"

"It looks like I'm the one who drove you to the resolution, and I feel badly. Apparently, you really like him, but you can't do anything about it because you wrote that resolution. If there was a way I could help you get out of it, I would . . ."

Sabrina was genuinely touched. How unusual for Eric to

think of someone besides himself, for a change. Although it was quite presumptuous of him to assume that he was the sole reason behind her resolution not to fall in love.

She smiled. "Wow. Thank you."

But she didn't want to discuss this situation with anyone until after the *Morning Coffee* interview was over.

Knowing that Eric would take the bait, she changed the subject.

"Tell me how the book's coming along," she suggested.

"The book is actually done. I'm writing a new one. But the really exciting news is that I found an agent."

"Congratulations," she said, and she meant it.

Eric had been searching for a literary agent since she'd first met him.

"I guess I should actually thank you," he admitted. "The agent saw my story in the magazine and called me. If you hadn't made the resolution, I wouldn't have done that interview and the agent wouldn't even know who I am."

Sabrina hardly felt flattered that he'd done the interview in the first place, but she chose to be gracious. "No need to thank me. I'm sure you would have found an agent without my story."

"Do you think so? That's good, because . . ." Eric launched into another of his long stories. Not too much had changed about him.

She got up and peeked out the window. The reporters were still there.

Sitting back on the bed, she stifled a yawn.

"You're tired?" Eric asked.

"I am," Sabrina answered truthfully. She and Maris had stayed up late talking the night before. Now the lack of sleep was beginning to catch up with her.

"I'll let you go so you can get some sleep," he said.

Sabrina didn't protest. In fact, she was grateful. "All right, thanks for calling. I'll talk to you later . . . Bye."

She hung up the phone and lay down. Too tired to think about *Morning Coffee*, Avery, Stephan, or even Darci, she closed her eyes. Within minutes, Sabrina fell asleep.

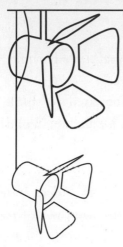

Chapter Twenty-Six

Someone knocked at the door. Sabrina was too exhausted to move, let alone open it.

"Sabrina?" Maris's voice called out from the other side of the door.

Sabrina struggled to open her eyes. "Yeah?" she answered.

"Can I come in?"

"Sure." She managed to sit up as Maris swung the door open.

Maris's eyes were full of excitement as she walked in. "You'll never guess what happened," she said, sinking into the over-stuffed chair in the corner of the room.

Sabrina rubbed her eyes. "What?"

Maris looked at her carefully. "You were sleeping. I didn't mean to wake you up."

Sabrina shrugged. "I just needed a short nap. I'm fine now." A glance at the bedside clock revealed that she'd only been asleep for twenty minutes or so.

"Sid's mom called me," said Maris.

Sabrina braced herself for bad news. Maris and Sid's mom were like oil and vinegar without a whisk. Sabrina had been praying for both of them, but Maris still was no fan of the woman.

"What happened?" Sabrina asked, feeling wary.

"We actually talked." Maris's eyes were wide, and she had a huge grin on her face.

"You talked? About what?"

"Everything. At first I was upset because she called and started giving me a lecture about this whole situation with the reporters outside. But I remembered how you kept telling me to forgive her, so I started praying while she talked.

"A few minutes into the conversation, I felt like I needed to apologize for something I'd said to her a long time ago—back when Sid and I first got married."

"So did you do it?"

"I didn't want to, but the harder I tried not to think about it, the more it stood out in my memory. So I took a chance and told her I was sorry about it."

"What did she say?"

"I think she was surprised, but she accepted my apology." Maris leaned forward in her chair. "*Then,* get this. She apologized to me for a bunch of stuff *she* did. The next thing I knew, we were swapping apologies back and forth." She stood up and paced the length of the room. "Sabrina, I don't know if you understand how unbelievable this is. I think I'm in shock."

Sabrina grinned. "I understand how unbelievable it may seem, but I also understand the power of prayer."

Maris turned and stared at her, wide-eyed. "Prayer. You're right. It does work." She shook her head, an awestruck expression on her face. "It really worked."

"Thank God it works," Sabrina said. "Otherwise, I'd be a nervous wreck right now."

Maris stopped pacing and sat on the edge of the bed. "Do you really think God will work this out for you?"

"I know He will. There's a verse in the Bible that says, 'In all things God works for the good of those who love Him, who have been called according to His purpose.'"

Maris shrugged. "So what does that mean?"

"It means that everything that happens to a Christian will work out for good, according to God's will."

"So you think God made all of this happen to you?"

Sabrina had seen that one coming. "Everything that happens, God either allows it or prevents it. But sometimes these circumstances will help draw a person closer to God—if they put their full trust in Him."

"Define 'Christian' for me," said Maris.

Sabrina blinked at the question. That one she hadn't seen coming. "Well . . ." she began slowly, haltingly, looking for just the right words. "I'm not sure what exactly you mean. Can you clarify a bit for me?"

Maris sighed. "Your friend Jasmine almost fainted when I told her I never prayed that salvation prayer the preacher leads every week. But I do believe in God and I do believe in prayer. So does that qualify me for the eternal life in heaven part?"

Sabrina relaxed a little, finally understanding what Maris was getting at. "Let me ask you a question. How long have you and Sid been married?"

"Twelve years," Maris answered promptly.

"Tell me about your wedding," Sabrina said.

"Tell you about the wedding?" Maris looked confused. "I thought I was the one asking the questions here."

Sabrina grinned. "Humor me. I'm going somewhere with this."

Maris sighed. "It was a big wedding. Four hundred people.

We got married in the gorgeous cathedral downtown. You've seen the pictures."

"Why'd you invite all the people?"

"For one thing, Sid's mother and my parents insisted on having every person they knew there, but Sid and I invited all of our friends because . . ." She trailed off. "Well, because they'd been there for us when we were dating . . . They knew how much we loved each other, and we wanted them to be there when we tied the knot. For sentimental reasons, I guess."

"But you could have gotten your marriage license, walked into the preacher's office, and said your vows on a Monday morning with just the church secretary as a witness."

Maris gave her a look. "Our parents would have had a conniption."

"But, legally, you'd be married."

"True."

"You and Sid love each other, right?"

Maris looked up at the ceiling and sighed. "Yes, Sabrina. Is 'twenty questions' almost over?"

"I'm getting there."

"Okay. Yes, we love each other."

"Then why'd you even get married at all? Why not just say, 'We love each other and that's good enough for us'? Why go to church and say vows?"

Maris looked at Sabrina as if she had lost her mind. "Look, Ms. Holy, I *know* you're not advocating living together without being married."

"Then answer my question."

Maris blew out a sigh. "Because . . . that made it all . . . real. We have legal rights to each other's property, insurance benefits, and things like that."

"Benefits you can't have in a common-law marriage," Sabrina said.

"Exactly."

Sabrina took a deep breath. "Okay. You want me to define a Christian?"

Maris nodded. "That's what I've been waiting for."

"A Christian is someone who hears what the Bible says about God and believes it.

"A Christian believes that a life without God will lead to eternity in hell, and they choose to spend eternity in heaven.

"A Christian commits to trying to obey the rules God lays down for us in the Bible, and will devote the rest of their life to learning how to depend on God for everything."

Maris looked Sabrina in the eye. "I think I fit that description, so I don't see why Jasmine got so upset with me. You never said a Christian has to go to the front of the church and pray that prayer."

"I haven't got to that part yet," Sabrina said. "Remember the legal rights of marriage?"

"Yes."

"Why did you and Sid have to go to the front of the church and say your vows out loud, in front of everyone? Couldn't it have been just as legal if Sid had stood in front and you sat in one of the pews and quietly said the vows?"

"Sabrina, that would be ridiculous. Nobody would even believe you were married."

"Bingo."

"Bingo, what? We're talking Sid and God here. Big difference, Sabrina," said Maris.

"Being a Christian requires such commitment that it's sometimes compared to marriage in the Bible. There are special rights and privileges that God promises to those who commit to serve and obey Him.

"Getting up in front of the church and pledging your life to God makes it like going up to say 'I do' to Sid. It shows you're just as serious as you were the day you married Sid."

Maris nodded. "You make some good points."

Sabrina chuckled. "I didn't make this up. It's all in the Bible—I'm just kind of paraphrasing."

Maris looked at her watch. "I think I'll start dinner."

Sabrina got off the bed. "I'll help."

Maris and Sabrina were getting ready to leave for church the next morning when Sid joined them in the kitchen.

"You're a little overdressed for breakfast," she said, taking in his business-casual attire. "We're on our way out the door, but I've got pancakes on a plate in the microwave."

Sid nodded but didn't sit down at the table.

Maris arched an eyebrow at him. "I hope you're not planning to go out there and do anything embarrassing while we're at church."

He winked. "You'll get the whole story when Stephan does his special report tonight."

Maris felt her pulse speed up. "Your mother will think I put you up to it. Please don't go out there and make things worse."

Sid tossed his head back and laughed. "Scared you, didn't I?" He pulled her close to him and kissed her. "I'm sick of being housebound, so I thought I'd come to church with you and Sabrina."

Maris nearly dropped her orange juice. Sid wanted to go to church? "You want to come with us?"

"Why not?" he said. "I don't want to be stuck inside all day if you and Sabrina get to go out."

Maris chuckled and hoped she didn't look as rattled as she felt. Of course she didn't mind Sid coming to church, but part of her wished he didn't have to be there the day she planned to go up front and make the big commitment.

Sid had tolerantly listened to her confession of praying about his mother. He was happy that the two of them had patched things up, but Maris knew that alone wouldn't be enough to convince him to really believe in God—the way she did now.

When they pulled out of the garage, Stephan came running toward the car with a microphone. Sid rolled down the window.

"Sid, what are you doing?" Maris said through clenched teeth.

Sid winked. "Having a little Sunday morning fun." He turned to Stephan. "Well, hello, hello, Mr. Frazier. Isn't this lovely weather we're having? It appears that spring has sprung."

Stephan Frazier seemed to be speechless for the moment.

Maris hoped his trusty cameraman was getting *that* on tape.

Sid thrust his hand out the window and waited for Stephan to shake it.

Stephan shook the proffered hand and seemed to recover his wits. "And who might you be, sir?"

"Why, I'm Sid Russell—Mr. Maris, if you will."

"Mr. Russell," Stephan repeated.

"Yes. I'm surprised you haven't already figured that out— using your investigative skills and all."

Stephan flushed a deep shade of red.

Sid chuckled. "Well, we will see you all later. We must be on our way."

Stephan's reporter voice returned. "And where might you be going?" he asked, peering into the back window, where Sabrina sat. "Ms. Bradley, we received your and Mr. Benjamin's statements yesterday," he called, trying to get her attention.

"Let's go, Sid," Maris said.

Sid backed out of the driveway.

Stephan followed, calling for Sabrina. "Do you have anything you'd like to add to that statement, Ms. Bradley?"

Once they were on the street, driving toward church, Sid chuckled. "At least I get to be on the dramatic footage for the day."

Maris shook her head.

During the remainder of the ride to church, Sabrina and Sid chatted and joked, but Maris was quiet. She truly wished Sid were still at home. She had been all set to go forward in church and pray that prayer, but she couldn't do it with Sid sitting right next to her. He would look at her as if she were crazy. He might even laugh.

When they got to church, Jasmine was waiting in the foyer for Sabrina, along with an older lady named Erma.

Sabrina introduced Sid to both women, and Maris felt relief when Sid didn't crack any jokes.

All through the service, Maris could hardly focus on what the preacher was saying. As the end of the service drew near, she debated whether she should still go forward. She wanted to make the commitment that Sabrina had talked about, but she didn't want to upset Sid.

He had never been enthusiastic about religion; in fact, he tended to laugh at people who walked around quoting Bible verses. He said he liked Sabrina because, even though she sermonized from time to time, she didn't pretend to be perfect. That was the kind of Christian Maris wanted to be—one who could acknowledge her shortcomings.

Maris could hardly believe her thoughts.

She wanted to be a Christian.

A year ago she wouldn't have believed it.

". . . Don't wait." The pastor's voice interrupted her thoughts. "Some of you are sitting in your seats, wondering what the person next to you will think if you come up here right now." He shook his head. "Don't worry about what they think. You feel God calling you to come and take that step—just do it."

That was all Maris needed to hear.

I'm going.

She put her purse down on the floor and suddenly realized that Sid was standing up.

What is he doing? Maris worried that he might be getting ready to say something completely inappropriate.

She looked up at him, and he shrugged.

"I'm going up there," he whispered. He wore a serious expression—the one he normally reserved for weddings and preparing income tax returns.

He felt it, too.

"I'm coming with you," she whispered. She didn't even know what had been said that convinced him to go, but she was glad he'd heard it.

He took her hand, and they went together.

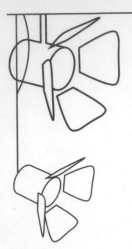

Chapter Twenty-Seven

Sabrina went home Sunday night. Since Stephan and his crew had located Maris's house, it didn't make much sense for her to stay there any longer.

Either way, they would sit outside the front door and watch her every move.

She was on an emotional high after witnessing both Maris and Sid go forward and accept Jesus.

She'd been praying for them since Maris befriended her on her first day at *The Daily Dose*, and it was exciting to be there when her prayers were answered.

Now she prayed and waited for a positive outcome to the situation at work.

Avery had come to church yesterday morning, but Darci was conspicuously absent. Sabrina made eye contact with him from a good distance away, but they didn't speak to each other.

Sunday evening, Sabrina felt the pangs of cabin fever again, only this time she didn't have Maris and Sid with her to help lessen the strain.

She picked up the phone, wanting to call Avery but unsure of what to say.

I know I said I didn't want to date you, but I lied.

No way. He was already frustrated with her decision to stick with the resolution.

It was easy for him to be angry because he didn't know the whole story. Sabrina was tired of carrying around this secret. She wanted the promotion; she wanted the bonus; but she wanted Avery, too.

Right now she really missed him.

Is this really worth it? she wondered.

Sabrina remembered her conversation with the woman in the grocery store. She'd told Sabrina to forget the resolution if true love came her way.

Did she love Avery?

Sabrina thought about it. The idea was both exciting and scary. She certainly cared for him a lot more than she had ever cared for Eric—and she'd thought she loved Eric.

Sabrina decided she didn't want to think about love. Not right now. It was only the beginning of April. That meant eight more months of keeping her resolution.

There was no need to call Avery. It would only make things more painful for both of them.

She put the phone back in its cradle and went to bed.

Monday morning, Darci waited for Avery to arrive at work. When he passed by her office door, she called to him.

He entered the room, a wary look on his face. Poor man.

Look what Sabrina had done to him. The usual spring in his step was gone. His shoulders were stooped, and there were bags underneath his eyes.

"You look tired," she said.

"I love it when people state the obvious."

Darci decided not to beat around the bush. She had a mission, and she would complete it.

"We need to talk."

He sighed and shook his head.

"No, please, before you say anything, hear me out."

He stood unmoving for several moments. Darci held her breath.

Just sit down.

He sat.

Showtime.

Darci stood, crossed to the other side of the room, and closed the door. But she left the blinds open.

Avery slouched in the chair, waiting. Darci stood behind him and placed her hands on his shoulders.

He tensed up.

She laughed.

"Relax, Avery."

He didn't relax.

"I have work to do, Darci. What did you want to talk about?"

"About us."

"There is no 'us.'"

She ignored his tenseness and began kneading his shoulders.

He shook his head. "You don't have to do that," he said, pushing her hand away.

"I want to," she said, and continued the massage. "Besides, you need this. I can feel knots all around your shoulder blades. What have you been doing to yourself?"

He seemed tense at first, but relaxed into the chair after several moments.

"See? I don't bite," she said.

Avery closed his eyes. Now she had a captive audience.

"I'm curious as to why there can't be an 'us.' Is it because you and Sabrina are an 'us'?"

Avery's eyes popped open. He shifted in the chair, but Darci kneaded even harder.

"No, Darci. I'm not dating Sabrina. You know what happened."

"If you guys like each other so much, then why not have her stop the resolutions program? Seems to me that you'd both be a lot happier."

"That won't happen. She'll never quit the program. She's gotten obsessive about sticking to it. Every time I talk to her, she's always warning me that she won't let me distract her from her goal."

"Hmm," Darci said. So Sabrina was trying to keep her part of the bargain.

"In fact, I'm not sure she even liked me in the first place," Avery said. "I did most of the asking and pursuing. Maybe she only went on that date because I wore her down."

"Sabrina's a very ambitious young woman," Darci said, keeping her voice smooth and mellow.

"Yeah, she is. So are you."

"I am," she agreed.

She didn't say anything, but let what she didn't say wash over him.

He took the bait. "What are you saying?"

"Nothing in particular."

"You're thinking something."

"I'm always thinking something," she said lightly. She didn't want to sound rehearsed.

Avery opened his eyes and looked up at her. "Tell me what you're thinking."

Darci stole a glance out her windows and across the hallway. The office door remained closed, blinds shut tight.

What a day for Sabrina to be late. If the plan was going to work, Sabrina would have to show up soon.

Avery might be enjoying this massage right now, but Darci couldn't hold him here all day.

"Okay, I'll tell you what I'm thinking. But don't read anything into this. I'm not saying this to get you back—it's just my observation of another member of my own sex."

"A woman-to-woman observation," Avery said.

"Right." She took a deep breath. "Sabrina's progressed rapidly these past few months, and maybe it's been too much too fast."

"But she's been here for three years. Don't you think that's enough time for her to adjust to the responsibility?"

Darci paused. "Maybe. But consider the fact that until January of this year, she was pretty much a glorified secretary for Maris. Now she's learning how to do Maris's job, in addition to being on TV once a week for the resolutions program."

"She's got a good head on her shoulders, though," Avery protested.

"Of course she does. We wouldn't have hired her otherwise. But then you decided that you liked her, and that may have compounded things for her."

"How so? She's a grown woman and she knows how to make her own decisions," he said.

"Yes, she is and she does. But you're the boss. In fact, you're the big boss. Imagine what she could be thinking. Just as she starts getting more job responsibilities, you come along, saying that you like her."

Darci saw movement in her peripheral vision. Annette and Sabrina arrived at the same time.

Perfect.

Sabrina's desk faced Darci's office, so she would get a bird's-eye view of what was going on.

Provided Annette did what she was supposed to do and got those blinds open. That was pretty much all she ever asked of Annette—keep the blinds open during working hours. If that girl messed this up, Darci would get rid of her this very week.

Some of Darci's helpers—spies, as Avery had called them—had a more innate sense of how to move around the office and gather information and carry out various other duties.

Others, like Annette, had potential but needed more help and guidance. But Darci wasn't in the mood to give any extensive training right now. At this crucial stage, she needed someone who could get the job done.

Seconds later, the blinds were open. Darci let out a sigh of relief.

Good girl.

Darci had intentionally let the conversation drop in order to give Avery some time to think.

"Do you think I scared her?"

Darci shrugged. "I don't know. It's a toss-up."

"Between what?"

"Either she got nervous and figured you would demote her if she didn't date you . . ."

"Or . . ."

Darci paused, taking a moment to work on a particularly savage knot on his left shoulder. "Or she's more ambitious than we both judged, and she manipulated you into liking her, in the hope that it would lead to bigger and better things job-wise."

Avery stilled and didn't say anything.

Darci sneaked a sideways glance to see what was going on across the hall. Sabrina was watching. Time to make her move.

Darci continued to rub his shoulders, then said, "I could be totally wrong, so don't get too wrapped up in thinking about it." She bent over and lightly kissed the top of his head.

She knew he would take off after that, so she moved first and sat back down at her desk.

He stood up, thanked her for the massage and the advice. "I'll give that some thought," he said.

In a moment he was gone, headed to his own office.

Darci pretended to stare at her computer screen but was really watching the office across the hall.

Less than a minute later, Sabrina took off down the hallway.

Darci had a feeling she knew where Sabrina was headed.

She stood up. It was time to visit the ladies' room. She was growing tired of trying to keep two steps ahead of that girl.

She opened her door and stepped into Sunny's workspace. Where was that woman? She needed to send her on an errand, but there was no telling where she might be.

"Honestly, she spends more time roaming around this building than anyone else," Darci mumbled as she strode down the hall.

Sabrina barely made it to the ladies' room before the sobs erupted. Thankfully, the room was quiet, sparing her the embarrassment of being caught crying by one of her coworkers.

Moments later, she managed to calm down a bit. She grabbed some paper towels and doused them with cool water, then dabbed at her eyes.

Staring at her reflection in the mirror, Sabrina felt as pitiful as she looked.

She felt angry and betrayed. Couldn't Avery make up his

mind? Last Friday he was telling her how much he liked her. Monday morning he was in Darci's office getting a shoulder massage and a kiss.

But why was she upset about it? Maybe she had lied to herself.

I guess I do love him, she realized.

Darci pushed open the door.

Just as she suspected, Sabrina was wiping away the telltale signs of a sob session.

"Are you all right?" Darci asked.

Sabrina locked gazes with her. Darci was impressed. There was some new spark in those brown eyes of hers. Sabrina was a hard one to figure out. One minute she seemed weak and sniveling; the next, she was surprisingly bold and stoic.

"I'm fine," Sabrina said.

Darci smirked. "How are those resolutions coming along?"

"I'm keeping them."

"Good for you," Darci said. "I'm glad to hear it. You'll really feel a sense of accomplishment if you manage to keep them all year long."

"Yeah, I'm sure I will. Besides, I don't have a choice, do I?" Sabrina asked.

Time to burst her little bubble.

Darci leaned against the countertop. "Actually, you can do whatever you want to do. It really doesn't matter to me anymore."

Sabrina took a step back. "What?"

"I said, I don't really care if you keep them or not."

Sabrina nodded. "I see. The deal is off?"

Darci laughed. "Oh, come on. Did you really think I was going to pay you ten thousand dollars to keep those ridiculous resolutions?"

"I . . . I guess not."

"You guessed right. All I needed was a way to keep you away from Avery while I was deciding whether or not I wanted him back. You were distracting him, taking his focus away from me, so I prevented you from focusing on him."

"It worked well, I see."

"Really?" Darci leaned close to the mirror and smoothed some stray hairs. "Do you think so?"

Sabrina shrugged nonchalantly, but her tone was steely. "I'd say so, judging from the little chiropractic session I just saw in your office."

Darci turned to face Sabrina again. She lifted an eyebrow. "Avery loves to have his shoulders massaged. But then, if you *really* knew him, you would already know that."

Sabrina cleared her throat. "I could go in there and tell Avery about the deal right now."

"Go ahead, but he won't believe you. I have his ear now, not you."

"Then I guess you don't need me anymore."

"Right again. You might want to dust off your résumé because—" She stopped mid-sentence.

Was someone else in here?

Darci looked toward the stalls. She hated the idea of actually bending over to see if any were occupied, but she had to know. If someone had overheard, she would probably have to shell out some big bucks to keep her quiet.

Either that or she could work overtime to discredit Sabrina and whoever it was.

Swallowing her pride, Darci leaned over and checked for feet. All clear.

She stood up, sighing in relief.

"Like I was saying," she told Sabrina, "get your résumé ready. I predict that you will go on *Morning Coffee* and make yourself look completely stupid. By the time you get back, Avery will be fully convinced that you are anything *but* an asset to this company."

"Was that your plan? The entire time?"

Sabrina was giving her way more credit than she deserved, but Darci wouldn't turn away a compliment.

"What? Get rid of you and get Avery back? It worked out well, don't you think?"

Sabrina was quiet. Then she took a step closer and pointed her finger at Darci. "You won't get away with this, Darci."

"I already have." Darci laughed.

Sabrina shook her head. "No. I mean this. I don't know how or when, but God won't allow you to do this and get off scot-free."

Leave it to Sabrina to go dragging God into something. Darci rolled her eyes. "Then I guess we'll wait and see what happens."

Chapter Twenty-Eight

Sabrina sat in the green room of *Morning Coffee Live,* praying the butterflies away.

If there was a bright side to things, it was the fact that Stephan Frazier hadn't followed her here.

Her cell phone beeped. She had voice mail.

She pulled the phone from her purse and pressed the mailbox icon.

Avery's voice greeted her.

"Hey, it's me. I know you're not speaking to me—why, I'm not sure, but I thought it would be best not to press the issue until after you got back from *Morning Coffee.*

"Just wanted to call and tell you I'm praying for you. I'll be watching, and I know you'll do a great job. And don't forget—'Preach the gospel at all times, and when necessary, use words.'"

The message ended, and Sabrina listened to it again, feeling a mixture of encouragement and confusion. She was probably going to lose her job because of him, and yet he called and left nice messages for her.

She didn't have time to dwell on it, because the production

assistant came and told her it was time to get in her place backstage.

"Let's move," he said. "We've got about three minutes till they introduce you."

"Welcome to *Morning Coffee Live.* I'm Daphne McGuire . . ."

"I'm Gordon Mitchell . . ."

"And I'm Renee Phillips. Thanks for joining us. Right now I'm happy to introduce the most talked about woman in television. Please welcome Sabrina Bradley!"

Sabrina said one last prayer and headed out to the coffee table, where Daphne, Gordon, and Renee sat waiting for her.

Sunny Harris watched as the printer spit out the letter she'd just typed.

She read over it for mistakes and signed her name with a flourish. Writing the words "Sunny Harris" gave her pause. Not exactly true, but it would have to do.

She folded the letter into thirds, placed it in an envelope, sealed it, and left it on Darci's desk.

A fleeting sensation of guilt washed over her. Proper etiquette dictated giving at least two weeks' notice in such situations. Leaving a letter of resignation on the boss's desk instead of delivering the news in person was definitely a breach of protocol.

But at sixty-three years old, Sunny didn't feel much like following proper etiquette.

She emptied the last of her personal items into the cardboard box and left the office.

Sunny Harris was no more.

Avery grinned as Sabrina made it safely to the coffee table. She'd been so worried about tripping in those shoes.

He stretched out on his couch and settled in to watch. He'd opted to go in to work later and watch *Morning Coffee* at home.

Sabrina was confident and articulate as she waded through the "fluff" part of the interview.

Avery found himself holding his breath when Daphne got to *the question.*

"Now, Sabrina, we have to ask. What is the real story behind these photos of you and your boss that just recently surfaced? Did you break your resolution not to fall in love?"

Sabrina looked Daphne in the eye without flinching. "In some ways, I did. Avery is a wonderful man, and I guess he swept me off my feet—no matter how hard I tried to keep them on the ground."

"So," asked Renee, "you're saying that you did fall in love?"

Sabrina looked into the camera. "I think I fell in 'like.' I hadn't known Avery long enough to love him, but I definitely saw things in him that I was attracted to."

"So where do things stand now with the two of you?" Gordon wanted to know.

"Well, it was a difficult decision, but I decided that I needed to stay true to my original resolution—for the sake of the show. I didn't want to lie to the public."

"Now, that's loyalty," said Daphne.

"I'm curious, though," said Renee. "What happens if you and

Avery do decide that you're in love? Or if you meet someone else before the year ends and it turns out to be love at first sight. What will you do? Ignore love just to say you kept your resolution?"

Sabrina shook her head. "If I truly fall in love, I'll let everyone know. I met a lady one day in the grocery store who told me not to get caught up in keeping the resolutions just to prove that I could."

"Well, I think the public agrees with you," said Gordon. "Several of our viewers have called or written to say that making a resolution not to fall in love doesn't mean you shouldn't be able to talk to a man or go on a few dates."

"Exactly," said Daphne. "In fact, a lot of people wrote just to say that they wished you would get rid of that resolution altogether. They think it's an unrealistic expectation."

Sabrina laughed. "I'll be the first to admit that I wrote that resolution after a bad day. I was upset about something my ex-fiancé had done, and it sounded like a good idea at the time."

"So you had second thoughts about it from the beginning?" said Gordon.

"Yes."

"Then why didn't you get rid of it early on?" asked Renee.

Sabrina took a deep breath. "I'll just say that I had my own personal reasons for doing so. There were circumstances beyond my control that prevented me from getting rid of it."

"Sounds mysterious," said Daphne.

Sabrina smiled.

"I'm curious to know what these circumstances might be," added Gordon.

Avery wondered what those circumstances might be, as well.

Renee's face filled the television screen. "Mysterious circumstances or not, it appears that Sabrina's lips are sealed. I don't think we'll be able to get anything out of her."

"Thank you, Sabrina, for coming to chat with us," said Gordon. "We wish you the best of luck in keeping those resolutions—but I don't think there's a person in this country who really doesn't want you to fall in love."

"Please come back and see us again—soon," said Renee.

"We're going to take a commercial break," said Daphne. "But when we come back, we're going to bring you a spring fashion show live from our outdoor studio. Don't miss out on this season's hottest new looks."

Avery clicked off the television. Sabrina had done a fine job. Stephan Frazier and his cronies should pack up and go home now. There was nothing to investigate.

Resign?

Darci stared at the letter again.

How could Sunny quit like this with no warning? How rude.

She needed someone to pick up her dry cleaning. Annette was at home, sick with a cold. Sabrina was in New York, on *Morning Coffee.* And Sunny had quit.

What was she going to do?

Darci went to her door and opened it.

"Maris!" she yelled.

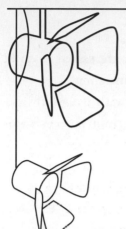

Chapter Twenty-Nine

Avery awoke the next morning to the sound of the phone ringing.

"Hello?"

"Avery, it's Maris. We have a serious issue on our hands."

He chuckled. "More serious than Sabrina's secret boyfriend?"

Maris didn't laugh. "Turn on the news. And get your hands on a copy of this week's *Journal New York*."

He rubbed his eyes. "Does Sabrina know about this—whatever it is?"

Maris sighed. "I don't think so. She had a late flight home last night, and she told me she planned to go in late this morning. The reporters aren't saying exactly what's going on, so I thought I'd wait until I had more details before I called her."

"Good idea," said Avery. "She's been through so much lately—no use in getting her needlessly upset."

"Oh, gotta go. They're breaking in for an update."

"All right, Maris," he said. "Calm down and let me handle this. I'll find out what's going on, and if Sabrina needs to know, I'll tell her."

Maris hung up.

Avery stumbled out of bed, looking for the television remote. What did *Journal New York* have to do with his show?

The weekly New York newspaper frowned on the very things *The Daily Dose* thrived on: fashion, home decorating, even the resolutions program.

Journal New York was a prestigious newspaper of the highest order, and its writers devoted themselves to hard-hitting social commentary and human-rights activism.

Surely they hadn't stooped to the level of Stephan Frazier and his cronies to speculate about "scintillating secrets" and "heartbreakers."

He found the remote and flipped to one of the news channels.

Who else but Stephan Frazier would be on, doing a live report, no less?

"I'm Stephan Frazier, with the *Inside Entertainment* investigative team. Behind me is the St. Louis home of Darci Oliver, host of the popular television show *The Daily Dose.*

"We're here hoping for a comment from Ms. Oliver about the stunning accusations brought against her by Iris Davenport, the well-respected investigative journalist on staff at *Journal New York.*"

Avery's jaw dropped. Iris Davenport? Everyone had heard of Iris Davenport. But she didn't dabble in celebrity gossip. What could she possibly have against Darci?

He glanced at the television, where Stephan was still babbling on and on about . . . absolutely nothing.

There was only one way to find out what was going on: Avery needed to get his hands on a copy of that paper.

Sabrina was in the kitchen, finishing the last of her cereal, when she heard a car pull up outside.

She wondered if it was Maris. Thankfully, Stephan and his crew hadn't been here last night after she got home from the airport.

She felt like a free woman again.

She was ready for work but didn't exactly feel like going in. *Maybe I should take the day off.*

Would missing one day be so horrible? Darci had basically told her that she wouldn't have a job after she got back from *Morning Coffee.*

A knock sounded at the door.

Sabrina went and looked through the peephole. It was Avery. Was he coming to fire her before she even got to work? She hesitantly opened the door. She had never seen him look this harried.

"Can I come in?"

"Sure." Sabrina swung the door open a bit wider and allowed him inside.

He held up a copy of *Journal New York.* "Have you read this?"

Sabrina shook her head. She subscribed to it, but her mail hadn't arrived yet.

"Have you seen the news?" he asked.

Sabrina shook her head. Lately, nothing good ever came after the words "Have you seen the news?"

Avery handed her the magazine, open to a specific page. "Maybe you'd better sit down," he suggested.

Sabrina went into the living room and sat on the sofa.

Avery followed.

She glanced at the title caption on the page:

BEAUTY AND THE TYRANT, *by Iris Davenport*

"Iris Davenport?" she said. "You came to my house at nine in the morning to show me an Iris Davenport article?"

"You're a fan of hers?"

Sabrina nodded. "Big-time. But I don't read Iris Davenport reports first thing in the morning. She writes heavy stuff."

Avery inclined his head back to the paper. "Trust me, you'll want to read this one. It's about you."

About me?

Sabrina turned her attention back to the page and began to read.

I have a confession to make: I am an incurable snoop.

Snooping isn't always a bad thing for a journalist; in fact, my ability to snoop got me the job I've had for the last twenty years.

Some of you are probably licking your chops, wondering what injustice Iris Davenport has uncovered in our cruel world. I have to warn you. The story that follows isn't my usual fare. In fact, I have a feeling that even some of my most faithful readers will turn up their noses at it. You may write it off as sensational celebrity drivel, and I wouldn't blame you. Iris Davenport writes about child welfare, you might say. Iris Davenport goes undercover to study women's rights and risks life and limb in third world countries to show the world how people are being mistreated.

Iris Davenport doesn't write about American celebrities.

Seven months ago, I would have agreed with you. The world doesn't need one more reporter to tell us what designer gown so-and-so wore to such-and-such awards ceremony.

But seven months ago, in my quest to study how senior citizens were treated in the workplace, I unwittingly stumbled upon a story of another kind of injustice—a story that just happens to involve celebrities . . .

Sabrina looked up from the paper. "I don't understand where this is going. I love Iris Davenport's investigative exposés, but what does this article have to do with me?"

Avery pointed to the paper. "Keep reading."

Sabrina sighed and forged ahead, this time reading a bit faster.

My next assignment was to find a job in corporate America. On a whim, I applied for an executive assistant position at the *Daily Dose* offices. I didn't really expect to land it, but my parents always taught me to aim high. Miraculously, I landed the job. I became Darci Oliver's personal assistant. My alias was Sunny Harris . . .

"Sunny?" Sabrina stared at Avery. "I can't believe Iris Davenport was at work with me every day for over half a year and I didn't know it."

"That's the meaning of the word 'undercover,'" Avery said, chuckling. "Besides, I don't think the *Journal* has ever run her photo."

"Yeah," Sabrina agreed. "I've always heard she's really camera-shy."

Avery nodded in agreement. "She's one of those journalists we know by her words, not her looks."

"True."

Sabrina continued to skim through the rest of the article. It filled an entire page and a half and detailed Iris's experiences working at *The Daily Dose.*

Sabrina realized that Sunny had indeed been up to some-

317

thing, just as Avery and Maris suspected. But she wasn't working for Darci; instead, she'd been working for herself.

Not only did she tell the truth about how Darci treated her employees, but she also went into detail about the negative effects of office gossip and backstabbing.

And true to form, Iris didn't waste her ammunition on the obvious story about Sabrina, Avery, and Darci. In the course of running Darci's endless string of errands, Iris had gotten to know several of the employees in all the *Daily Dose* departments.

The article recounted story after story about how everyday people in all areas of the company were affected by workplace disagreements with their fellow workers and bosses.

Toward the end of the piece, Sabrina stopped skimming and read more slowly.

> In all my years of zipping here and there to remote countries and trying to find the most underprivileged areas of our own America, I am saddened to say that there seems to be a serious problem where I least expected to find it: posh, affluent corporate America.
>
> The workers arrive every morning in droves to complete their assigned tasks. I would liken them to worker bees in a hive. They are all subject to the queen.
>
> In a corporate setting, the queen is the boss, the supervisor, the manager. The boss outlives them all, and the workers labor tirelessly to see that the boss is happy.
>
> The workers are often belittled, betrayed, and bullied. And many times they have no recourse. There is a constant struggle among the employees themselves, and going to a supervisor is often out of the question.
>
> Those in management can wield their power like a

sword, forcing others beneath them to do their work for them or taking ideas that they didn't create.

The workers don't want to lose their security, their regular paycheck, their dental plans, and their 401(k)s, so they try to dodge trouble by doing as they are told.

When they have negative encounters with their fellow employees, they are apt to go home and worry over it, telling their friends and family about what happened in great detail. But they are reluctant to take their complaints to the higher-ups, fearing they may be seen as nagging tattletales . . .

Sabrina looked up and found Avery watching her intently.
"Is it true?"
"What?"
"The part about the deal you made with Darci?"
Sabrina's face grew warm. How did Iris know about that?
She skimmed forward to the end of the article. Iris recounted the entire conversation between Sabrina and Darci.

When I found myself crouched in a stall in the ladies' room, raptly listening to the most astonishing conversation I could imagine, I knew my time at *The Daily Dose* had ended. I had a story to tell, before it was too late—too late for Sabrina Bradley and who knows how many other people in similar situations around the country.

As I'm typing this, people are up in arms, wondering if Sabrina broke her resolution by going on a date with Avery.

I say, who cares?

Sabrina, Avery, if you're reading this—no, I was not a spy for Darci. I'd prefer that you think of me as a secret agent— an agent for what is right and just.

I do have some advice for both of you, like it or lump it.

Sabrina: Ditch the resolution and tell Avery how much you care about him. It may not be love yet, but give it a chance.

Avery: Get rid of Darci. She's a real smooth talker and comes across as a saint on television. But in the real world, she's a terror—take it from me, her personal slave for seven months. If you let her go unchecked, it'll only be a matter of time before she turns on you—if she hasn't already.

Everyone else: Be fair to the person at the desk next to you. When you see workplace injustice (and you know you have), speak up. It only takes one person to make a difference.

Signing off for now,

Iris Davenport.

Sabrina looked at Avery.

"It's true, isn't it?" he said. "Why didn't I see? Why didn't you tell me?"

She shrugged. "I wanted the promotion and the money."

"And Darci threatened to fire you if you did anything different."

Sabrina nodded. He had no idea how relieved she was that this was all out in the open.

He moved closer so that he was sitting right next to her. "Let's pretend, for five minutes, that there is no Darci, no resolutions program, and no Stephan Frazier peeking in your windows."

Sabrina laughed.

"I'm going to ask you a question, and I want an honest answer."

"Ask away."

"Will you let me take you on a date—a real date—tonight?"

She grinned at him. "I was hoping you'd ask that."

Sabrina stood in the wings of the *Daily Dose* set. Those butter-flies had taken up permanent residence in her stomach for the past few days.

She closed her eyes. *Lord, I need your help. Tell me what to say. Show me how to touch people's lives.*

Peace settled over her almost as soon as she finished.

Maris's voice came through her earpiece. "One minute, Sabrina. And I'm praying for you."

Sabrina grinned.

Avery came and stood next to her. "Are you nervous?"

"Trying not to be," she said.

He gave her a hug and kissed her gently. "Watch the lip-stick," she told him.

"Twenty seconds," said Maris.

Sabrina looked at Avery. "Here goes."

"You'll do fine. And don't forget what I told you."

Sabrina nodded and said it along with him: "When necessary, use words."

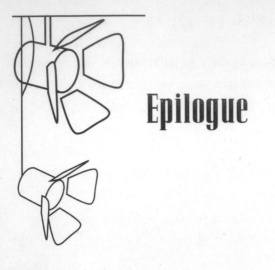

Epilogue

Welcome back to *Morning Coffee.* I'm Daphne McGuire, and we're privileged to have Iris Davenport, the famed investigative reporter, with us this morning." Daphne paused, and Gordon picked up the baton.

"As we all recently learned, Iris served several months as executive assistant to Darci Oliver, former host of the hit talk show *The Daily Dose.*"

Renee began the interview. "Now, Iris, you initially set out to do a story on how people over the age of sixty were treated on the job. First you worked at a fast-food franchise; then you served a stint at a chain bookstore. But it's become apparent that you hit pay dirt when you interviewed for a position at the *Daily Dose* offices."

Iris nodded her head. "Correct. In fact, when I began, I thought I would only hold the position for a month or two. After that, I had planned to try retail sales."

"But you noticed some things that got your investigative juices flowing," said Daphne.

"I certainly did. As you mentioned earlier, I wanted to do a piece about discrimination against people my age in the workplace. But other issues took over, and, well, here we are."

Gordon leaned closer. "Tell us, Iris, was it really that difficult working for Darci?"

Iris shrugged. "For me, it actually wasn't. I did what she told me to do and we got along quite famously. But it wasn't such a picnic for most of her other employees."

"Employees like Sabrina Bradley," Renee prompted.

"You mentioned in your article that Darci treated you like royalty in contrast to her interactions with Sabrina," said Daphne.

"She did. But then again, I wasn't young enough or pretty enough to catch the eye of the very handsome and accomplished Avery Benjamin."

"The man Sabrina broke her resolution for," said Renee.

"Yes," Iris agreed. "It's so refreshing to see true love prevail even in the midst of so much turmoil."

"Now, Iris," said Gordon, "can you tell us what it was like to work in such a fast-paced environment? Was it anything like you'd expected?"

"Yes and no. In fact, my son told me I'd be making a mistake to work in a corporate setting. He didn't like the idea of me nosing around too much. He worried that I was too much of a granny to handle all of the backstabbing and such."

"Are you surprised at the state of what you saw?"

Iris shook her head. "Not really. When I was eighteen years old, I went to work for a big insurance company as a secretary. I'm ashamed to admit that there was still a great deal of gossip and general workplace politics."

"So it's not that much different?" asked Daphne.

"Not much. The slang and fashion have changed, but people's attitudes are quite similar. It's every man for himself, rather than teamwork."

Gordon nodded solemnly. "Such a shame."

Daphne spoke up. "We've got to take a commercial break in a moment, but before we go, Iris, would you answer the question America is clamoring to know?"

She paused dramatically, then continued: "Is Sabrina Bradley, the new host of *The Daily Dose,* as nice in person as she is on television?"

Iris grinned wide. "First of all, let me say this, Daphne. Since my article broke, I think we've all learned a thing or two about putting ordinary people up on pedestals just because we watch them in movies or listen to their music or even see them on television every day.

"People are just that: people. In my sixty-three years of life, I've yet to meet a perfect person. We all have our bad days and we all lose our tempers. But, to answer your question . . ."

Iris looked into the eye of the camera and nodded. "Yes, America, she is. She really is."